Bertolt Brecht Poems & Songs from the Plays

Edited and
mainly translated by
John Willett

Methuen

*First published in Great Britain in 1990 by Methuen London.
Published by arrangement
with Suhrkamp Verlag, Frankfurt am Main.*

*First published in paperback in Great Britain in 1992
by Methuen London.*

I S B N 0 413 66830 4

*Printed in Great Britain by
Richard Clay Ltd, Bungay, Suffolk*

Contents

The extra dimension

In 1976 we published a selection of some five hundred Brecht poems in English versions which has remained in print in both Britain and the United States. With one important limitation it represented the widest choice of that author's poems then possible; and the general introduction with which it opened still holds good for the 171 additional poems which make up the present book. The limitation was that we were not including those songs and poems that would (or already could) be found in our edition of the plays, which still had a long way to go. Now we are publishing the majority of them as a separate book, using much the same chronological divisions and editorial principles but with a greater emphasis on performance. We have taken all that can be read or sung independently of their theatrical context, going back sometimes to the pre-theatrical versions; added one or two from Brecht's other writings, grouped them in much the same chronological divisions as before and followed the same editorial principles. The result is a structurally similar book with about a third as many poems, ranging from famous items like 'Legend of the dead soldier' (2) to the splendid but virtually unknown 'Anne Smith relates the conquest of America' (28), an unused speech from a posthumously published fragment.

The basic difference from our original selection is one of function. Whether or not he originally intended them as such, Brecht felt these poems to be theatrically usable, either as part of the play text, as songs, as prologues or spoken 'arias'; or as aids to production or comment. Many were intended to be set to music; others were not so but proved to be settable, often to great effect. Yet even in translation they are recognisably the work of the same writer as the *Poems* proper (which also included theatre poems and texts that were set to music); the borders between the different categories become blurred by the similarities of style and tone. In one respect only there is a sharp contrast, for whereas roughly two-thirds of *Poems 1913–1956* had been unknown before the poet's death, five-sixths of the present selection were by then already published. Moreover some of the more private genres which he used are missing: the sonnet for example, the classical epigram and the poetry for children. But looking at the two volumes together, even the most practised critic would find it hard to say at first sight which items were private and which public: which form part of a play, which are meant for singing and which are to be read on the page, let alone how often their function was changed.

For so many of the same qualities run through all Brecht's writing. The same literary influences can be seen at work – Villon, Rimbaud, Kipling, the translations of Arthur Waley – and so can the same attitudes to politico-economic factors. Thus the songs of *The Threepenny Opera* and *Happy End* criticise the boom of the mid-1920s; the militant songs with Eisler (75 ff.) look to a German revolution that never materialised; the *Fear and Misery* verses (114) review Hitler's Reich on the eve of war; the 'German Miserere' (138) and other *Schweik* numbers and the new *Threepenny Opera* songs (154–5) react to the war itself; the (unused) American *Galileo* prologue and epilogue (157–8), to the first atom bomb; the *Antigone* hexameters (160), more obliquely to the disastrous situation of Germany after 1945. Once again Brecht's feelings about these things are bitten into the verse.

There are certain elements in his poetic writing which emerge more strongly than before, notably his expressions of faith in the USSR and the German Communist party (which have to be heard in the Eisler settings if the streak of quiet persuasiveness in them is to be understood). But once again we see here the now familiar impact of the cities on an intensely imaginative young Augsburg poet who overflowed with passionate, irreverent, exotic ideas and phrases; then the iconoclasm of the satirist leading to an austere communism that often denied itself regular poetic forms; followed by a distancing and loosening up during the years of exile; finally the return to a new constructive role, concerned above all with the German theatre and its repertoire but also with the young people in the new state. At the same time the book contains poems relating to the less obviously dramatic categories within the 'straight' poems: the 'Reader for those who live in cities' for instance (e.g. 34–5), the 'Visions' (see the prose-poem 'Roll-call of the virtues and the vices', 122) and even the classic hexameters in imitation of Lucretius that so obsessed Brecht after the end of the Second World War (160). In such examples there is nothing self-evidently theatrical or song-like: it is just that he is drawing on many different categories of poem to give an extra dimension to his stage.

2

Brecht himself made very clear, in some of his statements included in our previous selection, that his early poems were 'nearly all supposed to be singable', while in his later writing too 'I was always thinking of actual performance'. It is less well known how very far he was prepared to cannibalise (or re-function) those poems and resituate them in his plays, sometimes years after the poem in question had been written. Roughly a quarter of those in the present volume had led an independent existence as poems before acquiring their role as songs or verse speech in the plays; indeed the process starts with the very first pair. Thus 'Lucifer's evening song' (1) was composed by Weill and incorporated in *Rise and Fall of the City of Mahagonny* (1929) where it shifted position at least once, then in the 1950s Brecht loaned it to Rudolf Wagner-Régeny for inclusion in his opera *Persische Legende*. 'Legend of the dead soldier' (2) was put into *Drums in the Night* as an interlude song, then printed separately in Brecht's first and second books of poems. As for the *Baal* songs that followed, they and 'The drowned girl' are something else, for they instantly become the kernel of that play (Brecht's first in time of writing, though not of performance), whose poetic character they have determined to this day. 'The drowned girl' later went on to become part of Weill's *Berlin Requiem* along with other Brecht texts, after that composer had first set three of the German-language and the two English-language 'Mahagonny Songs' to make the 1927 'Songspiel' version of his eventual opera.

Then with the full *Rise and Fall of the City of Mahagonny* Brecht went over to a deliberate policy of montage on two levels. Where the overall structure of the operatic work was concerned he proclaimed a new principle of 'separation of the elements', by which Weill's music, Caspar Neher's drawings (projected on a great screen behind the action) and his own text would make their separate contributions to the performance without attempting to fuse or blend. Within this novel combination the text itself was a patchwork of stylistically divergent poems written between 1917 and 1928 which greatly extended the nucleus of 'Mahagonny Songs' proper; most of them forming distinct 'numbers' within the generally 'durchkomponiert' score, though we also print one or two thematically related items which were not used. In *The Threepenny Opera*, whose writing and production overlapped *Mahagonny*, the even more distinctive singling-out of the song numbers was heightened by the use of special lighting, titles and (in the original intention) Neher's drawings to detach them from the narrative flow of the play; the songs themselves however were newly adapted from Villon or purpose-written, only two of them being products of the earlier kind of cannibalisation. In *Happy End* (1929) the relation to the narrative was even more oblique (the best-known item, 'Surabaya Johnny', being an unrelated cabaret song) while three of the numbers were in turn rejigged as part of the epic play *Saint Joan of the Stockyards* along with the central figure, the Chicago setting and the Salvation Army theme.

There are few plays by Brecht that are totally lacking in music and/or poetry – *Señora Carrar's Rifles*, and some of the early one-acters seem to be the only examples – although there are a small number from all periods that include just one or two songs, while *Fear and Misery of the Third Reich* is a special case with its use of a long processional poem (cf. 'Legend of the dead soldier' and, in the earlier selection, 'Ballad on approving of the world' and 'The anachronistic procession') as a chain to link up an adjustable sequence of scenes. And from *Edward the Second* (1924) to the last adaptation of *Trumpets and Drums* (1956) Brecht often used a fluctuating mixture of the methods described – cannibalisation, texts written specially for the play or, more rarely, for a special dramaturgical reason within the play, poems for speech or singing, poems integral to the play or semi-detached. To take only two instances, *Man equals man* between 1926 and 1931 uses a mock-Kipling theme song, some verses relating to the *Mahagonny* and *Happy End* material, the refrain of the 'Cannon song' from *The Threepenny Opera*, a rhymed speech Interlude (sometimes switched to serve as a Prologue) and the dissected, partly spoken 'Song of the Flow of Things' in the vein of the 'Reader for those who Live in Cities' in the earlier selection. Similarly *Mother Courage* starts its career in 1939 with songs from *The Threepenny Opera* and *The Round Heads and the Pointed Heads*, the Kiplingesque 'Ballad of the Girl and the Soldier' (18), 'Surabaya Johnny' from *Happy End* and a new theme song to the tune of the early 'Ballad of the Pirates'; subsequently songs are added or dropped, while 'Surabaya Johnny' is refashioned as the 'Song of Fraternisation' after the end of the Second World War.

Brecht's only wholly and coherently purpose-written stage works appear to be the first two 'Lehrstücke', the three pieces written with Eisler between 1929–36, the radio play *Lucullus* (1939), *The Caucasian Chalk Circle* (1944) – which demands a particular Georgian or Azerbaijani approach to narrative singing – and Weill's sung ballet *The Seven Deadly Sins* (1933). In the last two of these perhaps the poetry is less easily appreciated in isolation from the theatrical context, though for various reasons it seemed advisable to include them here. The Eisler songs from *The Decision* and *The Mother* however already stand individually as poems in Brecht's second collection *Lieder Gedichte Chöre* of 1934, and thereafter several of them led a life outside the parent play. Certainly the montage process never again reached the complexity it had attained in *Rise and Fall of the City of Mahagonny*, and it is worth noting both that Brecht remained dissatisfied with its realisation in this work and that after 1929 communist aestheticians in Germany and the USSR began to discourage its use. Yet he never abandoned montage entirely – indeed it can be argued that the basic principle of his 'epic theatre' is the bolting-together of disjoined narrative episodes and songs – so that it still survives in so largely custom-written a play as *The Good Person of Szechwan* (1940–41) with its spoken verse 'arias'. Perhaps it is just this re-use of earlier material that shows the hidden connections and meanings in that work: for instance the underlying whiff of opium which was due to the origins of 'The Song of the smoke' (10 and 124) and finally reemerged as a powerful element in the 'Santa Monica version' of 1943, or the militant thread that leads from Lillian Holiday's 'God's little lieutenant' (55) to Shen Teh's 'Song of the Defencelessness' (127), as well as the transvestite thread running on from Shen Teh to Victoria Balance in one of the last songs.

3

For all the sense of continuity and renovation brought about by his ruthless refunctioning of many early poems, Brecht's attitude to the songs in his plays altered over the years. The change can be seen in his manuscripts, where the home-made, almost plainchant melodies to the *Baal* poems, with the music clearly following the spontaneous phrasing of the lines, give way to scansion schemes and tables of rhymes as the poet tries to hammer out a sound and a rhythm which his chosen composer can come along and set. Particularly in the drafts of such seemingly effortless rhymed songs as 'The Song of the Moldau' and 'The Ballad of the Waterwheel' we can observe how the inspiration of his early twenties had to be followed by hard, nagging work. Look then at the 'Key to major works' in the notes at the end, and you will see how his relations with his principal musical collaborators fall into three stages. Up to his move to Berlin in 1924 he was to a great extent writing (and himself singing) tunes of his own, several of which are given in an appendix to his first book of poems published in 1927; and these also served for the songs in his plays right up to the first performance of *Man equals man* in 1926. Briefly he then collaborated with the cabaret composer Franz Bruinier, who seems to have helped to polish up some of his melodic ideas in the months before he met Weill, and also with Piscator's musical director Edmund Meisel, who wrote settings for the radio broadcast of *Man equals man*. Both Bruinier and Meisel died young, but this was the beginning for Brecht of a ten-year spell of intensive collaboration with some of the most interesting composers of the day: Kurt Weill (1927–1933), Paul Hindemith (1929) and Hanns Eisler (1930–1937).

For Weill this originated in the impression made on him by Brecht's first book of poems and the radio performance of *Man equals man* (which he had to review); it finished when he began to feel cramped by the (slightly) older man's increasingly austere and uncompromising demands. For Hindemith it centred on a common interest in new didactic forms of art but soon ended in what seems to have been a mutual awareness of personal and political incompatibility. For Eisler it sprang no doubt from Brecht's adoption around 1929 of a communist standpoint that the composer himself already held, as well as from their shared interest in by-passing the established 'apparatus' of the arts. 'I functioned', said Eisler many years later, 'as the messenger of the workers' movement', in other words the German Communist Party. For all three of these musicians the process entailed working together with the writer at the planning stage, agreeing the whole thrust of the work in question and exchanging views about wording, rhythms, melodies, orchestration and the singing voice. Weill, we know, made use of at least one of Brecht's home-made tunes and was the first to spell out their joint concept of 'gestic' music. Eisler with his 'Kampflieder' or militant political songs brought Brecht close to agitprop and more than once got him to modify his texts for singing. Hindemith may well have given him his conception of the 'Lehrstück' or didactic cantata, though it was not long before their ideas diverged.

After 1937 this close interaction came virtually to a halt, and following Eisler's departure for the United States early in 1938 there came a four-year interlude during which Brecht was without any regular musical collaborator, though he continued to send Eisler scripts of his new plays. When the two friends did meet up again in Hollywood during the Second World War the old integrated way of working was reserved for individual songs such as the 'Hollywood Elegies' (in *Poems 1913–1956*), and from then on all the songs for the plays were written first and in most cases not set to music till an actual production had been arranged. Only Paul Dessau, yet another German émigré composer who had gone to America, was prepared in the case of *Mother Courage* and *The Good Person of Szechwan* to write settings in advance of any professional production and to do so in a way that met Brecht's requirements. The result was that in the later and larger Brecht plays, from *Galileo* on, the component songs and poems had generally become part of the script some years before the chosen composer sat down to it. No longer would he be named in the published text as a 'collaborator', as Weill had been for *The Threepenny Opera* and *Mahagonny* or Eisler for the three works in which he was involved. The process had become that much closer to orthodox theatre routine.

And yet it is difficult to tell, on hearing a given song, which method led to its composition. Not only will its text normally be recognisable at once as Brecht's work, but the setting too is likely to have characteristics that became common to all his main composers. Admittedly he allowed them some liberties in his last years: thus Eisler was able to use a full orchestra for the dream sequences in *Simone Machard* and to spurn the political marching song (which he had come to associate with the Nazis), while Dessau could write an operatic version of *Lucullus*, and later *Puntila*, for the despised grand opera 'apparatus'. But as late as the mid-1950s Eisler's settings for *Schweik in the Second World War* and Wagner-Régeny's (a Neher protégé) for *Trumpets and Drums* still show the 'Brechtian' hallmarks which have been resumed as

> thin, clear, slightly tart orchestration (concentrating on wind instru-
> ments and percussion); the use of jazz elements and the 1920s song
> (the only modern folk music Brecht found truly congenial); the
> writing for untrained singers; the shaping of the melody to fit and
> underpin the verbal rhythms; the audible importance of punctuation.
> This was the kind of music that Brecht needed in order to stimulate
> thought and make the audience prick up its ears.

Brecht worked in an artistically exciting time, and was lucky to find a choice of outstanding contemporaries who were very open to these requirements. All five of those whom we have mentioned – from Weill to Wagner-Régeny – were associated with the 'new music' experiments of Hindemith, which in turn derived from the French 'Les Six' group and its respect for vulgar popular music and that small-scale masterpiece of 1917, the Stravinsky/Ramuz *The Soldier's Tale*. But was this common affiliation enough to explain the similarity of their responses to Brecht's often insistent demands? Surely something more was involved. One factor must have been his preference for certain untrained actor-singers who showed the same concern for articulate performance as he himself had learnt from the clown Karl Valentin and the Munich poet/play-wright Frank Wedekind, greatest of the founders of German cabaret. Among them were Friedrich Holländer's wife Blandine Ebinger and, above all, Weill's wife the dancer Lotte Lenya who had largely made the success of the first *Mahagonny*. Yet not all the songs now indelibly associated with Lenya seem to have been conceived specifically with her in mind – 'Surabaya Johnny' for instance or 'Pirate Jenny' (which Polly, not Jenny was intended to sing) – while although Brecht wrote the *Seven Deadly Sins* poems and some of the *Schweik* songs for her he took no such steps for the proposed musical version of *The Good Person of Szechwan* which Weill hoped to make in America. As for Ernst Busch, the strong-voiced actor who sang many of the Eisler marching songs and played in *The Decision* and (as the son Pavel) in *The Mother*, it is interesting that in the former the singer was not him but the operatic tenor Anton Maria Topitz. For while Eisler often performed with Busch (even at the ceremony following Brecht's death in 1956) he never shared the poet's contempt for the conventionally 'beautiful' trained voice.

Secondly, there is also some evidence that Brecht's involvement in the setting of his words was not merely negative, in the form of rejection of Wagnerian tenors, stringed instruments (other than plucked ones) and everything else that he most disliked, but had its more constructive aspects. For instance one or two of Weill's settings of the 1920s do seem to contain echoes – rhythmic or melodic – of the preliminary work done by Brecht and Bruinier, whether for the publication of the 'Mahagonny Songs' in Brecht's first book of poems or for cabaret performance by artists such as Kate Kühl. With Eisler, who was personally and politically much closer to him than Weill, the boot was on the other foot as the composer persuaded him to cut and change the poetic text to meet the musical demands. With Dessau he apparently never hesitated to make suggestions about melodies and orchestration, all the more freely perhaps because Dessau by his marriage to Elisabeth Hauptmann had joined the inner Brecht circle. But in the end it seems that nothing counted so much in the evolution of a common musical approach as the unconscious aural qualities of the texts, whether rhymed, balladesque, or 'rhymeless verse with irregular rhythms' as Brecht termed it on the eve of the Second World War (the relevant essay is in *Poems 1913–1956*, pp. 463–71). For his language had a clarity, a directness, a rhythmic variety and an audible edge to it which even today provoke the composer to put it to music, the performer to speak or to sing it.

4

Many of us still find the songs, with their marvellous settings and their power to attract outstanding performers, the simplest and most direct way into all Brecht's work. Hear them, and at once you know the man was something very special; sense this *and* read some of his knottier essays – on the theatre, say – and you realise that it all adds up to a quite distinctive artistic personality, at once complicated, self-contradictory and close-knit. They thus form the principal key to a writer who today is fast becoming a world classic; so that one of the main objects of the present selection must be to make them intelligible to English-speaking readers yet capable at the same time of being effectively performed. This is a slightly different business from good literary translation, because it means that there is an additional aspect of the original whose claim on the translator is at least as urgent as the usual ones of sense, tone and style. It is not even mere 'singability' but what Weill and Brecht called the *Gestus* or gest, i.e. the attitude to be expressed by words, music and performer both overall and at any given point in the song: in short the underlying structure of its communicative message. Everything in the songs is geared to that; so the English text must be too, even if the niceties of literal meaning sometimes get a bit bent.

Fortunately Brecht's drafts show us that where the songs were concerned this was his attitude to his own language: look for instance at the 'Ballad of the waterwheel', that lovely song in which the bubbling underground Schubert in Eisler seems to surface for the first time – and you find the basic statement of the poem was first written out in prose, then turned bit by bit into increasingly lucid verse as rhymes were found that would convey it with a minimum of irrelevant embroidery. The result of such a process is bound to be some elaboration, however slight, of the bald statement, and in this marginal area the translator too is sometimes forced into other options in order to get a singable result. Of course the song translator is also concerned with the more normal literary criteria; all the poems which we have selected were and are meant to be read as verse. But in trying to balance this with the gestic aspect one's ear is haunted by the music that best conveys the latter as Brecht intended. It is more than a matter of mere rhyme and metre, as can be heard instantly if you try to fit a formally accurate rendering of one of these songs to its setting by Eisler or Weill: unless the stresses, the punctuation, the breathing pauses and even the little metric ir-regularities are right it will be curiously lifeless; it will lack the gest. This is what makes translation of the Brecht songs so difficult, and it may help to explain why performances of the plays in English often fall down in this respect. The songs which should be helping to power them – particularly in the case of works written between 1927 and 1937 – are failing to spark, and the whole contraption fails to take off.

Hence my concern to make a large proportion of the translations in this book gestically singable, though of course I have had to accept a number of editorial compromises, sometimes out of necessity, sometimes for what seemed to me good reasons. Four levels of translation are involved. Those versions marked (by the marginal sign ♭) as singable in the 'Notes on Individual Poems' (p. 215) have either been written to fit the gest and syllabic pattern of the music or, better still, been proved to do so in performance – performance sometimes by such outstanding singer-performers as David Bowie and Robyn Archer. Of the others, some are metrically accurate and can be adjusted to the music without too much problem (as was the case with many of the translations in *Poems 1913–1956* of texts that also serve as songs in various settings); others are freer and have been included because of more literary considerations. Among them are those Auden and Isherwood translations which would otherwise not have figured in our edition, since although Dessau's music for *The Caucasian Chalk Circle* need not, in my view, be seen as forming a unity with Brecht's words, that for *Mother Courage* does. In such cases I have accepted versions for the present selection which neither fit the music nor even follow the German rhythms; more gestically-accurate translations of the *Courage* songs will be found in our edition of that play.

5

The editorial material relating to Brecht's poetry as a whole will be found in the earlier selection; I have not repeated it here. This comprises the 'Texts by Brecht' setting out his views on poetry, its publication, analysis and delivery, as well as some thirty pages of editorial notes discussing the various categories and collections into which the main corpus of his poetry falls. In the present volume I have, as before, provided a (more or less) chronological list of the poems included, corresponding once again to the same chronological arrangement of the material, along with a similar section of 'Notes on the Individual Poems'. These have the additional purpose of making clear (in the briefest terms) the context of each poem or song: who delivers it, and at what point it comes in the given play or other work. Preceding this, and corresponding to the section on 'The Principal collections of Brecht's poems' in the earlier selection, there is a 'Key to major works and their constituent songs' for the benefit of interested readers. Here they can not merely see how to group the material as in the corresponding German volume (*Gedichte und Lieder aus Stücken*, which avoids chronological arrangement and makes a slightly different selection), but find at a glance which scattered earlier poems were cannibalised for each of the various plays. They can also get a general idea of the music for each work, along with names of the composers and publishers responsible. A much fuller key to the musical settings has been prepared by Joachim Lucchesi and Ronald K. Shull, and is published in both halves of Germany.

Work started on this book not long after the appearance of the earlier volume in London twelve years ago. It too has been subject to a great deal of revision and improvement, and once again I owe much to my various helpers. This time the poems have been read by Carol Stewart, Adrian Henri, Derwent May and the late John Cullen, and most of their suggestions have been incorporated in the final versions (so long as they do not conflict with the musical settings). Michael Morley, who has a particular knowledge of the music, has not only been over the editorial notes but did additional research for them on various visits to Germany; and I have also learned a good deal from Robyn Archer and Dominic Muldowney. A number of newer publications have been of use in addition to those listed on pp. 520–1 of the earlier volume, notably Günter Glaeser's two volumes of *Bertolt Brecht Briefe 1913–1956* whose English edition should appear more or less concurrently with the present book – Fritz Hennenberg's *Das Grosse Brecht-Liederbuch* (Henschel and Suhrkamp Verlage, 1984) with a selection of simplified musical settings, Albert Dümling's *Lasst euch nicht verführen* (also re the music: Kindler 1985) and volumes 11/12 and 2 of the new 'Grosse kommentierte Berliner und Frankfurter Ausgabe' of Brecht's work. These last have been edited respectively by Jan and Gabriele Knopf and Jürgen Schebera (Suhrkamp and Aufbau Verlag, 1988).

Without the kindness of the director and staff of the Brecht Archive in East Berlin much of this work would have been impossible, and once again Suhrkamp-Verlag have been generous with their publications, of which the pocket-sized *Die Gedichte von Bertolt Brecht in einem Band* published in 1982 is now much the most useful adjunct for those who want to refer to the German texts. Nearer home I would like to thank Nicholas Franglen for his very competent transcription of my typescript on to disc, and to express our gratitude and affection to Nick Hern who dealt with us on behalf of Methuen for several years. This edition owes much to his combination of enthusiasm, understanding and patience. We shall not forget his contribution.

I The Augsburg Years
1913–1920

(First versions of *Baal* and *Drums in the Night*.
One-act plays: *The Wedding, The Beggar, The Catch,
Driving out a Devil, Lux in Tenebris.*
Early poems and psalms.)

1 LUCIFER'S EVENING SONG

1

Let them not deceive you
There is no returning home.
The day is nearly over
The night wind makes you shiver
Tomorrow will not come.

2

Let them not mislead you
This life's a slight thing. So
Gulp it with urgent greed! You
'll find nothing else to feed you
When once you let it go.

3

Let them not console you
The time is getting late.
Leave the redeemed to moulder.
Life dazzles the beholder:
It isn't going to wait.

4

Let them not deceive you
Into drudgery and want.
No terrors now can reach you
You'll die like any creature
And nothing waits beyond.

2 LEGEND OF THE DEAD SOLDIER

1

And when the war reached its final spring
With no hint of a pause for breath
The soldier did the logical thing
And died a hero's death.

2

The war however was far from done
And the Kaiser thought it a crime
That his soldier should be dead and gone
Before the proper time.

3

The summer spread over the makeshift graves
And the soldier lay ignored
Until one night there came an offi-
cial army medical board.

4

The board went out to the cemetery
With consecrated spade
And dug up what was left of him
For next day's sick parade.

5

Their doctor inspected what they'd found
Or as much as he thought would serve
And gave his report: 'He's medically sound
He's merely lost his nerve.'

6

Straightway they took the soldier off.
The night was soft and warm.
If you hadn't a helmet you could see
The stars you saw at home.

7

They filled him up with a fiery schnapps
To spark his sluggish heart
And shoved two nurses into his arms
And a half-naked tart.

8

He's stinking so strongly of decay
That a priest limps on before
Swinging a censer on his way
That he may stink no more.

9

In front the band with oompah-pah
Intones a rousing march.
The soldier does like the manual says
And flicks his legs from his arse.

10

Their arms about him, keeping pace
Two kind first-aid men go
Or else he might fall in the shit on his face
And that would never do.

11

They daubed his shroud with the black-white-red
Of the old imperial flag
Whose garish colours obscured the mud
On that blood-bespattered rag.

12

Up front a gent in a morning suit
And stuffed-out shirt marched too:
A German determined to do his dut-
y as Germans always do.

13

So see them now as, oompah-pah
Along the roads they go
And the soldier goes whirling along with them
Like a flake in the driving snow.

14

The dogs cry out and the horses prance
The rats squeal on the land:
They're damned if they're going to belong to France
It's more than flesh can stand.

15

And when they pass through a village all
The women are moved to tears.
The trees bow low, the moon shines full
And the whole lot gives three cheers.

16

With oompah-pah and cheerio
And tart and dog and priest
And right in the middle the soldier himself
Like some poor drunken beast.

17

And when they pass through a village perhaps
It happens he disappears
For such a crowd's come to join the chaps
With oompah and three cheers.

18

In all that dancing, yelling crowd
He disappeared from view.
You could only see him from overhead
Which only stars can do.

19

The stars won't always be up there
The dawn is turning red.
But the soldier goes off to a hero's death
Just like the manual said.

Five Songs from 'Baal'

3 BALLAD OF THE ADVENTURERS

I

Sick from the sun, with rainstorms lashing him rotten
A looted laurel in his tangled hair
He called back the dreams of a childhood he'd long since
      forgotten
Forgotten the roof, yet the sky was always there.

2

O you who were kicked out alike from Heaven and from Hades
You murderers who've been so bitterly repaid
Why did you part from your mothers who nursed you as babies
Where it was quiet, and you slept, and there you stayed?

3

Still he'll explore, and scan the absinthe-green ocean
Though his mother has given him up for lost
Grinning and cursing, with a few odd tears of contrition
Always in search of that land where the life seems best.

4

Loafing through hells and flogged through paradises
Calm and grinning, with fast vanishing face
Sometimes he'll dream of a small field he recognises
With blue sky overhead and nothing else.

4 DEATH IN THE WOODS

I

And a man died in the primeval woods
Where the storm blew in torrents around him –
Died like an animal clawing for roots

Stared up through the trees, as the wind skimmed the woods
And the roar of the thunderstorm drowned him.

2

Several of them stood to watch him go
And they strove to make his passage smoother
Telling him: We'll take you home now, brother.
But he thrust them from him with a blow
Spat, and cried: And where's my home, d'you know?
That was home, and he had got no other.

3

Is your toothless mouth choking with pus?
How's the rest of you: can you still tell?
Must you die so slowly and with so much fuss?
We've just had your horse served up as steak to us.
Hurry up! They're waiting down in Hell.

4

Then the forest roared above their head
And they saw the treetrunk he was seizing
And they heard his screams and what he said.
Could not go to him, but stood and smoked instead
And, exasperated, watched him freezing:
So like them, and yet so nearly dead.

5

You're mad, useless, putrid! To your lair!
You're a sore, a chancre, you're excreta!
Selfish beast, you're breathing up our air!
So they said. And he, the cancer there:
Let me live! Your sun was never sweeter!
Ride in radiance all of us can share!

6

This is what no friend could understand:
How the horror made them quietly shiver.

Earth was holding his poor naked hand
In the breeze from sea to sea lies land:
I'm to lie in silence here for ever.

7
Yes, this poor life, by its prodigious weight
Held him so that even half-decayed
He thrust his dead body ever deeper:
At first dawn of day he fell dead in the grassy shade.
Numb with disgust they buried him, and cold with hate
Hiding him with undergrowth and creeper.

8
And they rode in silence from that place
Turning round to see the tree again
Under which their comrade once had lain
Who felt dying was too sharp a pain:
The tree stood in the light ablaze.
Then each made the mark of the cross on his face
And they rode off swiftly over the plain.

5   HYMN OF BAAL THE GREAT

Baal grew up within the whiteness of the womb
With the sky already large and pale and calm
Naked, young, endlessly marvellous
As Baal loved it when he came to us.

And that sky remained with him through joy and care
Even when Baal slept, blissful and unaware.
Nights meant violet sky and drunken Baal
Dawns: Baal good, sky apricot-like pale.

So through hospital, cathedral, bar
Baal trots coolly on, and learns to let things go.

When Baal's tired, boys, Baal will not fall far:
Baal will drag his whole sky down below.

Where the sinners herd in shame together
Baal lies naked, soaking up the calm.
Just the sky, but sky to last for *ever*
Hides his nakedness with its strong arm.

And that lusty girl, the world, who laughs when yielding
To the man who'll stand the pressure of her thighs
Gives him moments of a sweet ecstatic feeling.
Baal survived it; he just used his eyes.

And when Baal sees corpses all around
Then a double pleasure comes to him.
Lots of space, says Baal; they're not enough to count.
Lots of space inside this woman's womb.

Once a woman, Baal says, gives her all
She'll have nothing more, so let her go!
Other men would represent no risk at all.
Even Baal is scared of babies, though.

Vice, says Baal, is bound to help a bit
And so are the men who practise it.
Vices leave their mark on all they touch.
Stick to two, for one will be too much.

Slackness, softness – that's what you should shun.
Nothing's tougher than pursuing fun.
Powerful limbs are needed, and experience too:
Swollen bellies may discourage you.

Baal watches the vultures in the star-shot sky
Hovering patiently to see when Baal will die.
Sometimes Baal shams dead. The vultures swoop.
Baal, without a word, will dine on vulture soup.

Under mournful stars in our sad vale of trouble
Munching, Baal can graze broad pastures down to stubble.
When they're cropped, into the forest deep
Baal trots, singing, to enjoy his sleep.

And when Baal's dragged down to be the dark womb's prize
What's the world to Baal? Baal has been fed.
Sky enough still lurks behind Baal's eyes
To make just enough sky when he's dead.

Baal decayed within the darkness of the womb
With the sky once more as large and pale and calm
Naked, young, endlessly marvellous
As Baal loved it when he came to us.

6 BAAL'S SONG

If a woman's hips are ample
Then I want her in the hay
Skirt and stockings all a-rumple
(Cheerfully) – for that's my way.

If that woman bites in pleasure
Then I wipe it clean with hay
My mouth and her lap together
(Thoroughly) – for that's my way.

If the woman goes on loving
When I feel too tired to play
I just smile and stroll off waving
(Amiably) – for that's my way.

7 ORGE'S SONG

Orge told me that:

In all the world the place that he liked best
Was not the grass mound where his loved ones rest

Was not the confessional, nor some harlot's room
Nor yet the warm white softness of the womb.

Orge thought the best place known to man
In this world was the lavatory pan.

Here is a place to set the cheeks aglow
With stars above and excrement below.

A place of refuge where you have a right
To sit in private on your wedding night.

A place of modesty, where you admit
You are a man, and have to do your bit.

A place of wisdom, where your gut turns out
To gird itself up for another bout.

Where you are always doing good by stealth
Exerting tactful pressure for your health.

At that you realise how far you've gone:
Using the lavatory – to eat on.

8 BALLAD OF CHASTITY IN A MAJOR KEY

See them melting with desire!
Mine! he thought. If she is free.
And the darkness fanned their fire.
And she thought: just him and me.
And he said: 'I'll never hurt you'.
Not a girl of easy virtue
And she didn't want to be.

Oh, their fingers' sweet sensations
As with beating heart she lay!
What about his hesitations?
Each of them could only pray.
And he said: 'I mustn't hurt you'.
Not a girl of easy virtue
And she hadn't learnt the way . . .

Sooner than profane that moment
Off he went to find a tart
Who could show him what to come meant
Helping nature out with art.
Lovely bodies, though, are killing:
Once he had been very willing
Now he swore to stay apart.

Still red-hot but still unsullied
Quick release was now *her* prayer
So she found herself a solid
Chap who didn't have a care.
(And who beat her something horrid
Laying her across the stair.)
Being manhandled rejoiced her –
Not for her the holy cloister.
Now at last the urge was there.

So he sees his hesitation
To have been entirely right:

Thinks it was an inspiration
Not to hurt her that May night.
She's all vice and he's all virtue:
Each is anxious to alert you
Not to play with dynamite.

9 THE DROWNED GIRL

1
Once she had drowned and started her slow descent
From streams to where the great rivers broaden
The opal sky shone most magnificent
As if it had to be her body's guardian.

2
Wrack and duckweed cling to her as she swims
Slowly their burden adds to her weight.
Cool the fishes play about her limbs
Creatures and growths encumber her in her final state.

3
And in the evening the sky grew dark as smoke
And at night the stars kept the light from falling.
But soon it cleared as dawn again broke
To maintain her sequence of evening and morning.

4
As her pallid body decayed in the water there
It happened (very slowly) that it gently slid from God's
          thoughts:
First her face, then her hands, and right at the end her hair.
Leaving those corpse-choked rivers just one more corpse.

II The Mahagonny Myth
1920–1925

(Production of *Drums in the Night* and *Baal*.
Writing and production of *In the Jungle of Cities*
and *Edward II*. First drafts of *Man equals man*.
The later Devotions and the first city poems.)

1

The girl:
In those distant days of loving-kindness
Which they say are now forever gone
I adored the world, and sought for blindness
Or a heaven, the very purest one.
Soon enough, at dawn, I got my warning:
Blindness strikes the inquisitive offender
Who would see the heavens' pure bright dawning.
And I saw it. And I saw its splendour.
How can scrounging crumbs make people happy?
What's the good if hardships last forever?
Must we never pluck the crimson poppy
Just because its blooms are sure to wither?
    And so I said: drop it.
    Breathe in the smoke twisting black
    Towards colder heavens. Look up: like it
    You'll not come back.

2

The Man:
My enemy who 'mid the poppies moulders –
I think of him when lighting up the drug.
And my bull? I've harnessed his great shoulders
And I've marched before a crimson flag.
By midday I'd tired of strife and rancour
Thought they offered nothing much to go on
You meantime were being so much franker
Saying they could be of use to no one.
Why smite enemies? I have no doubt mine
Nowadays could smite me without trying.
Nobody grows fatter than his outline.
Why then put on weight when you are dying?
    And so I said: drop it.
    Breathe in the smoke twisting black.

Towards colder heavens. Look up: like it
You'll not come back.

3
The Man:
Ever since those distant days I've hurried
Sown my millet, reaped it where it grew
Lain with women, cried to gods when worried
Fathered sons who now sow millet too.
Late enough, at night, I got the lesson:
Not a cock will crow – they're all ignoring
My end – nor will the most complete confession
Rouse a single god where he lies snoring.
Why keep sowing millet on this gravel
Soil whose barrenness can't be corrected
If my tamarisk is doomed to shrivel
Once I'm dead and it is left neglected?
   And so I said: drop it.
   Breathe in the smoke twisting black
   Towards colder heavens. Look up: like it
   You'll not come back.

II TAHITI

1
The booze had been flushed away down the toilet
We'd lowered the pink venetian blind
Enjoyed our tobacco – there'd been nothing to spoil it –
And went running before the Tahiti wind.

2
On our horsehair sofa we kept high and dry
Stormy the night and the waves roll high
The ship was tossing, the night struck rocks
Six of us three were as sick as dogs.

3
With tobacco and booze, and a whirling spray too
Topp managed the sheets amid cries like these:
Hey, Gedde, take 'em off, the Equator's in view!
Or: Hold your hat, Bert, 'ware the Gulf Stream breeze!

4
They rounded Cape Good Horn and rolled past Rio.
What battles with pirates and the ice-green moon!
What tropical storms! Such a murderous trio
Sang 'Nearer, my God' in a Java typhoon.

5
Past Java the booze once more flowed undiluted
As B.B. had Topp tried and then executed.
Two days later a seagull got Gedde with child
Till the trade winds found them all three reconciled.

12 WHEN PARIS ATE THE BREAD OF MENELAUS

When Paris ate the bread of Menelaus
And salt in Menelaus's house, he slept –
Or so the ancient chronicles relate –
With Menelaus's wife, and on the ship
That took him back to Troy, she shared his bed.
Troy laughed. To laughing Troy and Greece as well
It seemed good sense to give that willing flesh
That bore the name of Helen, back to her Greek
Husband, because she was a whore.
Only Lord Paris, understandably
Objected. Said she was unwell. Meanwhile
Greek ships turned up, and multiplied like fleas.
One morning Greeks came barging into
Paris's house, intent on seizing the
Greek strumpet. Paris shouts
Out of the window: This place is my house

My castle; and the Trojans, thinking
Him not entirely wrong, grin and applaud.
The Greeks lower their sails, lie down and fish
Till one day in an ale-house in the port
Someone punches someone on the nose
And explains that it was done for Helen.
And in the next few days, before
Anyone realised what was happening
Too many hands reached for too many throats.
From shattered ships men speared the drowning
Like tuna fish. And as the moon waxed
More and more men were missing from their tents.
Many were found headless in the houses. The crabs
Grew fat that year in the Skamander River
But no one ate them. Men who in the morning
Looked out for signs of storm, thinking of nothing
But whether the fish would bite that afternoon
Had fallen by midnight through confusion and purpose
Every last one.
Seen at ten o'clock
With human faces
By eleven o'clock
Forgetting the language of their country
Trojan sees Troy and Greek sees Greece no more.
Instead they feel human lips
Turned into tiger jaws. At noon
Beast sinks its fangs into the flanks
Of moaning beast.
But if on the beleaguered walls one man
Had kept his wits and
Called them by name and species, many
Would even then have frozen in their tracks.
Better if they had gone down fighting
Aboard a vessel suddenly grown old
Sinking beneath their feet at nightfall
Nameless.
They were to kill each other more horribly:

That war dragged on ten years –
The Trojan War it's called –
And it was ended by a horse.
And so if reason, by and large, were not inhuman
And human ears not plugged
Regardless of whether Helen was a whore
Or grandmother to a flourishing line
Troy, which was four times bigger than our London
Would still be standing, Hector would not
Have died in the blood of his genitals, dogs
Would not have spat upon the aged hair
Of tearful Priam, an entire race
Would not have perished in its prime.
Quod erat demonstrandum. True
We would not have had the Iliad.

'Mahagonny songs' 1 to 5

13 MAHAGONNY SONG NO. 1

Off to Mahagonny!
The air is cool and fresh.
There's horses there and poker dice
Whisky and women's flesh.
   Cleaner, greener
   Moon of Alabama
   Guide us in!
   Here we come with stacks of notes
   Underneath our overcoats
   For a great big welcome
   From your stupid empty grin.

Off to Mahagonny!
The wind is in the east

There's prime selected sirloin steak
And neither king nor priest.
  Cleaner, greener
  Moon of Alabama
  Guide us in!
  Here we come with stacks of notes
  Underneath our overcoats
  For a great big welcome
  From your stupid empty grin.

Off to Mahagonny!
It's time we went on board.
The over syph-syph-syphilised
Can go there to get cured.
  Cleaner, greener
  Moon of Alabama
  Guide us in!
  Here we come with stacks of notes
  Underneath our overcoats
  For a great big welcome
  From your stupid empty grin.

14 MAHAGONNY SONG NO. 2

Every Mahagonny man
Had to have five dollars daily
Then, when once the fun began
Had to have some extra maybe.
In those days they all stayed boozing
In Mahagonny's poker drink saloon
And they all ended up by losing
But it passed an afternoon.

1
Both at sea and on land
Everyone gets skinned now irrespective of his talents

So they all take off their collars
And they hawk their skins for dollars
'Cause these skins when weighed are always shown as dollars on
      the balance.
   Every Mahagonny man
   Had to have five dollars daily
   Then, when once the fun began
   Had to have some extra maybe.
   In those days they all stayed boozing
   In Mahagonny's poker drink saloon
   And they all ended up by losing
   But it passed an afternoon.

2

Both at sea and on land
This means consumption of prime skins is now intensive
Oh, your flesh has often prickled
But who pays when you get pickled?
Since your skins may be a bargain but your whisky comes
      expensive.
   Every Mahagonny man
   Had to have five dollars daily
   Then, when once the fun began
   Had to have some extra maybe.
   In those days they all stayed boozing
   In Mahagonny's poker drink saloon
   And they all ended up by losing
   But it passed an afternoon.

3

Both at sea and on land
You can hear God's mills a-grinding with their slow relentless
      clatter
That's why you'll find all those persons
Hawking skins there in their dozens
Since to cut a dash is nice but to pay cash's another matter.

Any man who stays at home
Need not spend five dollars daily
And suppose he's got a dame
He can have himself a baby.
Nowadays you find them boozing
In Almighty God's economy saloon
Where there's no question of them losing –
Might as well be on the moon.

15 MAHAGONNY SONG NO. 3

One gloomy morning as we sat
Sipping our whisky
God came to Mahagonny
God came to Mahagonny.
Sipping our whisky
We caught sight of God in Mahagonny.

1
All you spongers mopping
Up My yearly bounty of good rye
Didn't think you'd ever see Me drop in
Shall I find you've drunk the whole place dry?
Looks were exchanged by the men of Mahagonny.
Yes, answered back the men of Mahagonny.
    One gloomy morning as we sat
    Sipping our whisky
    God came to Mahagonny
    God came to Mahagonny.
    Sipping our whisky
    We caught sight of God in Mahagonny.

2
Was it Friday night I heard you joking?
I was watching Mary Weeman then
Silent as a sprat, in salt seas soaking:

Will she ever dry out, gentlemen?
Looks were exchanged by the men of Mahagonny.
Yes, answered back the men of Mahagonny.
    One gloomy morning as we sat
    Sipping our whisky
    God came to Mahagonny
    God came to Mahagonny.
    Sipping our whisky
    We caught sight of God in Mahagonny.

3
What are those cartridge-cases?
Did you shoot My preacher good and true?
I can't stand your raddled boozer's faces.
Must I share My heavenly home with you?
Looks were exchanged by the men of Mahagonny
Yes, answered back the men of Mahagonny.
    One gloomy morning as we sat
    Sipping our whisky
    God came to Mahagonny
    God came to Mahagonny.
    Sipping our whisky
    We caught sight of God in Mahagonny.

4
You can all go to hell now
Stuff your wet cigar-butts up your bum!
There's a hell for you to go to, fellows
Down to My black hell, you filthy scum!
Looks were exchanged by the men of Mahagonny.
Yes, answered back the men of Mahagonny.
    One gloomy morning as we sat
    Sipping our whisky
    You'll come to Mahagonny
    You'll come to Mahagonny!
    Sipping our whisky
    While you deal with Mahagonny.

5
So let nobody budge now!
All out on strike! We shall never
Go to hell, though Your wild horses drag us:
For, You see, we've been in hell for ever.
God got a look from the men of Mahagonny.
No, answered back the men of Mahagonny.

16 MAHAGONNY SONG NO. 4

1
Now Johnny, you can't be
A wretched mollycoddle
If you're to knock out Jack Dempsey
Like a hollow bottle.
Be a man
If you can
My son!
And when you've lasted fifteen rounds
Then come to Mahagon.
   And once you've joined the other
   Mahagonny cases
   You'll do like those folk
   And from out your yellow faces
   Puff smoke.
   Sky like an ivory skin
   Thick golden shag!
   Once Frisco's flames begin
   All you can hope to win
   Must end up shovelled in –
   To a big bag.

2
Now Johnny, when you get
That skyscraper of yours
Then you must railroad it express

Up thirty-seven floors
Be a man
Bridge the span
My son!
Mind you come down, then come around
And come to Mahagon.
     And once you've joined the other
     Mahagonny cases
     You'll do like those folk
     And from out your yellow faces
     Puff smoke.
     Sky like an ivory skin
     Thick golden shag!
     Once Frisco's flames begin
     All you can hope to win
     Must end up shovelled in –
     To a big bag.

17 MAHAGONNY SONG NO. 5

                    Your legs were like billiard cues
                    An orangutan depraved them
                    In the pale clip-joints of Mahagonny.
                    Now tell us who shaved them.

1

We all know you lay with the fellows
In the yellow fever camps
In Mahagonny's sweltering nights –
A lady without lamps.
     It was always your legs, dear
     They always said the one thing
     Till the fellows found theirs, dear
     Were limp as old string.
     You may not want to wait till I've contracted your disease
     But wait at least, my darling, while my shirt dries in the
          breeze.

2

Oh, those old boys hunched over their card games
Used to shut their eyes and start shivering
And recall good times in Mahagonny
When poker was less fun than living.
   Across your body, dear
   They used to straddle
   But now to make love, dear
   They use a soup-ladle.
   You may not want to wait till I've been shrivelled by the
      freeze
   But wait at least, my darling, while my shirt dries in the
      breeze.

3

The girl heard her man pleading
When pickled on whisky:
Don't take me off to Mahagonny
Till I've pawned my knife for whisky.
   It was always your legs, dear
   They always said the one thing
   Till the fellows found theirs, dear
   Were limp as old string.
   You may not want to wait till he's been ravaged by disease
   But wait at least, my darling, while my shirt dries in the
      breeze.

18   BALLAD OF THE GIRL AND THE SOLDIER

The guns blaze away, and the bay'nit'll slay
And the water can't hardly be colder.
What's the answer to ice? 'Keep off!''s my advice.
That's what the girl told the soldier.
Next thing the solider, wiv' a round up the spout
Hears the band playing and gives a great shout:
Why, it's marching what makes you a soldier!

So it's down to the south, and then northwards once more;
See him catching that bay'nit in his naked paw!
That's what his comrades done told her.

Oh, do not despise the advice of the wise
Learn wisdom from those that are older
And don't try for things that are out of your reach –
That's what the girl told the soldier.
Next thing the soldier, his bay'nit in place
Wades into the river and laughs in her face
Though the water comes up his shoulder.
When the shingle roof glints in the light o' the moon
We'll be wiv' you again, not a moment too soon!
That's what his comrades done told her.

You'll go out like a light! And the sun'll take flight
For your courage just makes us feel colder.
Oh, that vanishing light! May God see that it's right! –
That's what the girl told the soldier.
Next thing the soldier, his bay'nit in place
Was caught by the current and went down without trace
And the water won't never be colder.
Then the shingle roof froze in the light o'the moon
As both soldier and ice drifted down to their doom –
And d'you know what his comrades done told her?

He went out like a light. And the sunshine took flight
For his courage just made 'em feel colder.
Oh, do not despise the advice of the wise!
That's what the girl told the soldier.

19 THE CANNON SONG

John was around then and Jimmy was there
And Georgie was up for promotion.
Not that the army gave a bugger what they were

When confronting some heathen commotion.
   The troops live under
   The cannon's thunder
   From Cork to Cooch Behar.
   Moving from place to place
   When they come face to face
   With a different breed of fellow
   Whose skins are black or yellow
   They quick as winking chop them into beefsteak tartare.

Johnny found his whisky too warm
And Jim found the weather too balmy
But Georgie took them both by the arm
And said: never let down the army.
   The troops live under
   The cannon's thunder
   From Cork to Cooch Behar.
   Moving from place to place
   When they come face to face
   With a different breed of fellow
   Whose skins are black or yellow
   They quick as winking chop them into beefsteak tartare.

John is a write-off and Jimmy is dead
And they shot poor old Georgie for looting
But young blokes' blood goes on being red
And the army goes on recruiting.
   The troops live under
   The cannon's thunder
   From Cork to Cooch Behar.
   Moving from place to place
   When they come face to face
   With a different breed of fellow
   Whose skins are black or yellow
   They quick as winking chop them into beefsteak tartare.

Three songs from 'Man equals man'

Hey, Tom, have you joined up too, joined up too?
'Cos I joined up just like you, just like you.
And when I see you marching there
I know I'm back on the old barrack square.
Have you ever seen me in your life?
'Cos I ain't never seen you in my life.
   That ain't the plan
   For man equals man
   Since time began.
   Tommy boy, let me tell you, it really ain't the plan!
   Man equals man!
   There's no other plan.
   The red sun of Kilkoa shines
   Upon our regimental lines
   Where seven thousand men can die
   And not a soul will bat an eye
   'Cos the whole lot are better gone.
   So who cares where Kilkoa's red sun shone?

2

Hey, Tom, was there rice in your Irish stew?
'Cos I had rice in my Irish stew
And when I found they'd left out the meat
The army didn't seem such a treat.
Hey, Tom, has it made you throw up yet?
'Cos I've not stopped throwing up yet.
   It ain't the plan
   For man equals man
   Since time began.
   Tommy boy, let me tell you, it really ain't the plan!
   Man equals man!

There's no other plan.
The red sun of Kilkoa shines
Upon our regimental lines
Where seven thousand men can die
And not a soul will bat an eye
'Cos the whole lot are better gone.
So who cares where Kilkoa's red sun shone?

3
Hey, Tom, did you see Jenny Smith last night?
'Cos me I saw Jenny Smith last night.
And when I look at that old bag
The army don't seem half such a drag.
Hey, Tom, have you been and slept with her?
'Cos you know I been and slept with her.
   That ain't the plan
   For man equals man
   Since time began.
   Tommy boy, let me tell you, it really ain't the plan!
Man equals man!
There's no other plan.
The red sun of Kilkoa shines
Upon our regimental lines
Where seven thousand men can die
And not a soul will bat an eye
'Cos the whole lot are better gone.
So who cares where Kilkoa's red sun shone?

4
Hey, Tom, have you got your kit packed up?
'Cos I have got my kit packed up.
And when I sees you with your kit
I feel the army's fighting fit.
But did you have bugger all to pack in yours?
'Cos I find I've got bugger all to pack in mine.
   That ain't the plan
   For man equals man

Since time began.
Tommy boy, let me tell you, it really ain't the plan!
Man equals man!
There's no other plan.
The red sun of Kilkoa shines
Upon our regimental lines
Where seven thousand men can die
And not a soul will bat an eye
'Cos the whole lot are better gone.
So who cares where Kilkoa's red sun shone?

5
Hey, Tom, are you quite ready to move off?
'Cos me I'm quite ready to move off
And when I sees you march I guess
I'll march just where the army says.
Have you got a clue where we're marching to?
'Cos I ain't got no clue where we're marching to.
    That ain't the plan
    For man equals man
    Since time began.
    Tommy boy, let me tell you, it really ain't the plan!
Man equals man!
There's no other plan
The red sun of Kilkoa shines
Upon our regimental lines
Where seven thousand men can die
And not a soul will bat an eye
'Cos the whole lot are better gone.
So who cares where Kilkoa's red sun shone?

21 THE SONG OF WIDOW BEGBICK'S DRINKING TRUCK

In Widow Begbick's drinking truck
You smokes and swigs and sleeps your time away.
You buys your beer and tries your luck

From Jubbulpore to Mandalay.
  From Halifax to Hindustan
  Horse, foot and guns, the service man
  Wants what the widow has to sell.
  It's toddy, gum and hi, hi, hi
  Bypassing heaven and skirting hell.
  Shut your big mouth, Tommy, keep your hair on, Tommy
  As you slides down Soda Mountain into Whisky Dell.

In Widow Begbick's drinking tank
You always gets the things that you likes best.
That's where the Indian Army drank
When you was drinking at Mummy's breast.
  From Halifax to Hindustan
  Horse, foot and guns, the service man
  Wants what the widow has to sell.
  It's toddy, gum and hi, hi, hi
  Bypassing heaven and skirting hell.
  Shut your big mouth, Tommy, keep your hair on, Tommy
  As you slides down Soda Mountain into Whisky Dell.

And when war comes to Cooch Behar
We'll stock ourselves with gum and smokes and beer
And climb on Begbick's drinking car
To show those wogs who's master here.
  From Halifax to Hindustan
  Horse, foot and guns, the service man
  Wants what the widow has to sell.
  It's toddy, gum and hi, hi, hi
  Bypassing heaven and skirting hell.
  Shut your big mouth, Tommy, keep your hair on, Tommy
  As you slides down Soda Mountain into Whisky Dell.

22 WHAT A BIT OF ALL RIGHT IN UGANDA!

What a bit of all right in Uganda!
Seven cents a seat on the verandah.
And the poker hands we played with that old tiger –
No, I've never played as well as that.
When we beat the hide off old pa Kruger
He bet nothing but his battered hat.
How peacefully the moon shone in Uganda!
Through the cool night we sat about
Until sunrise
And then pulled out.
A man needs money to be able
To sit at the poker table
With a tiger in disguise.
(Seven cents a seat on the verandah.)

Five more songs from 'Mahagonny'

23 THE CHEWING-GUM SONG

Many women could see no one in the world but Johnny
Who was the hardest man in Mahagonny.
This same Johnny was many people's chief impression in the
       world
His whole philosophy was that he chewed gum.
Very simple, very simple.
    Johnny was in all sorts of situations.
    Why not, why not?
    But whatever the situation Johnny chewed his gum.

Yes, a lot of men took pot shots at Johnny
Who was the handsomest man in Mahagonny
But Johnny himself shot seldom, and then only in the back

Because unlike a woman a bullet can't be had for nothing.
Very simple, very simple.
   Johnny only shot when it was really fun.
   Why not, why not?
   But behind his Browning too Johnny chewed his gum.

Yes, many women only put on their make-up for Johnny
Who was the meanest guy in Mahagonny
But Johnny himself loved seldom, and only when clothed at
         that
Likewise on Sunday morning with the door open and taking his
         time.
Very simple, very simple.
   Johnny was just as keen on made-up girls as we are
   Why not, why not?
   But he never did it without chewing gum.

It turned out that many people would have liked to see the end
         of Johnny
Who was the only man in Mahagonny
And Johnny died, but no, he hadn't really wanted to
For dealing with death, gentlemen, is unlike dealing with a
         woman
Not so simple, not so simple.
   But Johnny was soon in the picture dying
   And why not, yes why not?
   And even on his deathbed Johnny chewed gum.

24 THE JOHNNY-DOESN'T-WANT-TO-BE-HUMAN SONG

The secrets of the cocktail list are yours
You've seen the moon rise and the darkness fall.
The Mandalay Bar's had to close its doors
And so far nothing has happened at all.
Boys, why the hell has nothing happened at all?

1

I guess I would like to eat my hat
I guess I should do so too.
For why should a man not eat his hat
If it's all he's got to do?
    The secrets of the cocktail list are yours
    You've seen the moon rise and the darkness fall.
    The Mandalay Bar's had to close its doors
    And so far nothing has happened at all.
    Boys, why the hell has nothing happened at all?

2

I guess I had better get rid of my woman
I guess she and I are through.
For why should a man be stuck with his woman
When he's stuck for money too?
    The secrets of the cocktail list are yours
    You've seen the moon rise and the darkness fall.
    The Mandalay Bar's had to close its doors
    And so far nothing has happened at all.
    Boys, why the hell has nothing happened at all?

3

I guess I shall push on to Georgia
I guess there are cities there too.
For why shouldn't a man push on to Georgia
When he's got nothing else to do?
    The secrets of the cocktail list are yours
    You've seen the moon rise and the darkness fall.
    The Mandalay Bar's had to close its doors
    And so far nothing has happened at all.
    Boys, why the hell has nothing happened at all?

25 ALABAMA SONG

Oh, show us the way to the next whisky-bar
Oh, don't ask why, oh, don't ask why
For we must find the next whisky-bar
For if we don't find the next whisky-bar
I tell you we must die! I tell you we must die!
> Oh! Moon of Alabama
> We now must say good-bye
> We've lost our good old mamma
> And must have whisky
> Oh! You know why.

2

Oh, show us the way to the next pretty girl
Oh, don't ask why, oh, don't ask why
For we must find the next pretty girl
For if we don't find the next pretty girl
I tell you we must die! I tell you we must die!
> Oh! Moon of Alabama
> We now must say good-bye
> We've lost our good old mamma
> And must have a girl
> Oh! You know why.

3

Oh, show us the way to the next little dollar
Oh, don't ask why, oh, don't ask why
For we must find the next little dollar
For if we don't find the next little dollar
I tell you we must die! I tell you we must die!
> Oh! Moon of Alabama
> We now must say good-bye
> We've lost our good old mamma
> And must have dollars
> Oh! You know why.

26 BENARES SONG

1

There is no whisky in this town
There is no bar to sit us down
Oh!
Where is the telephone?
Is here no telephone?
Oh, sir, God damn it:
No!
   Let's go to Benares
   Where the bars are plenty
   Let's go to Benares!
   Jenny, let us go.

2

There is no money in this town
The whole economy has broken down
Oh!
Where is the telephone?
Is here no telephone?
Oh, sir, God damn it:
No!
   Let's go to Benares
   Where there's money plenty
   Let's go to Benares!
   Jenny, let us go.

3

There is no fun on this old star
There is no door for us ajar
Oh!
Where is the telephone?
Is here no telephone?
Oh, sir, God damn it:
No!
   Worst of all, Benares

Is said to have perished in an earthquake!
Oh! our good Benares!
Oh, where shall we go!
Worst of all, Benares
Is said to have been punished in an earthquake!
Oh! our good Benares!
Oh! where shall we go!

27 POEM ON A DEAD MAN

They can bring vinegar for him
They can wipe his forehead for him
They can take surgical forceps
They can pull his tongue out with them –
None of it is going to help a dead man.

They can come and talk to him
They can start yelling at him
They can just leave him lying
Take him along with them –
None of it is going to help a dead man.

They can stuff cash into his pockets
They can dig a hole for him
They can shove him into it
They can snatch his spade away from him –
None of it is going to help a dead man.

They can talk about his very finest moments
They can see that those moments get forgotten
They can live much better lives or worse ones –
None of it is going to help a dead man.

III The Impact of the Cities
1925–1928

(Completion and first production of *Man equals man*. Revision and Berlin production of *Baal*. Writing and production of *The Little Mahagonny* and *The Threepenny Opera*. Compilation of the *Berlin Requiem*. Work on the opera *Rise and Fall of the City of Mahagonny* and on the *Fatzer* project.)

In the beginning
It was grassland from the
Atlantic ocean to the still pacific sea
Bears and buffalo
Ran along the nameless Mississippi
And the red man
Ate their bloody flesh and his horse
The grass.
One day a man with white skin came
He roared and spewed out chunks of iron
When he was hungry and he was
Always hungry.
Red man murdered red man
Still on the river Mississippi but already
The white man passed by, some white men
With fiery water chunks of iron and the good book bible
And soon
There were chunks of iron in red men and bears and buffalo.
Three times one hundred years between the
Atlantic ocean and the silent pacific sea
The red man died
But
The rivers divided and the white man
Lifted the yellow metal out of them
And the ground tore apart under his hand
And out of it ran
The golden oil and all around
Wooden huts grew out of rotting grass and
Out of the wooden huts grew mountains of stone they were
Called cities. Into them went
The white people and said on the earth
A new age had broken out that is called: the Iron.
But the cities
Burned all night long
With the golden electricity

And by day
The decaying woods fell thundering upward: the trains.
Buffalo and red man
Had died out; however
There were oil and iron and gold more than water
And with music and shrieking the white people sat
In the eternal prairies of stone.
But the states that were there were called:
Arkansas, Connecticut, Ohio
New York, New Jersey and Massachusetts
And today still
There are oil and men and it is said
It is the greatest race on earth
That lives now and they all
Build houses and say
Mine is longer, and are there when there is oil
Ride in iron trains to the ends of the world
Grow wheat and sell it across the sea
And die no longer unknown but are
An eternal race in the earth's
Greatest age.

Six songs from the opera 'Rise and Fall of the City of Mahagonny'

29 DEEP IN ALASKA'S

Deep in Alaska's snow-covered forests
My three comrades and I used to cut down the mighty
Trees together and float them down the rivers.
We ate uncooked meat there and piled up money.
Seven years it took me in all
To make it to this place.

There stood the cabin where for seven winters
Our sharp knives hacked into the table our Goddams.
And we discussed where we'd best like to go to
Where we'd best like to go once we'd got enough money.
I endured the greatest hardships
To make it to this place.

When our time was over and we'd made our money
We felt we'd prefer Mahagonny to all other cities
And we came here just as quick as we could
By the shortest route.
What met our eyes was all this.
Nothing worse could occur to us
And nothing stupider cross our minds
Than to make it to this place.

30 ON THE CITIES

Underneath our cities lie sewers
With nothing in them. Overhead smoke hangs grey.
We live there still. The whole thing means nothing to us.
We're decaying fast, and slowly they too will decay.

31 MAHAGONNY THEME SONG

Never forget that food's the first thing
Second comes the sexual act
Thirdly don't forget there's boxing
Fourthly booze. It's in your contract.
But first and foremost one thing's true:
You all do all you want to do.

32 WONDERFUL IS THE FIRST APPROACH OF EVENING

Wonderful is the first approach of evening
And soft are the male exchanges in the dusk.
But it's not enough.

Soft is the solitude and stillness
And consoling the sense of concord.
But it's not enough.

Splendid is the simple existence
And beyond compare the grandeur of our world.
But it's not enough.

33 A DAMNABLE DAY WILL DAWN

Once the sky grows lighter
Then a damnable day will dawn.
But the sky is still covered up by darkness.
Just the night
Must not end yet
Just the day
Must not come.

I am afraid they will soon be here.
I must lie on the ground when once they've

Really got here.
They'll drag me off the ground then if they
Want to take me along.
Just the night
Must not end yet
Just the day
Must not come.

Put that in your pipe, old mate
And smoke it
Burn it up.
What is past and gone
Was good enough for you.
But what comes next –
Put it in your pipe, mate.
Surely the sky will long remain in darkness.
It can't get light yet
For then a damnable day will dawn.

34 BLASPHEMY

If you know of some
Thing that you can have for cash
Then you must get the cash.
If someone goes walking past who's got cash
Hit him on the head and take his cash:
Just do it!

If you'd like to live in a house
Then enter a house
And lie down on a bed.
If the wife comes in, let her live there as well.
But if the roof caves in you should go away:
Just do it!

If you come across any thought
Which you don't know

Think that thought in your head.
Though it costs you cash, takes over your house:
Think it out! Think it out!
Just do it!

For the sake of good order
And aiding the State
For the future of mankind
And promoting your own well-being
Just do it!

35   SONG OF THE FLOW OF THINGS

Often as you may see the river sluggishly flowing
Each time the water is different.
What's gone down can't come up again. Not one drop
Ever flows back to its starting point.
   Don't try to brush away the wave
   That's breaking against your foot: so long as
   It stands in the stream fresh waves
   Will be always breaking against it.

I was seven years in one place, had a roof over
My head
And was not alone.
But the man who kept me fed and who was not like anyone else
One day
Lay unrecognisable beneath a dead man's shroud.
All the same that evening I ate my supper.
And soon I let off the room in which we had
Embraced one another
And the room kept me fed
And now that it no longer feeds me
I continue to eat.
I said:

Don't try to brush away the wave
That's breaking against your foot: so long as
It stands in the stream fresh waves
Will be always breaking against it.

In this way I too had a name
And those who heard that name in the city said 'It's a good name'
But one night I drank four glasses of schnapps
And one morning I found chalked on my door
A bad word.
Then the milkman took back my milk again.
My name was finished.
Like linen that once was white and gets dirty
And can go white once more if you wash it
But hold it up to the light, and look: it's not
The same linen.
So don't speak your name so distinctly. What is the point?
Considering that you are always using it to name a different
        person.
And wherefore such loud opinions? Forget them.
What where they, did you say? Never remember
Anything longer than its own duration.
    Don't try to brush away the wave
    That's breaking against your foot: so long as
    It stands in the stream fresh waves
    Will be always breaking against it.

I spoke to many people and listened
Carefully and heard many opinions
And heard many say of many things: 'That is for sure'.
But when they came back they spoke differently from the way
        they spoke earlier
And it was something else of which they said: 'That is for sure'.
At that I told myself: of all sure things
The surest is doubt.

Don't try to brush away the wave
That's breaking against your foot: so long as
It stands in the stream fresh waves
Will be always breaking against it.

36 THE HORROR OF BEING POOR

I write off
(Lightly cancelling them without bitterness)
All those I know, myself included.
None of them will ever again
In future
Make me bitter.

The horror of being poor!
Many claimed they could bear it, but just look
At their faces a year or so later.
Lavatory smells and mouldy wallpaper
Overthrew those broad-shouldered men like bulls.
Watery vegetables
Thwart plans that will make a people strong.
Without bathwater, solitude and tobacco
Nothing can be demanded.
The public's contempt
Breaks one's backbone.
The poor man
Is not on his own. Everyone keeps
Peering into his room. Gnawing
At his plate. He wonders where to go.
The heavens are his roof, it rains on him.
The earth shrugs him off. The wind
Knows him not. The night makes a cripple of him. The day
Strips him naked. There is nothing to the money a man has. It
    will not save him.
But nothing helps the man
Who has no money.

37 THE SONG OF SURABAYA JOHNNY

1

I was just past my sixteenth birthday
When you drops in one day from the blue
And you says to come wiv' you to Burma
And to leave all the fixin' to you.
I asks you what job you was doing
And I swear that you answered to me
You was something to do with the railway
And 'ad nothing to do with the sea.
You talked a lot, Johnny
A lot of lies, Johnny
You took me for a ride, Johnny, all along the line.
I 'ates you so, Johnny
Your grinnin' there, Johnny –
Take that pipe out of your mouth, you swine.
   Surabaya Johnny, done the worst that you know.
   Surabaya Johnny, ah gawd, I love you so.
   Surabaya Johnny, where can I 'ide or go?
   You've got not 'eart, Johnny, yet I do love you so.

2

At first I was walkin' on roses
Till the day when I went off wiv' you
But I got on your nerves in a fortnight
And I guessed we was just about through.
We went 'iking all over the Punjab
Then driftin' downstream to the sea
Till I looks to meself in the mirror
Like a middle-aged 'ore on a spree.
You didn't want love, Johnny
You wanted cash, Johnny
I watched your mouth, Johnny, I knew the sign.
You asked a lot, Johnny
I gave you more, Johnny –
Take that pipe out of your mouth, you swine.

Surabaya Johnny, done the worst that you know.
Surabaya Johnny, ah gawd, I love you so.
Surabaya Johnny, where can I 'ide or go?
You've got no 'eart, Johnny, yet I do love you so.

3
I 'adn't the sense to wonder
'Ow you'd earned that particular name
But that coastline consisted of places
Where it turned out you often came.
One mornin' we'll wake in our lodgin's
And we'll hear the sea poundin' the rocks
And you'll get up and walk off in silence
'Cos your ship will be down at the docks.
You've got no 'eart, Johnny
You're no damn good, Johnny
You've gone away, Johnny, without a line.
I'm still in love, Johnny
Like at the start, Johnny –
Take that pipe out of your mouth, you swine.
Surabaya Johnny, done the worst that you know.
Surabaya Johnny, ah gawd, I love you so.
Surabaya Johnny, where can I 'ide or go?
You've got no 'eart, Johnny, yet I do love you so.

38 JENNY'S SONG

1

Now, you gents, hear what my mother told me.
She thought me a shocking case:
I'd end on a slab in the mortuary
Or in some even more shocking place.
Well, that's the sort of thing a mother says.
Yes, but I'm telling you it doesn't count.
It won't put me off in the least.
If you want to know what comes of me, just wait!
A girl's not a beast.
    You lies in your bed as you made it
    For the law of the jungle is strict
    And it's me what is doing the kicking
    And it's you what is going to get kicked.

2

Now, you gents, hear what my fellow told me.
He gave me a look and said:
'Of all things on earth love's the greatest'
And 'Tomorrow's a long way ahead'.
Oh, 'love's' such an easy word to speak
But when you're growing older day by day
It's no longer love that you seek.
So best use the little time that's left you.
A girl's not a beast.
    You lies in your bed as you made it
    For the law of the jungle is strict
    And it's me what is doing the kicking
    And it's you what is going to get kicked.

Thirteen songs from 'The Threepenny Opera'

39 PIRATE JENNY

My fine gentlemen, to-day you may see me wash the glasses
And see me make the beds each morning.
And I thank you for your penny and you think I'm pleased as hell
For you only see my ragged frock and this dirty old hotel
And there's no one to give you a warning.
But one fine night there'll be yelling in the harbour
And they'll ask: Who is making all the row?
And they'll see me smiling as I wash my glasses
And they'll say: What's she smiling at, now?
    And a ship with eight sails
    And with fifty big cannon
    Will be moored to the quay.

Someone'll say: Go and dry your glasses, child.
He'll give me a penny, like the rest.
And the penny will be taken
And the bed be made, all right,
But nobody's going to sleep in it that night
And who I really am they still won't have guessed.
And that evening there'll be a din in the harbour
And they'll ask: What is making all that din?
And they'll see me standing watching at the window
And say: Why has she got that nasty grin?
    And the ship with eight sails
    And with fifty big cannon,
    Will shoot at the town.

My fine gentlemen, that'll wipe the smiles off your faces,
For the walls will open gaping wide
And the town will tumble down flat to the ground
But a dirty old hotel will stay standing safe and sound
And they'll ask: What big swell lives inside?

All night long there'll be a yelling round about that hotel
And they'll ask: Why is it treated with such care?
And then they'll see me stepping from the door in the morning
And they'll say: What! Did *she* live there?
   And the ship with eight sails
   And with fifty big cannon
   Will beflag her masts.

And at midday there'll be coming a hundred men on land
And the hunt in dark corners will begin
And they'll enter every house, take every soul they see
And throw them into irons and bring them straight to me
And ask: Which of these shall we do in?
And that midday it will be quiet down by the harbour
When they ask who has got to die.
And then they'll hear me answer: All of them!
And as the heads fall I shall cry: Hoppla!
   And the ship with eight sails
   And with fifty big cannon
   Will vanish with me.

40 BARBARA SONG

When I was only a simple little girl –
For I once was simple just like you –
I thought: perhaps some day there'll come someone
And then I'll have to know what to do.
And if he's got money
And if he's a nice boy
And if his workday collar's white as snow
And if he knows how a lady should be treated
Then I shall tell him: 'No'.
For you must talk about the weather.
And never let your feelings show.
The moon will shine all night, as before;
Certainly the boat will be tied to the shore.
But that's as far as it may go.

O, a girl can't afford to make herself too cheap!
O, a girl must keep her man well in tow.
Or else all sorts of things might happen!
Ah, the only answer is: No.

The first one who came, he was a man from Kent
And all that a man should be.
The second owned three steamers in the harbour
And the third was wild about me.
And as they'd got money
And as they were nice boys
With their workday collars white as snow
And as they knew how a lady should be treated
I said to all three: 'No'.
So I talked about the weather,
Never let my feelings show.
And the moon shone all night, as before;
Certainly the boat was tied to the shore,
But that was as far as it could go.
　　O, a girl can't afford to make herself too cheap!
　　O, I had to keep my man well in tow.
　　Or else all sorts of things might have happened!
　　Ah, the only answer was: No.

But then one fine morning, when the sky was blue,
Came a man who did not sigh
But just hung his hat up on the peg in my bedroom
And I let him, and didn't know why.
And as he had no money
And as he wasn't a nice boy
And even his Sunday collar wasn't white as snow
And as he didn't know how a lady should be treated
To him I couldn't say No.
Then I didn't talk about the weather
And I let my feelings show.
Ah, the moon shone all night, as before;
But the boat was cast loose and put out from the shore,

It all had to be just so!
    O, sometimes a girl must make herself cheap!
    O, sometimes she can't keep her man in tow.
    But then, ah, anything may happen!
    And there's no such word as No.

41 BALLADE OF GOOD LIVING

I've heard them praising single-minded spirits
Whose empty stomachs show they live for knowledge
In rat-infested shacks which once held forage.
I'm all for culture, but there are some limits.
The simple life is fine for those it suits.
I'm not the type that sort of life attracts.
There's not a bird from here to Halifax
Would peck at such unappetising fruits.
        What use is freedom? In a world like this
        Only the rich can know what living is.

The dashing sort who cut precarious capers
And go and risk their necks just for the pleasure
Then swagger home and write it up at leisure
And flog the story to the Sunday papers –
If you could see how cold they get at night
Sullen, with chilly wife, in clammy bed
And how they dream they're going to get ahead
And see their future stretching out of sight –
        Now tell me, who would choose to live like this?
        Only the rich can know what living is.

There's plenty that they have. I know I lack it
And ought to join their splendid isolation
But when I gave it more consideration
I told myself: my friend, that's not your racket.
Suffering ennobles, but it can depress.
The paths of glory lead but to the grave.

You once were poor and lonely, wise and brave.
You ought to try to bite off rather less.
> The search for happiness boils down to this:
> Only the rich can know what living is.

42   BALLAD OF IMMORAL EARNINGS

There was a time, now very far away
When we set up together, I and she.
I'd got the brains, and she supplied the breast.
I saw her right, and she looked after me –
A way of life then, if not quite the best.
And when a client came I'd slide out of our bed
And treat him nice, and go and have a drink instead
And when he paid up I'd address him: Sir
Come any time you feel you fancy her.
Those days are past, but what would I now give
To see that whorehouse where we used to live?

That was the time, now very far away
He was so sweet and bashed me where it hurt.
And when the cash ran out the feathers really flew
He'd up and say: I'm going to pawn your skirt.
A skirt is nicer, but no skirt will do.
Just like his cheek, he had me fairly stewing
I'd ask him what the hell he fancied he was doing
Then he'd lash out and knock me down the stairs.
I had the bruises off and on for years.
Those days are past, but what would I now give
To see that whorehouse where we used to live.

That was the time, now very far away –
Not that the bloody times seem to have looked up
When afternoons were all I had for you
(I told you she was generally booked up.
The night's more normal, but daytime will do).

Once I was pregnant, so the doctor said.
So we reversed positions on the bed.
He thought his weight might make it premature.
But in the end we flushed it down the sewer.
That could not last, but what would I now give
To see that whorehouse where we used to live?

43 BALLAD IN WHICH MACHEATH
BEGS ALL MEN FOR FORGIVENESS

You fellow men who live on after us
Pray do not think you have to judge us harshly
And when you see us hoisted up and trussed
Don't laugh like fools behind your big moustaches
Or curse at us. It's true that we came crashing
But do not judge our downfall like the courts.
Not all of us can discipline our thoughts –
Dear fellows, your extravagance needs slashing
Dear fellows, I've shown how a crash begins.
Pray then to God that He forgive my sins.

The rain washes away and purifies.
Let it wash down the flesh we fed too well
We, who saw so much more than we could tell –
The crows will come and peck away our eyes.
Perhaps ambition used too sharp a goad
It drove us to these heights from which we swing
Hacked at by greedy starlings on the wing
Like horses' droppings on a country road.
Oh brothers, learn from us how it begins
And pray to God that He forgive our sins.

The girls who flaunt their breasts as bait there
To catch some sucker who will love them
The youths who slyly stand and wait there
To grab their sinful earnings off them

The crooks, the tarts, the tarts' protectors
The models and the mannequins
The psychopaths, the unfrocked rectors
I pray that they forgive my sins.

Not so those filthy police employees
Who day by day enflamed my anger
Thought up new troubles to annoy me
And chucked me crusts to feed my hunger.
I'd call on God to come and choke them
Yet now a softer mood begins:
I realise how that might provoke them
And pray that they forgive my sins.

Someone must take a giant crowbar
And batter in their ugly chins
But now I know the whole thing's over
I pray that they forgive my sins.

44 SOLOMON SONG

You saw sagacious Solomon
You know what came of him.
To him complexities seemed plain.
He cursed the hour that gave birth to him.
And saw that everything was vain.
How great and wise was Solomon!
    The world however couldn't wait
    And quickly saw what followed on.
    It's wisdom that had got him in that state –
    How fortunate the man with none!

You saw the lovely Cleopatra
You know what she became.
Two emperors slaved to serve her lust.
She whored herself to death and fame

Then rotted down and turned to dust.
How beautiful was Babylon!
  The world however couldn't wait
  And quickly saw what followed on.
  It's beauty that had got her in that state –
  How fortunate the girl with none!

You saw the gallant Caesar next
You know what he became.
They deified him in his life
Then had him murdered just the same.
And as they raised the fatal knife
How loud he cried, 'You too, my son!'
  The world however couldn't wait
  And quickly saw what followed on
  It's courage that had got him in that state –
  How fortunate the man with none!

And now look at Macheath and me
The sands are running out.
If only he'd known where to stop
And stuck to crimes he knew all about
He surely would have reached the top.
But suddenly his heart was won.
  The world however couldn't wait
  And quickly saw what followed on.
  His sexual urges got him in that state –
  How fortunate the man with none!

45 BALLAD OF SEXUAL OBSESSION

There goes an evil man who loves a battle:
The butcher, he. And all the others, cattle.
The cocky sod! No decent place lets him in.
Who does him down, that downs all others? Women.
Want it or not, he can't ignore that call.
Sexual obsession has him in its thrall.

He doesn't read the Bible, sniggers at the law.
Sets out to be an utter egotist
And knows a woman's skirts are what he must resist
So when a woman calls he locks his door.
So far, so good, but what's the future brewing?
As soon as night falls he'll be up and doing.

Thus many a man observed the sad conclusion:
A mighty genius, stuck on prostitution!
While as for those whose urges were exhausted
Once they'd collapsed, who paid the funeral? Whores did.
Want it or not, they can't ignore that call.
Sexual obsession has them in its thrall.
    Some fall back on the Bible. Some set out to change the law.
    Some turn to Christ, and some turn anarchist.
    At lunch you pick the best wine on the list
    And then you meditate on what life's for.
    At tea: what noble aims you are pursuing!
    Then soon as night falls you'll be up and doing.

There stands a man. The gallows loom above him.
They've got the quicklime mixed in which to shove him.
They've put his neck just under where the noose is
And what's he thinking of, the idiot? Floozies.
They've all but hanged him, yet he hears the call.
Sexual obsession has him in its thrall.
    She's sold him down the river, shopped him heart and
        soul
    He's seen the filthy money in her hand.
    And bit by bit begins to understand:
    The pit that covers him is woman's hole.
    Then he may rant and roar and curse his ruin –
    But soon as night falls he'll be up and doing.

46   APPEAL FROM THE GRAVE

Hark to the voice that's telling you to weep.
Macheath lies here, not under open sky
Not under treetops, no, but good and deep.
Fate struck him down in outraged majesty.
God grant his dying words may reach a friend.
The thickest walls encompass him about.
Are none of you concerned to know his fate?
Once he is gone the bottles can come out
But do stand by him while it's not too late.
D'you want his punishment to have no end?

Come here and see the shitty state he's in.
This really is what people mean by bust.
You who set up the dirty cash you win
As just about the only god you'll trust
Don't stand and watch him slipping round the bend!
Go to the Queen and say her subjects need her
Go in a group and tell her of his trouble
Like pigs all following behind their leader.
Say that his teeth are wearing down to rubble.
D'you want his punishment to have no end?

47   SECOND THREEPENNY FINALE

You gentlemen who think you have a mission
To purge us of the seven deadly sins
Should first sort out the basic food position
Then start your preaching. That's where it begins.
You who prescribe restraint and watch your weight as well
Should learn for all time how the world is run:
However much you twist, whatever lies you tell
Food is the first thing. Morals follow on.
So first make sure that those who now are starving
Get proper helpings when we start the carving

What keeps mankind alive? The fact that millions
Are daily tortured, stifled, punished, silenced, oppressed.
Mankind can keep alive thanks to its brilliance
In keeping its humanity repressed.
You gentlemen must learn to face the facts:
Mankind is kept alive by evil acts.

You say that girls may strip with your permission.
You draw the line dividing art from sin.
So first sort out the basic food position
Then start your preaching, that's where we begin.
You men who bank on your desires and our disgust
Must learn for all time how this world is run:
Whatever lies you tell, however much you twist
Food is the first thing. Morals follow on.
So first make sure that those who now are starving
Get proper helpings when we start the carving
　What keeps mankind alive? The fact that millions
　Are daily tortured, stifled, punished, silenced, oppressed.
　Mankind can keep alive thanks to its brilliance
　In keeping its humanity repressed.
　You gentlemen must learn to face the facts:
　Mankind is kept alive by evil acts.

48 LOVE SONG

MAC: Look at the moon over Soho.
POLLY: I see it, dearest. Feel my heart beating, my
　　　beloved.
MAC: I feel it, my beloved.
POLLY: Where'er you go I shall be with you.
MAC: And where you stay, there too shall I be.
BOTH:
　　　　And though we've no licence to say we're wed
　　　　And there's no altar covered with flowers

And no one can tell for whom your dress was made
And even the ring is not ours –
That platter, off which you are eating your bread
Give it one brief look; fling it far.
For love will endure or will not endure
Regardless of where we are.

49 SONG OF THE INADEQUACY OF HUMAN ENDEAVOUR

Mankind lives by its head
Its head won't see it through
Inspect your own. What lives off that?
At most a louse or two.
　For this bleak existence
　Man is seldom sharp enough.
　Hence his weak resistance
　To all its tricks and bluff.

Aye, make yourself a plan
They need you at the top!
Then make yourself a second plan
Then let the whole thing drop.
　For this bleak existence
　Man is seldom bad enough
　Though his sheer persistence
　Can be lovely stuff.

Aye, race for happiness
But don't you race too fast.
When all chase after happiness
Happiness comes in last.
　For this bleak existence
　Man is never reticent enough.
　All his loud insistence
　Is a load of guff.

Man could be good instead
So slug him on the head
If you can slug him good and hard
He may stay good and dead.
   For this bleak existence
   Man's not good enough as yet.
   Don't expect assistance.
   Slug him on the head.

50   THE CRIMES OF MAC THE KNIFE

See the shark with teeth like razors.
And he wears them in his face.
And Macheath has got a knife, but
Not in such an obvious place.

See the shark, how red his fins are
As he slashes at his prey.
Mac the Knife wears white kid gloves which
Give the minimum away.

By the Thames's turbid waters
Men abruptly tumble down.
Is it plague or is it cholera?
Or because Macheath's in town?

On a shining sky-blue Sunday
See a corpse stretched in the Strand.
See a man dodge round the corner –
Mackie's friends will understand.

And Schmul Meier, posted missing
Like so many wealthy men:
Mac the Knife acquired his cash box
God alone knows how or when.

Jenny Towler turned up lately
With a knife stuck through her breast
While Macheath walks the Embankment
Nonchalantly unimpressed.

Where is Alfons Gleet the cabman?
Who can get that story clear?
Someone may lay information
But Macheath has no idea.

And the ghastly fire in Soho –
Seven children at a go –
In the crowd stands Mac the Knife, but he
Isn't asked and doesn't know.

And the child-bride in her nightie
Whose assailant's still at large
Violated in her slumbers –
Mackie, how much did you charge?

51 CHORALE

Injustice must be spared from persecution:
Soon it will freeze to death, for it is cold.
Think of the blizzards and the dark confusion
The cries of pain that echo through this world.

IV Songs of the Crisis Years
1929–1933

(Writing and production of *Happy End*: end of involvement at the Theater am Schiffbauerdamm. First 'Lehrstücke' with Weill and Hindemith followed by *The Decision* and *The Mother* with Eisler. Evolution of the 'Kampflied' or militant communist song. Films: Pabst's *Threepenny Opera* and the collectively made *Kuhle Wampe*.)

52 RED ROSA

Red Rosa also, it seems, has gone.
She is dead
And where she now lies is quite unknown.
She told the poor the truth, with such persistence
The rich expunged her from this existence.
Rest in peace.

53 THE LOVERS

See those wild cranes in a great circle sweeping!
The clouds that lie behind them, soft and gentle
Started to drift with them as they were leaving
Their old life for a new one. Thus they went, all
At the same height and with the same haste soaring
Both of them seeming merely incidental.
That cloudbank and wild bird should thus fly sharing
The lovely sky which each so quickly covers
That therefore neither lingers in this clearing
And neither see a thing except how wavers
The other in the wind which both feel brush them
Who now in flight lie alongside each other.
So into nothingness the wind may thrust them
If neither of them alters or disperses
So long will nothing have the power to touch them
So long can they be chased away from all these places
Where storms are threatening or shots re-echo.
So, under sun's and moon's but slightly differing faces
They fly away, each merging in his fellow.
Where going? . . Nowhere much . . Away from whom? . . All of
      you.
That is a loving pair.
You may ask: how long have they been together? . . A short
      while.
And how will they go on after? — Apart.
So lovers find in love a firm support.

Eight songs from 'Happy End'

54 IN THOSE GOLDEN DAYS

In those golden days of childhood
Mother's hand was warm and kind.
Now she's gone, and left us stranded
And we've left those days behind.

Once we heard the church bells tolling –
Golden echoes far away –
Gently chiding and cajoling
And we hear their tones today.

55 GOD'S LITTLE LIEUTENANT

I
Watchful, be watchful.
Look! there's a man going down.
There's a child in need of rescue.
There's a girl about to drown.
Stop all those motorcars, hold up that tram
So many people sinking and no one gives a damn.
Keep your eyes open wide
Remember all your brothers for whom you must provide.
Abandon your good dinner
Remember you're a sinner
And thousands wait outside.

I hear you saying nobody can change this
For inequality is ours from birth.
But now I'm telling you it's time we acted
And set ourselves to sweep it from the earth.
So now let's get tanks to move up here
And warships we'll mobilise

And bombers shall blacken the skies
All to gain a bowl of soup to make the poor man's supper.
Yes, it's now that we have to go forward
Let no one ignore our call.
Don't forget the poor are
The mightiest army of all.
　By the right! 'Tention! Let's hear those rifles slam!
　So many people sinking and who gives a damn?

2

Watchful, be watchful.
We've seen you, man going down.
We hear you calling for rescue.
We see you, girl who could drown.
Stop all those motorcars, hold up that tram
We've come to stop you sinking, we do give a damn.
You who may not survive
Behold us now, my brothers, we're hurrying to your side.
Sit up and eat the dinner
That we have come to bring you
As you wait there outside.

So never say that nobody can change this
That inequality is ours from birth.
Once you decide to join in and march forward
And set yourselves to sweep it from the earth
And get all those tanks to move up here
Get warships to mobilise
And bombers to blacken the skies
Then, my brother, you will have potatoes for your supper.

No, don't forget that you poor are
The mightiest army of all
That's why we should now move forward
Till everyone hears our call.
　By the right! 'Tention! Let's hear those rifles slam!
　Courage, all you who were sinking! We're coming. Here I am.

56 BILBAO SONG

Bill's Ballroom in Bilbao
Was the best in any transatlantic port.
You paid a dollar there for bliss and rumpus
And for a bit of indoor sport.
Just imagine someone tempted you to walk in
(I can't say how much you'd reckon that was worth)
Oh
Brandy lay in puddles on your chair.
There was grass growing up the stair.
Through the ceiling you could see the moon
While the band drowned all the sound of talking
And of mirth.
Joe, can you remember that old tune?
  Good old Bilbao moon
  You should have heard me croon –
  Funny old words
  It's all so long ago.
  I'm not so sure what you would think all that was worth, but–
  It was the finest
  It was the finest
  Place on earth.

2
Bill's Ballroom in Bilbao . . .
When in 1908 towards the end of May
Four guys got in from Frisco with their bankrolls
They smashed the place to pieces one fine day.
Just imagine they'd persuaded you to walk in:
(I can't say how much you'd reckon that was worth)
Oh
Brandy lay in puddles on one's chair
There was grass growing up the stair.
Through the ceiling one could see the moon.
You'd have heard those four guys get their Brownings barking.

How's your nerve?
Well, then, try to pick up this old tune:
   Good old Bilbao moon
   Love in a cheap saloon –
   It won't come back to me
   It's been too long, you see –
   I'm not so sure what you would think all that was worth, but
   It was the finest
   It was the finest
   Place on earth.

3
Bill's Ballroom in Bilbao . . .
Oh, they run it more discreetly nowadays
With palm trees and an icecream soda fountain . . .
Like a perfectly average place.
But suppose you chose to pop in for a minute
You might hope at last to get your money's worth.
Pooey!
All that grass has been cut and cleared
And the brandy has disappeared
And the moon must have been strangled at birth
And the band is making such a filthy din, it
Costs the earth.
Joe, would you just play us that old tune?
   Good old Bilbao moon
   That's what I used to croon
   You should have seen them swoon.
   It went something like that – So sorry
   Good old Bilbao moon
   It's too long ago . . .
   I'm not so sure what you would think all that was worth, but
   It was the finest
   It was the finest
   Place on earth –
   It was too long ago.

57   THE SAILORS' SONG

I

Ahoy! we're sailing off to Burma this morning
Whisky by the gallon at our elbow all day
As we smoke our fat cigars – Henry Clay
And I'm through with bloody girls ('scuse me yawning).
So at last we're really under way.
For other brands of cigar mean nothing to us
And we've only just enough smoke to take her to Burma
And as for God, we think He's not worth the fuss
And of religion you won't hear a murmur.
So now it's goodbye!

Then we'll sail where we will, and let's hope we survive
As for God, He's much too far above it
And I don't suppose He'll give a damn if we don't arrive.
If He does, then He knows where He can shove it.
So now it's goodbye!

With 'I'm all right, Jack' and it's 'Up yours, my dear!'
Write and tell when there's something amusing.
As for delicate feelings, we don't want them here
For what's left for us now, but boozing?
    And the sea is blue as blue
    And everything's as right as rain
    And when the whole thing's over
    You bet we'll start again.

2

Ahoy! Supposing we went off to see the cinema —
Better than read all those books on the shelves.
We're not the sort of blokes to let the time slip by.
Got to have entertainment to keep us out of mischief
For we write the bloody rules ourselves.

Errata

Page 51, poem 37, last line of first stanza. For 'not 'eart' read 'no 'eart'.

Page 71, poem 53, line 10. For 'see' read 'sees'.

Page 94, poem 71, section II, line 13. For 'statesmen, statesmen' read 'statesmen, statesman'.

Page 114, poem 94, first line. For 'But he went' read 'But when he went'.

Page 192, poem 160, line 9. For 'on' read 'in'.

Page 204, poem 169, line 3. For 'The' read 'Then'.

Page 266, chronological list, under 122 bracketed date should be '1939'.

Page 267, list of translators, under Christopher Isherwood add '39, 40'.

Cigars for less than five cents are no use to us
And rye bread affects the digestion.
Other people's affairs are just not worth the fuss
And our own we would sooner not question.
We look after ourselves.

So let's do what we will, and let's hope we survive
As for God, He's much too far above it
And I don't suppose He cares a damn if we don't arrive.
If He does, then He knows where he can shove it.
Yes, live and let live!

With 'I'm all right, Jack' and it's 'Up yours, my dear!'
Write and tell when there's something amusing.
As for delicate feelings, we don't want them here
For what's left for us now, but boozing?
    Oh, the sea is blue as blue
    And we'll sail the Spanish Main
    And when the whole thing's over
    You bet we'll start again.

3
(Now all we want is for a storm to start blowing.)
My God, I see the docks of Burma!
Idiot, it's only a vast black wall of cloud!
What, with waves like that? They shouldn't be allowed.
Hey, man, those waves could gulp us down without a murmur!

Yes, this will put paid to all our crowd.
Yes, it's putting paid to all our crowd.
Quickly the ship goes down, the sea washes over
None but the sharks will see the men who die today.
They'll have no use for whisky or for Henry Clay
They're off to where no girl follows her lover
So now it really is goodbye.

And the sea's whipping up, and the ship's going down
As the black wrath of heaven squats above it

Just a ship that won't float, just some men that will drown
Well, at last they'll find where they can shove it.
So now it's goodbye.

Then suddenly all that bragging talk will disappear
Until all of them seem like little midgets
And you will hear them try to articulate a prayer
In order to tell us that they never did it.

So now that is it.
And now hear what I've got to tell you: your type are well
     known
You're all piss and wind, your body rotten with liquors
But once you appear before God's throne
Just won't you be wetting your knickers!
    Oh the sea is blue as blue –
    And everything is right as rain.
    But when the whole thing's over
    It cannot start again.
    Oh the sea is blue as blue
    As the poets all maintain
    Oh the sea is blue as blue, yes, the sea is blue.

58   THE SONG OF MANDALAY

Mother Goddam's House in Mandalay
Dirty little hut beside the bay
Goddam, the finest knocking-shop you ever saw
With fifteen randy men in a queue outside the door
Watches in their hands, hip hip hooray!
Are they short of tarts in Mandalay?
    Tarts are just the greatest thing on earth
    And you always get your money's worth.
    Yes, in my opinion life would be ideal
    If the bloke before me weren't so bloody slow.
    Better fire your pistol through the keyhole –

Make him realise he's holding up the show.
Quicker, Johnny, hey! Quicker, Johnny, hey!
While we sing the song of Mandalay:
Love is a sport to be kept within limits.
Johnny, be quick, for we're counting the minutes
And the moon won't shine forever on you, Mandalay.
And the moon won't shine forever on you.

Mother Goddam's House in Mandalay
Now it's at the bottom of the bay.
Goddam, the finest knocking-shop you ever saw
But where there was a queue once, there ain't a queue no more—
No more watches, no hip hip hooray.
All the tarts have gone from Mandalay.
When you used to see tarts walk the earth
Then you'd always get your money's worth.
Now they've gone it's simply shattered our ideal
Knocking-shops like this one got dealt a mortal blow.
Same goes for the gun and for the keyhole:
Take away the tarts and you've wrecked the show
Quicker, Johnny, hey! Quicker, Johnny, hey!
While we sing the song of Mandalay:
Love is a sport to be kept within limits.
Johnny, be quick, for we're counting the minutes
And the moon won't shine forever on you, Mandalay.
And the moon won't shine forever on you.

59 SONG OF THE TOUGH NUT

If you want to be a big shot
Better toughen up your nut
'Cause you'll never hit the jackpot
If your nut starts going phut.
See the big shot strip for action
As he stoops to take his cut
Then the small man's sole protection

Is the toughness of his nut.
So don't you weaken
Just never let yourself weaken
But take a cosh and coolly slug him on the nut.
He may be neck-deep in the mire and sinking deeper
But don't you fret, old boy, you're not your brother's keeper
And don't you weaken
Just never let yourself weaken.
First catch him defenceless
Then you bash him till he's senseless.

60 BALLAD OF THE LILY OF HELL

1
When you watch the hellfire licking
Round my feet down in the pit
You may think 'That's one more chicken
Getting roasted on the spit' –
Wait for it:
     That won't come until tomorrow
     And tomorrow's not my sorrow.
     What's tomorrow? I don't care
     (You can stuff it you know where.)
     Thoughts for the morrow never pay
     Tomorrow you regret what you did today –
     Sooner or later you'll die anyway.
     Good thing too, if I may say.
     (You can stuff it you know where.)

2
But once you begin believing
That you're treating me too well
It's yourselves you'll be deceiving
For I really am in hell –
Wait for it:

Don't let that be ground for sorrow
Sure, you'll put it right tomorrow
But don't kid yourselves I'll care
(You can stuff it you know where.)
Thoughts for the morrow never pay
Tomorrow you regret what you did today –
Sooner or later you'll die anyway.
Good thing too, if I may say.
(You can stuff it you know where.)

3
As I raise my eyes in yearning
Up to God's last Judgement Seat
P'raps he'll make me go on burning.
P'raps he may turn off the heat.
Wait for it:
    We can leave it till tomorrow
    And tomorrow's not my sorrow.
    What's tomorrow? I don't care
    (You can stuff it you know where.)
    Thoughts for the morrow never pay
    Tomorrow you regret what you did today –
    Sooner or later you'll die anyway.
    Good thing too, if I may say.
    (You can stuff it you know where.)

61 HOSANNA ROCKEFELLER

Treat Thou the rich to Thy treasure
Hosanna! Hosanna!
And virtue and leisure
Hosanna! Hosanna!
Give him that hath: a hand

Hosanna!
Give him the state and the land
Hosanna!
Give to the winner in full measure!
Hosanna! Hosanna!

Hosanna Rockefeller
Hosanna Henry Ford
Hosanna coal and steel and oil
Hosanna God's own Word.

Grant to the rich man Thy pity
Hosanna! Hosanna!
Take him into Thy City
Hosanna! Hosanna!
Temper Thy wrath
Hosanna!
Do not chastise him that hath
Hosanna!
Look on the well-fed with pity
Hosanna! Hosanna!

Hosanna Rockefeller
Hosanna Henry Ford
Hosanna coal and steel and oil
Hosanna God's own Word.

All to gain a bowl of soup to make the poor man's supper.

Help Thine own Class which hath helped Thee
Hosanna! Hosanna!
Not stinting Thy spending
Hosanna! Hosanna!
Destroy the roots of hate
Hosanna!
Smile with the smilers, and may't
Lead all their crimes to a happy ending
Hosanna! Hosanna!

Hosanna Rockefeller
Hosanna Henry Ford
Hosanna coal and steel and oil
Hosanna God's own Word
Hosanna sex appeal
Hosanna Duke and Lord
Hosanna Faith and ten per cent
Hosanna fire and sword.

62 IDEOLOGY

1

Many say time is ancient
But I always knew this was a new time.
I tell you it is no accident
That for twenty years buildings have shot up like bronze
        mountains
Many move each year expectantly to the cities.
And on the laughing continents
The word gets round that the great and awful ocean
Is a tiny puddle.
Today I am making the first flight across the Atlantic
But I am convinced: by tomorrow
You will be laughing at my flight.

2

Yet it is a battle against what is backward
And a strenuous effort to improve the planet
Like dialectical economics
Which will change the world from the bottom up.
So now
Let us battle with nature
Till we ourselves have become natural.
We and our technology are not natural as yet

We and our technology
Are backward.
The steamer competed with the sailing ship
Which had left the rowing boat far behind.
I
Am competing with the steamer
In the struggle against what is backward.
My aeroplane, weak and tremulous
My equipment with all its defects
Are better than their precursors, but
In flying I
Struggle with my aeroplane and
With what is backward.

3
So I struggle with nature and
With myself.
Whatever I may be and whatever idiocies I believe
When I fly I am
A true atheist.

During ten thousand years, unimpeded
Where the waters grew dark in the sky
Between light and twilight, there arose
God. And in the same way
Over the mountain top, whence the ice came
Did ignorant people, incorrigible
Glimpse God, and in the same way
In the deserts he arrived in a sandstorm and
In the cities he was produced by the disorder
Of the different classes, for there are two kinds of men due to
Exploitation and ignorance; but
The revolution abolishes him. But
Build roads through the mountains and he disappears.
Rivers drive him out of the desert. The light
Shows up voids and
Scares him away at once.

Therefore take part
In the battle against what is backward
In the abolition of the other world and
The scaring away of any kind of god, where-
Ever he crops up.

Under more powerful microscopes
He collapses.
Improved equipment
Is driving him from the skies.
The clearing-up of our cities
The removal of poverty are
Causing him to vanish and
Chasing him back to the first millennium.

4
Thus there may still remain
In our improved cities confusion
Which comes from lack of knowledge and resembles God.
But the machines and the workers
Will battle against it, and you too
Take part in
The battle against what is backward.

63   DO MEN HELP EACH OTHER

One of our kind across the sea went sailing and
There he discovered an unknown continent.
But many came after and
Built in that place mighty cities with
Boundless effort and cunning.
The price of bread did not get cheaper.

One of our kind once made an engine
In which the pressure of steam made a wheel turn; and that was
The mother of many more engines.

Yet many laboured a lifetime to
Make them perfect.
The price of bread did not get cheaper.

Many of us have been drawn to meditate
On the passage of the earth through the solar system, and on
A man's inner feelings, and the laws
Governing all people, and the properties of air
And the fish in the ocean.
Very many
Great things they have discovered.
The price of bread did not get cheaper.
Rather did
Poverty and need increase inside our cities
And long years have passed since
Anyone asked what a man is.

64 THE SONG OF THE LAWCOURTS

After the thieves and bandits
The law comes scavenging.
When an innocent man has been destroyed
The judges collect round his body to condemn him.
The law will destroy
His innocence and his rights.

The words of the court at work
Cast the shadow of a slaughterer's knife.
That slaughterer's knife
Is quite sharp enough
Without the attachment called a verdict.

Vultures darken the sky.
Where are they flying?
The desert has starved them out
But the lawcourts will have plenty to nourish them.

To the courts come murderers in flight
Persecutors congregate there in safety
And there in the lawcourts
Thieves hide their stolen goods
Wrapped in a piece of paper
On which is written
The law.

65 THE 'NOTHING COMES FROM NOTHING' SONG

1
See how he rises! He comes
Irresistible, the sun in his hands.
Now he rises up
His name is: Caesar!
Hear what he says!
He is saying: I will help you.
But in reality
He helps only himself, and you
He crushes, and you
Fear him.
Who is he?
    Don't be afraid!
    Look at him.
    Wait.
    He is nothing!
    He will not last long
    He has lost his bearings
    Nothing on his own, that's him:
    He is nothing!

2
See how he rose! He came
Irresistible, the sun in his hands.

Often he rose up
Each time his name was different.
Often he said: I will help you.
But in reality
He helped only himself, and you
He crushed, and you
Feared him.
Who was he?
   He did not last long
   He had lost his own bearings
   Nothing on his own, that was him:
   He was nothing!

3

See how he descends! He goes
Irresistible, the world in his hands.
Now he descends downwards
Hear what he says!
He is saying; Who'll help me?

4

Soon you will again hear he is coming
Irresistible, the sun in his hands.
Soon he will rise up
Soon his name will be: Who knows?
Soon he will say: I will help you.
   Don't be afraid!
   Look at him.
   Wait.
   He is nothing!
   He will not last long
   He has lost his bearings
   Nothing on his own, that's him:
   He is nothing!

66 AGAIN AND AGAIN IN RENEWED CONFLICTS

Again and again in renewed conflicts
Always unfinished, always untidy
Exhausted he stands
With no prospect.

Again and again
The ground recedes
Friends fall away
Many grounds, all sorts of friends.
So he uses up all the
Meagre trust placed in him.

And he who endured endless night
Involved in conflicts
Often checking to see whose
The blood on his cheek might be
Observes
As light dawns
Facing him
Too countless to number
The young, barely diminished but
Well rested squads, his
Real enemy.

And
So stripped is he of
All means of conflict
(For he, who set out with thousands, cannot find
An evening meal for himself)
That his best and
Only hope now is
Once again
To confront all this, and to his previous
Setbacks once more to
Add a fresh one.

Four songs from the 'Breadshop' project

67 THE UNEMPLOYED

You who have just
Come from your food
Permit us to tell you of our
Unceasing concern with food like yours
(Not that something more modest would not do).

We ask you: observe us
In our unceasing search for work.
Too bad that food and work
Are subject to immutable laws
Unknown ones.

Yet ever are falling
Downwards
Through gratings in the metalled streets
All kinds of people without marks
Or description to identify them, downwards
Suddenly, silently, quickly downwards
Snatched out of the mainstream of humanity according to
No clear principle
Six out of seven downwards, but the seventh
Enters the food room.

Which of us is it? Who
Has been detailed to be saved?
Who is marked out?
Where is the grating that's nearest?
– Unknown.

68 ROUND FOR THE UNEMPLOYED

And if no wood gets chopped, then
The baker can't bake his bread
And if he cannot bake it
The woodchoppers fall down dead

And if the woodchoppers die, then
Who's he to bake it for?
And if no bread gets baked, then
Wood won't get chopped no more

69 THE WAY DOWNWARDS

Don't ask, brother
Where your way leads.
Your way leads
Downwards.

When you were one year old, brother
You began to walk
You walked –
Downwards.

You walked to school
You walked to work
You walked easily
You walked with effort
Brother, don't walk too fast
You are walking downwards.

You take a wife, brother
You and she have children
You and she together walk the way
Downwards.

On Sundays, however, you walk in procession with your
        brothers
Singing, bearing your flag before you
You walk to the pulse of a drum
Downwards.

We have marched together, brothers
We have demonstrated
We have talked about new times
We disperse.
Where
Shall we meet?
Down below.

For even you, brother
Will not always walk
Downwards.
When you are lying below the soil
You will no longer walk downwards.

70 BUT EVEN BELOW US

But even below us there are
Further levels
Below which it seems
There are
Yet further levels, and even
We unfortunates
Will one day be termed
Fortunate
By others.

71 HOLD TIGHT AND SINK

I
Leave your post.
The victories have been fought out. The defeats have been
Fought out:
Leave now your post.
Plunge back down into the depths, victor.
The acclaim gathers where the fighting was.
Do not remain there.
Await the cry of defeat at the place where it is loudest:
In the depths.
Leave your old post.

Draw in your voice, speaker.
Your name is erased from the tables. Your orders
Are not carried out. Allow
That new names appear on the tables and
New orders are obeyed.
(You who no longer give orders
Do not call for disobedience!)
Leave your old post.

You were found wanting
You were not finished
Now you have the experience and are not wanting
Now you can begin:
Leave your post.

You who controlled offices
Heat your stove.
You who had no time to eat
Cook yourself soup.
You about whom much has been written
Learn your ABC.
Start in at once:
Take up your new post.

The beaten man cannot escape
From wisdom.
Hold tight and sink! Be afraid! But sink! At the bottom
The lesson awaits you.
You who were asked too many questions
Partake of the invaluable
Teaching of the masses:
Take up your new post.

II
The table is finished, carpenter.
Allow us to take it away.
Stop that endless planing now
Leave off painting it
Speak of it neither well nor ill:
We'll take it just as it is.
We need it.
Give it up.

You are finished, statesman
The state is not finished.
Allow us to alter it
According to the needs of our life.
Allow us to be statesmen, statesmen.
Under your laws stands your name.
Forget the name
Obey your laws, lawgiver.

Accept the rules, ruler.
The state needs you no longer
Give it up.

Three songs from the 'Threepenny Opera' film treatment

72 THE WHITEWASH SONG

Once the rot sets in and all your walls start peeling
You will need to act without delay
Or the damp could spread and reach the ceiling
Till you want to turn your eyes away.
So it's whitewash you need, lovely whitewash you need.
When the roof falls in it will be far too late.
Yes, it's whitewash you need, so let's give a new lead
And restore the whole thing to its pristine state.

But you'll soon see even vaster
Patches of damp on the plaster.
That's not so gay. (None too gay.)
Look, that crack needs raking
Where the paint is flaking.
Better take steps to fix it today.
They say things should start improving
But to feel your walls are moving
Won't be gay. (Far from gay.)
So it's whitewash you need, lovely whitewash you need.
When the roof falls in it will be far too late.
Yes, it's whitewash you need, so let's give a new lead
And restore the whole thing to its pristine state.

Here's your whitewash. Don't make such a fuss.
You'll get your whitewash, never mind just how.
Here's the whitewash, leave the rest to us
And you'll see your brand-new future now.

73 SONG OF THE COMMISSIONER OF POLICE

O, they are such charming people
If you'll leave them well alone
While they're fighting to recover
What has never been their own.

When the poor man's lamb gets butchered
Several butchers are involved
So the fight between those butchers
By the police must be resolved.

74 SONG TO INAUGURATE THE
NATIONAL DEPOSIT BANK

Don't you think a bank's foundation
Should be cause for jubilation?
Those without a wealthy mother
Must raise cash somehow or other.
To that end shares serve you better
Than a swordstick or Biretta.
What might land you in the cart
Is getting capital to start.
If you're short of this, conceal it
Otherwise you'll need to steal it.
Sure, all banks get started thanks to
Doing as the other banks do.
How did so much money come there? –
They'll have taken it from somewhere.

Eight songs from 'The Decision'

75 PRAISE OF THE USSR

All the world was telling of
Our misfortune.
But still there sat at our
Bare board
The hope of the numberless exploited which
Lives on water alone.
And our teacher was Knowledge, who
Behind our broken-down door
Gave clear lessons to all those present.
Once the door's been broken, we
Sit on inside, plainly visible
Whom no frost can kill off, nor hunger
Ever tireless, debating
The future of the world.

76 PRAISE OF ILLEGAL ACTIVITY

Good it is
Raising your voice for the working class
Loud and clearly calling on the masses to struggle
Stamping firmly on all oppressors, freeing all victims of
        oppression.
Useful and difficult are all those small routines
Secret and obstinate knots in
That mighty net the Party weaves
Under the rifle barrels of the bosses.
Speaking, but
Without betraying the speaker.
Winning, but
Without betraying the winner.

Dying, but
Without declaring the death.
Who would not do a lot for fame? who
Would do as much for silence?
But it is just the poorest of all that make Honour their guest
It's out of the meanest hovel that comes forth
Irresistible greatness.
And when Fame asks who did
The great deed, it will ask in vain.
Show yourselves
For an instant, you
Unknown men; you can cover your face while we
Utter our thanks.

77 SONG OF THE RICE-BARGE HAULIERS

In the town further upstream
There'll be a bowl of rice for us.
– Only the barge we're hauling is heavy
And the water's flowing downhill.
We'll never get this barge up there.
    Pull harder, men's mouths are
    Waiting for the next meal.
    Pull steadily, don't push
    The man in front.

Now night's almost come. A bunk
That would seem too cramping for a dog's ghost
Costs as much as half a bowl of rice.
And this bank is so slithery
We can't budge from this spot.
    Pull harder, men's mouths are
    Waiting for the next meal.
    Pull steadily, don't push
    The man in front.

We know we'll never
Outlive the rope that cuts our shoulders.
The whip which he wields has seen
Four generations like us
Nor are we the last one.
    Pull harder, men's mouths are
    Waiting for the next meal.
    Pull steadily, don't push
    The man in front.

First our fathers shifted the barge from the river mouth
Just a bit upstream. And our sons will
Get to the head springs, but our place is
In between them.
    Pull harder, men's mouths are
    Waiting for the next meal.
    Pull steadily, don't push
    The man in front

This barge bears rice. The farmer who
Sowed and gathered it was paid
With a heap of small change. Our
Payment is even less, because we
Are too many. One ox costs more.
    Pull harder, men's mouths are
    Waiting for the next meal.
    Pull steadily, don't push
    The man in front.

Once the rice has arrived at last
And the children want to know just
Who hauled the heavy barge, they'll hear: That's
A barge that got hauled here.
    Pull harder, men's mouths are
    Waiting for the next meal.
    Pull steadily, don't push
    The man in front.

The foodstuff from downstream reaches
The eaters upstream. Those
Who hauled it have not
Had their food yet.

78 STRIKE SONG

Comrade, come and join us, and risk
Your penny that's worth nothing at all
Your sleeping-place that's always sodden
And your place of work which you'll lose any day.

Join us in the coming struggle!
Surely you can't want us to fail.
Help yourself by giving us help. Let
Solidarity prevail.

Comrade, come and join us. Confront their rifles
And insist you get your pay.
Once you know that you've not all that much to lose
Their police will find their rifles simply aren't effective.

Join us in the coming struggle!
Surely you can't want us to fail.
Help yourself by giving us help. Let
Solidarity prevail.

79 SUPPLY AND DEMAND

Rice can be had down the river.
People in the remoter provinces need their rice.
If we can keep that rice off the market
Rice is bound to get dearer.
Then the men who pull the barges must go short of rice
And I shall get my rice for even less.

Don't ask me what rice is.
Don't ask me my advice.
I've no idea what rice is
All I have learnt is its price.

In winter time the coolies need warm clothing.
Then you must buy cotton so that
You can keep cotton off the market.
When a cold spell comes, then clothes get more expensive.
Our cotton spinning mills pay too high wages.
And cotton's too plentiful in any case.
        Don't ask me what cotton is.
        Don't ask me my advice.
        I've no idea what the hell cotton is
        All I have learnt is its price.

Men like these need too much feeding
And this makes a man dearer.
To provide for their feeding you need more men.
The cooks may get it done cheaper, but look at
The eaters making it dearer.
And men are in short supply in any case.
        Don't ask me what a man is.
        Don't ask me my advice.
        I've no idea what a man is
        All I have learnt is his price.

80 ALTER THE WORLD, IT NEEDS IT

Whom would the just man fail to greet, in order to stop an
        injustice?
What medicine tastes too nasty to save
A dying man?
How much meanness would you not commit if the aim is
To stamp out meanness?
If you'd found a way to alter this planet, what would you

Refuse to do?
What would you refuse to do?
Sink deep in the mire
Shake hands with the butcher: yes, but
Alter the world, it needs it!
Who are you?

81 PRAISE OF THE PARTY

Who do you think is the Party?
Does it sit in a big house with a switchboard?
Are all its decisions unknown, all its thoughts wrapped in
        secrecy?
Who is it?
We are it.
You and I and them – all of us.
Comrade, the clothes it's dressed in are your clothes, the head
        that it thinks with is yours
Where I'm lodging, there is its house, and where you suffer an
        assault it fights back.

Show us the path we must take, and we
Shall take it with you, but
Don't take the right path without us.
Without us it is
The most wrong of all.
Don't cut yourself off from us!
We can go astray and you can be right, so
Don't cut yourself off from us!

That the short path is better than the long one can't be denied.
But if someone knows it
And cannot point it out to us, what use is his wisdom?
Be wise with us.
Don't cut yourself off from us!

One single man may have two eyes
But the Party has a thousand.
One single man may see a town
But the Party sees six countries.
One single man can spare a moment
The Party has many moments.
One single man can be obliterated
But the Party can't be obliterated
For its methods are those of its philosophers
Which are based on experience of reality
And are destined soon to transform it
As soon as the masses make them their own.

82 WE ARE THE SCUM OF THE EARTH

When they see us going inside
The exploited man's cabin
All the exploiters get their cannon to fire
Against that cabin and our country as a whole.

For when the hungry man
Groans and hits back at
His torturers:
They say we must have paid
Him to groan and to hit back.

Each of our faces says
That we think exploitation is wrong.
Each warrant for us says we
Help people who are exploited.

Those who help men in despair
Rank as the scum of the earth.
We are the scum of the earth
We can't afford to let them find us.

83　THE SICK MAN DIES AND THE STRONG MAN FIGHTS

The sick man dies and the strong man fights.
Why should the earth yield up its oil?
Why should the coolie carry my pack?
To get oil you must fight
With the earth and the coolie
And in this fight the law is:
The sick man dies and the strong man fights.

The sick man dies and the strong man fights
And a good thing too.
The strong man is cared for, the sick have no rights
And a good thing too.
He'll go under, so kick him before he alights
That's a good thing too.
The winner can feast for a number of nights
A good thing too.
And no cook has to cater for dead appetites
Which is a good thing too.
And the God of Things-As-They-Are created lord and lad
And a good thing too.
And the one with the goods is good; and he who feels bad is
　　　bad
And a good thing too.

84　THE VOICES

I
He who does not arrive
Can plead no excuse. The fallen man
Is not excused by the stone.
Let not even the one who does arrive
Bore us with reports of difficulties

But deliver in silence
Himself or what is entrusted to him.

2
We gave you orders
Our situation was critical
We did not know who you were
You could carry out our orders and you could
Also betray us.
Did you carry them out?

3
Where men are waiting someone must arrive!

4
The net with one torn mesh
Is of no use:
The fish swim through it at that point.
As though there were no net.
Suddenly all its meshes
Are useless.

85 THE SNOW'S BLOWING THIS WAY

The snow's blowing this way
So who would want to stay?
The same as always stayed before:
The stony soil and the very poor.

86 THE SPRING

The play of the sexes renews itself
In the springtime. That's when the young lovers come together.
Just one gentle caress from the hand of her loved one
Has the girl's breast starting to tingle.

Her merest glance can overwhelm him.

A new-found light
Reveals the countryside to lovers in springtime.
The air's turning warm.
The days start getting long and the
Fields stay light a long while.

Boundless is the growth of all trees and all grasses
In springtime.
And incessantly fruitful
Is the land, are the meadows, the forest.
And then the earth gives birth to the new
Heedless of caution.

87 A HORSE MAKES A STATEMENT

REPORTER:
Ghastly story from the Frankfurter Allee:
Humans launch attack on fallen horse!
Reduced to a skeleton in ten minutes flat!
Is Berlin arctic? Has barbarism set in?
Falada, Falada, there thou art hanging . . .
Had thy mother known
Surely her heart would have broken.
Kindly tell us all about the fearful incident.

HORSE:
I tugged at my waggon, though I felt so feeble
And stopped in a street in our East End.
I stood there and thought: My friend
You are so feeble. If you don't make an effort
You'll start collapsing in front of all these people –
Twenty minutes later I was nothing but a heap of bones
in the roadway.

REPORTER:

Was your waggon too heavy, then? Your fodder
    insufficient?
In times of great shortage it is not without pity
That we observe man and beast fighting against
    unbearable poverty.
Falada, Falada, there thou art hanging . . .
Stripped–right–down–to–the–bones!
In the midst of our giant city, at eleven a.m.!

HORSE:

And while I was lying collapsed in the darkness
(My driver ran to telephone)
A horde of hungry people appeared
Out of the doorways, started frantically trying
Each to be first to cut the meat from my carcase
And they saw that I was still alive, and very far from
    finished with dying.

REPORTER:

Falada, Falada, there thou art hanging . . .
But these aren't humans! But these are wild beasts!
Coming out of their houses with knives and cookpots
    and helping themselves to meat!
And when you're still alive! Cold-hearted blackguards!
Be so good as to describe these people to us right away.

HORSE:

But all these people, I thought, were once my familiars.
They used to bring sacks to help me keep off the flies
Gave me old crusts to eat, and came up to advise
My driver that he must not beat me.
Once so kind-hearted, and now they're turned to killers!
What one earth can they have been through that would
    make them change their ways so completely?

REPORTER:

It led me to ask: What sort of people are these?
Have they no human feelings left? No heart beating
In their breast? With cast-iron foreheads
     They dash forward, forgetting all human standards
Coldly forgetting discipline and control, they yield
     themselves up
To the basest instincts. How can we help, then?
Help ten thousand people? It can't be done.

HORSE:

That led me to ask: who has sent such coldness
Right into the heart of the human race?
What's blowing into their face
So as to make them grow so freezing?
Please come to their aid, and act now with boldness
Or the consequences could well be beyond all reason.

Twelve songs from 'The Mother'

88 AS THE RAVEN

Brush down his coat
Brush it again then!
Once it's had a good brushing
It'll be decently ragged.

Cook with devotion
Take no end of trouble!
If you're a kopeck short
All his soup will be water.

Work even harder than now
Cut down your expenditure
Reckon it more exactly!
If you're a kopeck short
You can do nothing.

Whatever you do
You'll still have to struggle
Your position is bad
It'll worsen.
This cannot go on, but
What is to be the answer?

As the raven who can find nothing
For her fledglings to eat
Battles helplessly with the winter blizzard
And gets no reply to her crying
You too know there's no answer
When you cry.

Vainly you work till you drop, devising ways
To replace the irreplaceable and

Taking endless trouble to afford the unaffordable.
If you're a kopeck short, hard work is not enough.
Don't think the question of why your kitchen's empty
Will be decided in the kitchen.

> Whatever you do
> You'll still have to struggle
> Your position is bad
> It'll worsen.
> This cannot go on, but
> What is to be the answer?

89   PRAISE OF COMMUNISM

It stands to reason, anyone can grasp it. It's not hard.
If you're no exploiter then you must understand it.
It is good for you, find out what it really means.
The dullards will say that it's dull, and the dirty will say that
        dirty.
It has no use for dirt and no use for dullness.
Exploiters will speak of it as criminal
But we know better:
It's going to stop them being criminal.
It is not a madness, rather
The end of all madness.
It is not the problem
But the solution.
It is that simple thing
Which is so hard to do.

90   PRAISE OF LEARNING

Study the easy things: nothing
Comes too late for those whose day's
About to dawn.

Study your A B C. True, it's not enough, but
Study it. Don't neglect your potential
But learn! Knowledge is essential.
You must be ready to take over.

Study, tramp on a bench!
Study, man under sentence!
Study, wife in the kitchen!
Study, man of seventy!
You must be ready to take over.
Back to the classroom, you displaced person!
Get hold of more knowledge, freezing man!
Hungry man, grab for a book: books will be your weapons.
You must be ready to take over.

Don't hesitate to question things, comrade.
Don't just accept them but
See for yourself.
What you yourself don't know
You don't know.
Check through the invoices.
You have to pay them.
Learn how to point to each single item
Ask how it came to be there.
You must be ready to take over.

91 PRAISE OF THE REVOLUTIONARY

Some get in the way.
When they've gone it's an improvement
But when he has gone you miss him.

When oppression is on the increase
Many become discouraged
But his courage grows greater.

He'll mount a campaign for a
Penny on wages and for hotter tea
And the right to control the State.

He'll say to property:
Where do you come from?
He'll ask opinions:
Whom do you serve?

Where no one has raised a voice
You'll find him speaking
And where men live under oppression and much talk of
      Fate is heard
He'll see the names are published.

Where he sits at table
Dissatisfaction's sure to sit there too.
The food will be bad
And the room be found too cramping.

Wherever they chase him, there
Will come disorder, and where they've expelled him
There will unrest remain.

92 TO BE SUNG IN PRISON

They've got all their statute books and all their precedents
They've got all those police stations and prison blocks
(Not to mention other institutes and homes).
They've got all those prison warders and judges
Who earn fat pay packets and don't have any scruples.
What's the purpose?
Do they imagine they can get us down like that?
   Before they vanish – which we are expecting –
   They'll have come to realise
   That the whole thing's bound to be in vain.

They've got their newspapers and their printing presses
To blacken our name and reduce us to silence
(Not to speak of the statesmen they employ).
They've got those clerics and academics
Who earn fat pay packets and don't have any scruples.
What's the purpose?
Are they so scared of the truth coming out?
Before they vanish – which we are expecting –
They'll have come to realise
That the whole thing's bound to be in vain.

They've got their tanks and artillery
They've got their machine guns and hand grenades
(Not to speak of those rubber clubs they wield).
They've got their policemen and soldiers
Who earn thin pay packets and don't have any scruples.
What's the purpose?
Are their opponents as strong as all that?
They're so sure the Lord won't reject them
Or let them go down the drain.
But the refuse cart will collect them
And they'll find that everything will have been in vain.
Neither money nor tanks will protect them
As their shouts of 'Stop!' are lost in screams of pain.

93 PRAISE OF THE THIRD THING

People keep telling you how
A son is soon lost to his mother. Not to me:
I kept touch with mine. D'you want to know how? Through
The third thing.
He and I lived as two, but a third thing
Was shared by us both; we pursued it in common. It brought
Us together.
Often I have listened to children

When they spoke with their parents.
What a contrast it was when we two spoke
Talking about the third thing that was common to us:
That tremendous cause that is shared by so many!
How close to each other we felt when close to
That cause! How good to each other when
Close to its goodness!

94 REPORT ON THE DEATH OF A COMRADE

But he went to the wall where they intended to shoot him
He went towards a wall which had been built by
Men of his own kind
And the rifles they aimed at his breast, and the bullets
Had been made by men like himself. Merely absent
Were they therefore, or dispersed; but for him were still there
And present in the work of their hands. Not even
Those who were ordered to shoot him differed from him or
                were for ever incapable of learning.
Truly he still went bound with chains, that had been
Forged by his comrades and laid by them on their comrade; yet
Closer grew the factories; as he passed by he could see them
Chimney on chimney, and since it was early dawn
For it is at dawn that they normally bring them out, there was
Nobody there, but he saw them crowded full
With that huge throng, whose numbers had always grown
And still grew.
Then he was taken off by men like himself
And he, who understood this, could not understand.

95 GET UP, THE PARTY'S UNDER THREAT

Get up, the Party's under threat!
You are sick, but the Party's dying.

You are weak, but you must help us.
Get up, the Party's under threat!

You had your doubts about us
No time for doubting:
We've reached our limit.
You made complaints about the Party
Don't knock the Party when they're
About to smash it.

Get up, the Party's under threat!
Get up now!
You are ill, but we have need of you.
Don't die, for you must help us.
Don't stay away, we're off to the fight.
Get up, the Party's under threat, get up!

96 SONG OF THE ONLY WAY

When there's no food on the shelf
It's hard to go on fighting
But that is the only way –
The whole unjust system needs righting –
Till there's plenty on the shelf.
And you can just help your own self.

When there is not a ghost of a job for you
You've got to keep on fighting
Yes, that is the only way –
The whole unjust system needs righting –
For when the workers are employers too
Then there will be plenty of jobs for you.

When they laugh because you are not strong
You must not lose one minute.
You must muster for the march

And all who are weak must be in it.
All together you will be strong.
Don't worry, they won't be long.

97 SONG OF THE PATCHES AND THE COAT

If you see that our coat's in tatters
You come along and complain 'That's not good enough.
We must hurry to his rescue
Do our best to help him.'
Off you go to buttonhole our boss
While we hang about and shiver
Back you come then, triumphantly set to show off
What you've managed to win for us:
Just some makeshift patches.
    Right, we've got the patches.
    What we need is
    A whole new coat.

If you hear us cry out in hunger
You come along and complain 'That's not good enough.
We must hurry to his rescue
Do our best to help him.'
Off you go and buttonhole our boss
While we wait and rub our stomachs
Back you come then, triumphantly set to show off
What you've managed to win for us:
One stale crust.
    Right, we've got a stale crust.
    What we need is
    A whole new loaf.

We don't only need the patches
We must have a brand-new coat.
We don't only need a stale crust
We must have a whole new loaf.
We need much more than a job to fill

We must have the whole of the works
And the coalmines and the steel
And control of the State.
   Right, all that's what we must have
   But what
   Have you to offer us?

98   BUT HE WAS VERY MUCH FRIGHTENED

But he was very much frightened by the misery
Which is plain for all to see in our cities.
What terrifies us is hunger and the depravity
Of those who feel it and those who cause it.
Do not fear death so much, fear an inadequate life!

99   PRAISE OF DIALECTICS

Those still alive can't say 'never'.
No certainty can be certain
It cannot stay as it is.
When the rulers have already spoken
That is when the ruled start speaking.
Who dares to talk of 'never'?
Whose fault is it if oppression still remains? It's ours.
Whose job will it be to get rid of it? Just ours.
Whoever's been beaten down must get to his feet.
He who is lost must give battle.
He who is aware where he stands – how can anyone stop him
     moving on?
Those who were losers today will be triumphant tomorrow
And from never will come: today.

100 CHORUS OF LANDED GENTRY

Perhaps the years to come will just slip by us
And all those nasty dreams start disappearing.
Perhaps the rumours we're so sick of hearing
Were never true, but only sent to try us.

Perhaps men will forget us, as, if able
We'd all forget the names of those that harm us.
Then we perhaps can once more join the table.
Perhaps they'll let us even die in our pyjamas?

Perhaps they'll cease to curse our names and make them
      bywords?
Perhaps the dark will humanise our faces?
Perhaps our moon will now stay full, with no more phases?
Perhaps in future rain will start falling skywards . . .

V–VI The First Years of Exile
1933–1938

(Writing and production of *Señora Carrar's Rifles*, *Fear and Misery of the Third Reich*, and the ballet *The Seven Deadly Sins*. Revision and production of *The Round Heads and the Pointed Heads*. Writing and publication of the *Threepenny Novel*. Work on the project *The Oilfield*. Publication of *Songs Poems Choruses* and the *Svendborg Poems*.)

101 WAR SONG

And now they're off to the war
And they all need cartridges badly
And of course there are plenty of nice kind people
Who'll find them the cartridges gladly
'No ammunition, no war!
Leave that to us, my sons!
You go off to the front and fight,
We'll make you munitions and guns.'

And they made munitions in piles
And there wasn't a war to be found
And of course there were plenty of nice kind people
Who conjured one out of the ground.
'Off you go, dear boy, to the front!
For they threaten your native sod
March, for your mothers and sisters
For your King and your God!'

102 SISTER, FROM BIRTH

Sister, from birth we may write our own story
And anything we choose we are permitted to do
But the proud and the insolent who strut in their glory –
Little they guess
Little they guess
Little they guess the fate they're swaggering to.

Sister, be strong! You must learn to say No to
The joys of this world, for this world is a snare;
Only the fools in this world will let go, the
Don't care a damn
Don't care a damn
Don't-care-a-damn will be made to care.

Don't let the flesh and its longings get you
Remember the price that a lover must pay
And say to yourself when temptations beset you –
What is the use?
What is the use?
Beauty will perish and youth pass away.

Sister, you know when our life here is over
Those who were good go to bliss unalloyed
Those who were bad are rejected for ever
Gnashing their teeth
Gnashing their teeth
Gnashing their teeth in a gibbering void!

Four songs from 'The Round Heads and the Pointed Heads'

103 SONG OF THE STIMULATING IMPACT OF CASH

1

People keep on saying cash is sordid
Yet this world's a cold place if you're short.
Not so once you can afford it
And have ample cash support.
No need then to feel you've been defrauded
Everything is bathed in rosy light
Warming all you set your eyes on
Giving each what's his by right.
Sunshine spreads to the horizon.
Just watch the smoke; the fire's alight.
  Then things soon become as different as they can.
  Longer views are taken. Hearts beat harder.
  Proper food to eat. Looking much smarter.
  And your man is quite a different man.

2

O you're all so hopelessly mistaken
If you think cash flow has no effect.
Fertile farms produce no bacon
When the water-pump's been wrecked.
Now men grab as much as they can collect.
Once they'd standards they used not to flout.
If your belly's full you don't start shooting.
Now there's so much violence about.
Father, mother, brothers put the boot in.
Look, no more smoke now: the fire's gone out.
  Everything explodes, incendiaries are hurled
  Smash-and-grab's the rule; it's a disaster.
  Every little servant thinks he's master
  And the world's a very bitter world.

3
That's the fate of all that's noble and splendid
People quickly write it off as trash
Since with empty stomach and unmended
Footwear nobody's equipped to cut a dash.
They don't want what's good, they want the cash
And their instinct's to be mean and tight.
But when Right has got the cash to back it
It's got what it takes to see it right.
Never mind your dirty little racket
Just watch the smoke now: the fire's alight.

    Then you start believing in humanity once more:
    Everyone's a saint, as white as plaster.
    Principles grow stronger. Just like before.
    Wider views are taken. Hearts beat faster.
    You can tell the servant from the master.
    So the law is once again the law.

104 BALLAD OF THE BUTTON

1
Crippled man comes up to me:
Will I tell him truthfully
Might my best girl let him marry her?
I reply: 'I've known such things occur.
But I quickly rip a button from his collar
And I say: This is your fortune-teller.
Now let's see:
If these holes here come down heads you
Can be sure she never weds you
Better then stay fancy free.
Let's find out if Lady Luck is smiling.
Then I toss it, and say: No go, darling.
When they tell me: but these holes all seem to
Go right through! You'll hear me answer: That's true.
    And I'll say: it's no good trying to buck the system.

There's a simpler way, so why not try it?
Nothing is for free in this existence
If you must have love, you'll have to buy it.

2

Silly man comes up to me
And he asks me doubtfully
Will his wealthy brother see him right?
I reply: Undoubtedly he might.
But I quickly rip a button from his collar
And I say: Here is your fortune-teller.
Now let's see:
If these holes here come down heads you
Can be certain he's misled you
And prefers his luxury.
So let's find if Lady Luck is smiling.
Then I toss it and say: No go, darling.
When they tell me: but those holes all seem to
Go right through, you'll hear me answer: That's true.
   And I'll say: it's no good trying to buck the system.
   Don't complain if you want peace and quiet.
   If you really hope for his assistance
   Tell your brother you're prepared to buy it.

3

Working man comes up to me
And he tells me angrily
Rich man's knocking down his garden fence
Do I think he can get recompense?
So I rip a button from his collar
And I say: Here is your fortune-teller.
Now let's see:
If these holes here come down heads you
'll never get the money paid you
So you'd better let things be.
But let's find if Lady Luck is smiling.
Then I toss it, and say: No go, darling.

When they tell me: but those holes all seem to
Go right through, you'll hear me answer: That's true.
    Then I'll say: it's no good trying to buck the system.
    That's the law, so go on and apply it.
    Justice is a fraud. You'd better listen:
    Right or wrong, you're going to have to buy it.

105 THE WHAT-YOU-HAVE-YOU-HOLD SONG

A man in days of old
Was waiting in the cold.
They told him go on waiting.
He did as he was told.
Which was excruciating.
    Hail our Leader! It's nowt
    But
    What you have you hold.

The man was passing out
He threw his weight about.
His manner was offensive.
They gave in to that lout
Although it came expensive.
    Hail our Leader! It's nowt
    But
    What you have you hold.

There was a man of old.
They wouldn't share their gold
So he just went and snatched it.
Now eats all he can hold
And says the rest is rat shit.
    Hail our Leader! It's nowt
    But
    What you have you hold.

106 BALLAD OF THE WATERWHEEL

1

Take mankind's outstanding figures
Don't their legends sound enthralling?
First they shoot up like a comet
Then tail off like comets falling.
What a comfort, and how well worth knowing!
As for us who have to keep them going
How are we to tell just what the difference is –
Upsurge or collapse, who pays the expenses?
 For the waterwheel must keep on turning
 And so what's on top is bound to fall.
 All the time the water underneath is learning
 It has to drive the waterwheel.

2

Oh, we've had so many masters
We've had tigers and hyenas
We've had eagles, we've had warthogs:
Fed the lot of them between us.
People tell us that all men are brothers
But each jackboot felt like all the others
And it crushed us. Which should serve to show one
That it's not a different master that we need, but no one.
 For the waterwheel must keep on turning
 And so what's on top is bound to fall.
 All the time the water underneath is learning
 It has to drive the waterwheel.

3

And they'll batter one another senseless
For the booty.
Each one will claim he's poor and defenceless
Acting from a sense of duty.
Watch them rip each other's hands to bits to prise off
Their adornments. But the consternation

When we say we're going to cut supplies off!
Then there is a total reconciliation.
 For the waterwheel has now stopped turning
 And the pendulum no longer swings
 As the water flows through, freely churning
 To apply its power to better things.

107   ONCE AGAIN MAN'S HANDIWORK CRUMBLES

Once again man's handiwork crumbles
That which cost so much effort.
That which caused so many tears
And for which so much blood was shed, those works
Are foundering.

The dwellings crumble. In them henceforward will live
Fungus. Into the machine-rooms
Moves the crack-up. Across the railway tracks
Goes the evening wind, for none but the wind still visits
The tottering derricks and once
Powerful cranes, now given over
To their last proprietor, the
All-consuming rust.

The goatherd
Takes his surviving goats round the barbed wire.
The peasant
Again tugs his spade from the soil, a peasant once more
But a peasant without land, no longer a peasant.
For the field that once grew hay
Has become a scrapheap and now grows nothing.

Once again the rock raises its mighty shoulder
The grass moves in again. The thickets tangle.
And yet
Were oil to be required in the cities and between cities
It would be lying where the grass grows.

You, though, who saw the battles that were fought
Ingenuity of men's brains, force that strikes
Saw great efforts on all sides, now you know
How much effort it cost not
To produce oil.

108   ALL OF US OR NONE

Slave, say who is going to free you.
Those in deepest darkness lying
Comrade, they will hear your crying
Through the blackness they will see you:
Slaves just like yourself will free you.
    Everything or nothing. All of us or none.
    None gets through without assistance.
    Surrender or resistance.
    Everything or nothing. All of us or none.

2
You who hunger, who will feed you?
If you want to get your ration
Turn to us who face starvation
Follow on where we shall lead you;
Hungry men like you will feed you.
    Everything or nothing. All of us or none.
    None gets through without assistance.
    Surrender or resistance.
    Everything or nothing. All of us or none.

3
If you're hit, who'll hit back for you?
You who have been roughly handled
Join the ranks of the abandoned.
Let our feebleness restore you:
Comrade, we will hit back for you.
    Everything or nothing. All of us or none.
    None gets through without assistance.

Surrender or resistance.
Everything or nothing. All of us or none.

4
If you're lost, why not be daring?
He whose misery's past bearing
Must join up with those preparing
In their need and in their sorrow
For today and not tomorrow.
Everything or nothing. All of us or none.
one gets through without assistance.
Surrender or resistance.
Everything or nothing. All of us or none.

109 LETTER TO THE NEW YORK WORKERS' COMPANY 'THEATRE UNION' ABOUT THE PLAY 'THE MOTHER'

1
When I wrote the play 'The Mother'
On the basis of the book by comrade Gorky and of many
Proletarian comrades' stories about their
Daily struggle, I wrote it
With no frills, in austere language
Placing the words cleanly, carefully selecting
My character's every gesture, as is done
When reporting the words and deeds of the great.
I did my best to
Portray those seemingly ordinary
Countless incidents in contemptible dwellings
Among the far too many-headed as historical incidents
In no way less significant than the renowned
Acts of generals and statesmen in the school books.
The task I gave myself was to tell of a great historic figure
The unknown early champion of humanity
To constitute an example.

2

So you will see the proletarian mother take the road
The long and winding road of her class, see how at the start
She feels the loss of a penny on her son's wages: she cannot
Make him a soup worth eating. So she engages
In a struggle with him, fears she may lose him. Then
Reluctantly she aids him in his struggle for that penny
Ever fearful now of losing him to the struggle. Slowly
She follows her son into the jungle of wage claims. Thereby
She learns to read. Quits her hut, cares for others
Beside her son, in the same situation as he, those with whom
      she
Earlier struggled over her son; now she struggles alongside them.
Thus the walls around her stove start to tumble. Her table
      welcomes
Many another mother's son. Once too small for two
Her hut becomes a meeting place. Her son, though
She seldom sees. The struggle takes him from her.
And she herself is among the throng of those struggling. The
      talk
Between son and mother grows into a rallying-cry
During the battle. In the end the son falls. No longer was it
Possible for her to provide him with his soup by the one
Available means. But now she is standing
In the thickest turmoil of the vast and
Unceasing battle of the classes. Still a mother
Now even more a mother, mother of many now fallen
Mother of fighters, mother of unborn generations, she embarks
On a spring-clean of the State. Gives the rulers stones
In their extorted feast. Cleans weapons. Teaches
Her sons and daughters the A B C of struggle
Against war and exploitation, member of a standing army
Covering the entire planet, harried and harrying
Untolerated and intolerant. Defeated and relentless.

3

So too we staged the play like a report from a great epoch
No less golden in the light of many lamps than the
Royal plays staged in earlier times
No less cheerful and funny, discreet
In its sad moments. Before a clean canvas
The players entered simply with the characteristic
Gests of their scenes, delivering their phrases
Precisely, authentic words. Each phrase's effect
Was awaited and exposed. And also we waited
Till the crowd had laid those phrases in the balance – for we
     had noticed
How the man who owns little and is often deceived will bite
A coin with his teeth to see if it is genuine. Just like coins then
Must the actors' phrases be tested by our spectators
Who own little and are often deceived. Small hints
Suggested the scene of the action. The odd table and chair:
Bare essentials were enough. But photographs
Of the great opponents were projected on the screens at the
     back
And the sayings of the socialist classics
Painted on banners or projected on screens, surrounded the
Scrupulous actors. Their bearing was natural
Yet whatever said nothing was left out in the
Carefully considered abridgement. The musical numbers
Were lightly presented, with charm. Much laughter
Filled the house. The unconquerable
Good humour of the resourceful Vlassova, grounded in the
     assurance of
Her youthful class, provoked
Happy laughs from the workers' benches.
Keenly they took advantage of this rare chance
To experience the usual incidents without urgent danger, thus
Getting the leisure to study them and so prepare
Their own conduct.

4

Comrades, I see you
Reading the short play with embarrassment.
The spare language
Seems like poverty. This report, you reckon
Is not how people express themselves. I have read
Your adaptation. Here you insert a 'Good morning'
There a 'Hullo, my boy'. The vast field of action
Gets cluttered with furniture. Cabbage reeks
From the stove. What's bold becomes gallant, what's historical
        normal.
Instead of wonder
You strive for sympathy with the mother when she loses her
        son.
The son's death
You slyly put at the end. That, you think, is how to make the
        spectator
Keep up his interest till the curtain falls. Like a business man
Investing money in a concern, you suppose, the spectator
        invests
Feeling in the hero: he wants to get it back
If possible doubled. But the proletarian audience
At the first performance never missed the son at the end.
They maintained their interest. Not out of crudeness either.
And then too we were sometimes asked:
Will the workers understand you? Will they renounce
The familiar opiate: the spiritual participation
In other people's anger, in the rise of others, the whole deception
That whips one up for two hours, to leave one still more exhausted
Filled with hazy memories and yet vaguer expectations?
Will you truly, offering
Knowledge and experience, get an audience of statesmen?

Comrades, the form of the new plays
Is new, But why be
Frightened of what's new? Is it hard to bring off?
But why be frightened of what's new and hard to bring off?

To the man who's exploited, continually deceived
Life itself is a perpetual experiment
The earning of a few pennies
An uncertain business which is nowhere taught.
Why should he fear the new rather than the old? And even if
Your audience, the workers, hesitated you should still
Not lag behind it but show it the way
Swiftly show it the way with long strides, its final power
     inspiring you
With unbounded confidence.

110 NANNA'S SONG

There was I, with sixteen summers
Prenticed to the trade of love
Ready to take on all comers.
Nasty things occurred
Frequently, I'd heard
Even so I found it rather rough.
(After all, I'm not an animal, you know.)
    Thank the Lord the whole thing's quickly over
    All the loving and the sorrow, my dear.
    Where are the teardrops you wept last evening?
    Where are the snows of yesteryear?

Certainly the passing summers
Simplify the trade of love
Let you take increasing numbers:
First it may feel nice
But you turn to ice
If you don't withhold yourself enough.
(After all, stocks can't last for ever, can they?)
    Thank the Lord the whole thing's quickly over
    All the loving and the sorrow, my dear.

Where are the teardrops you wept last evening?
Where are the snows of yesteryear?

Even once you've got the measure
Of the ways how love is sold
Making money out of pleasure
Isn't all that fun.
Well, it has been done
But it can't prevent you getting old.
(After all, you don't go on being sixteen always, do you?)
    Thank the Lord the whole thing's quickly over
    All the loving and the sorrow, my dear.
    Where are the teardrops you wept last evening?
    Where are the snows of yesteryear?

III MADAM'S SONG

Oh, they say to see the red moon shining
On the waters causes girls to fall
And they'll talk about a woman pining
For some lovely man. But not at all!
    If you want to know what makes them swoon
    It's his chequebook, not the moon.
    Try to look at it in this light:
    Decent girls won't take to bed
    Any gent whose wad is tight
    But they can be very loving
    If a fellow sees them right.
    It's a fact: cash makes you randy
    As I've learnt night after night.

What's the use of all those red moons shining
On the waters once the money goes?
Beauty can provide no silver lining
When you're broke and everybody knows.
    If you want to know what makes them swoon

It's the lining, not the moon.
Try to look at it in this light:
How can couples go to bed
With the proper appetite
If they've both got empty bellies?
Better get the order right.
Food is fuel, cash makes you randy.
As I've learnt night after night.

112 BALLAD OF KNOWLEDGE

The stupid man may work in a great hurry
But what he wants won't come from hurrying
And what he has stays with him: i.e. worry.
The trouble is: he doesn't know a thing.
The man without a horse gets trampled under
The man with one gets where he wants to go.
For knowledge helps in any job. No wonder.
You'll never get your cut, unless you know.

'Your shop's too small', I hear my friends maintaining
'Some bigger shark is sure to swallow you.'
I clutch at those few hairs I have remaining
And wonder how to be a big shark too.
Humble myself, I know how hard the humble
Have always worked for crusts and the odd blow
So I sit tight and count my cash, and mumble:
'I'm sure to get my cut, because I know'.

For instance, take a man with kidney trouble:
He sees a specialist who tests his pee.
The patient leaves the surgery bent double
But having paid. The doctor knows, you see.
He knows it by its textbook definition –
He knows too how the scale of charges goes.

Those who don't know can die of their condition
But Doctor gets his cut because he knows.

Love is a game in which one gains or loses
The lover, the beloved: who gets the breaks?
The one gets honey and the other bruises
One does the giving and the other takes.
Conceal your face, then, when you feel it flushing.
And hide your bosom if the bruising shows.
Give him a knife, he'll stab you till you're gushing
Love tells him where to cut. You see: he knows.

113 SHEEP MARCH

Led by the drummer the
Sheep trot in bleating.
Their skins make the drumskins
Which he is beating.
 The butcher calls. They don't look where he's leading
 But march like sheep with calm, relentless tread
 The sheep before them in the slaughterhouse lie bleeding
 And march in spirit even when they're dead.

They hold up their hands to show
The work that they do –
Hands that are stained with blood
And empty too.
 The butcher calls. They don't look where he's leading
 But march like sheep with calm, relentless tread
 The sheep before them in the slaughterhouse lie bleeding
 And march in spirit even when they're dead.

The crosses that go before
On big blood-red banners
Are angled to screw the poor
Like crooked spanners.

The butcher calls. They don't look where he's leading
But march like sheep with calm, relentless tread
The sheep before them in the slaughterhouse lie bleeding
And march in spirit even when they're dead.

114 THE GERMAN MARCH-PAST

When He had ruled five years, and they informed us
That He, who claimed to have been sent by God
Was ready for his promised war, the steelworks
Had forged tank, gun and warship, and there waited
Within His hangars aircraft in so great a number
That they, leaving the earth at His command
Would darken all the heaven, then we became determined
To see what sort of nation, formed from what sort of people
In what condition, what sort of thoughts thinking
He would be calling to his colours. We staged a march-past.

See, now they come towards us
A motley sight rewards us
Their banners go before
To show how straight His course is
They carry crooked crosses
Which double cross the poor.

Some march along like dummies
Others crawl on their tummies
Towards the war He's planned.
You hear no lamentation
No murmurs of vexation
You only hear the band.

With wives and kids arriving
Five years they've been surviving.
That's more than they will last.
A ramshackle collection

They parade for our inspection
As they go marching past

1
First the SS approaches.
Blown up with beer and speeches
They're in a kind of daze.
Their aim is a People, imperious
Respected and powerful and serious
Above all, one that obeys.

2
The next to be seen are the traitors
Who have betrayed their neighbours.
They know the others know.
If only the street would forget them!
They could sleep if their conscience would let them
But there's so far still to go.

3
Here come the brown storm-troopers
That keen-eyed squad of snoopers
To see where each man stands.
Their job's to put the boot in
And hang around saluting
With bloodstained empty hands.

4
While the storm-troopers are parading
The next lot are debating
What Bebel and Lenin meant.
They'll cling to the texts they've cited
Till they're forcibly united
By Nazi imprisonment.

5
The camps parade their warders:
Narks, butchers and marauders

The People's servants they.
They'll crush you and assail you
And flog you and impale you
For negligible pay.

6
The judges follow limply.
They've heard that justice is simply
What serves the People best.
And how are they to tell that?
They solve the problem so well that
The whole People's under arrest.

7
And as for the physicians
The State gives them positions
And pays them so much a piece.
Their job is to keep mending
The bits the police keep sending
Then send the result to the police.

8
Behold our local Newtons
Disguised as early Teutons
And none of them hook-nosed.
Their science will be barbarian
For they're getting an impeccably Aryan
State-certified physics imposed.

9
Then next you see men coming
Who've been forced to surrender their women
And bedded with blondes in their place.
It's no good them cursing or praying:
Once He catches them racially straying
He'll whip them back into the Race.

10

Here come the worthy school teachers.
The Youth Movement takes those poor creatures
And makes them all thrust out their chest.
Every schoolboy's a spy. So now marking
Is based not on knowledge but narking
And on who knows whose weaknesses best.

They teach budding traducers
To set hatchet-men and bruisers
On their own parents' tail.
Denounced by the sons as traitors
To Himmler's apparatus
The fathers go handcuffed to gaol.

11

The widows and orphans you're seeing
Have heard Him guaranteeing
A splendid time by and by.
But first they're to make sacrifices
While the grocers put up their prices.
The splendour is all in the sky.

12

To overcome class barriers
The poor are made fetchers and carriers
In Hitler's Labour Corps.
The rich serve a year alongside them
No differences divide them
Though they'd like to be paid a bit more.

13

Then the media, a travelling circus
Come to interview the workers
With microphone in hand.
But the workers can't be trusted
So the microphone is adjusted

To say what Goebbels has planned.

14
The coffins the S A carry
Are sealed up tight, to bury
Their victims' raw remains.
Here's one who wouldn't give in
He fought for better living
That we might lose our chains.

15
Questioned in torture cellars
These men were no tale-tellers
But held out through the night.
Maybe they never went under
Yet their wives and friends still wonder
What happened at first light.

16
With banners and loud drumming
The welfare men come slumming
Into the humblest door.
They've marched round and collected
The crumbs the rich have rejected
And feed them to the poor.

Their hands, more used to beatings
Now offer gifts and greetings.
They conjure up a smile.
Their charity soon crashes
Their food all turns to ashes
And chokes the uttered 'Heil!'

17
To bake their bread to our taste
The bakers arrive with flour paste

With which to practise their art.
They've cooked up our bread rations
From paste and regulations
And so they're in the cart.

18
Observe, further down the procession
The farmer's sour expression:
They've underpriced his crop.
Since what his pigs require
Is milk, whose price has gone higher
The farmer blows his top.

19
Next watch the voters troop in –
One hundred per cent in each grouping
As they vote to be led by the nose.
It's goodbye to bacon and porridge
It's goodbye to greatcoats and forage
Hitler is what they chose.

20
The Church's ten commandments
Are subject to amendments
By order of the police.
Her broken head is bleeding
For new gods are succeeding
Her Jewish god of peace.

21
Young boys learn it's morally healthy
To lay down their life for the wealthy:
It's a lesson that's made very clear.
It's much harder than spelling or figures
But the fists of their teacher look bigger
And they're fearful of showing fear.

22

The troops in His armed forces
Get meat and pudding courses
And can even ask for more.
This helps them to face the firing
And never dream of enquiring
Who profits from His war.

23

He sees that jobs are provided
The poor go where they are guided
And He likes them to be keen.
He'll permit them to serve the nation.
Their blood and perspiration
Shall fuel His war machine.

24

And as the column passes
We call with urgent voices:
Can none of you say No?
Your leaders say they need you.
This war to which they lead you
Will be your own death blow.

115 MARY, MARY SAT HER DOWN

Mary, Mary sat her down
Had a little old pink gown
Gown was shabby and bespattered
But when chilly winter came
Gown went round her just the same
Bespattered don't mean tattered.

VII The Darkest Times
1938–1941

(Writing of *Galileo* first version, *Mother Courage*, *Lucullus*, *The Good Person of Szechwan*, *Puntila*, and the *Conversations between Exiles*. Work on the *Messingkauf* project. The approach of war. Weill and Eisler both emigrate to the USA. Reduced links with the USSR.)

The other day I met my audience.
In a dusty street
He gripped a pneumatic drill in his fists.
For a second
He looked up. Rapidly I set up my theatre
Between the houses. He
Looked expectant.

In the pub
I met him again. He was standing at the bar.
Grimy with sweat, he was drinking. In his fist
A thick sandwich. Rapidly I set up my theatre. He
Looked astonished.

Today
I brought it off again. Outside the station
With brass bands and rifle butts I saw him
Being herded off to war.
In the midst of the crowd
I set up my theatre. Over his shoulder
He looked back
And nodded.

Five songs from 'Mother Courage'

117 MOTHER COURAGE'S SONG

You captains, tell the drums to slacken
And give your infanteers a break:
It's Mother Courage with her waggon
Full of the finest boots they make.
With crawling lice and looted cattle
With lumbering guns and straggling kit –
How can you flog them into battle
Until you get them boots that fit?
 The New Year's come. The watchmen shout.
 The thaw begins. The dead remain.
 Wherever life has not died out
 It staggers to its feet again.

Captains, how can you make them face it –
March to their death without a brew?
Courage has rum with which to lace it
And boil their souls and bodies through.
Their muskets primed, their stomachs hollow –
Captains, your men don't look too well.
So feed them up, and they will follow
And let you lead them into hell.
 The New Year's come. The watchmen shout.
 The thaw begins. The dead remain.
 Wherever life has not died out
 It staggers to its feet again.

And if you feel your forces fading
You won't be there to share the fruits.
For what is war but market trading
Which deals in blood instead of boots?

And some I saw dig six feet under
In haste to lie down and pass out.
Now they're at rest perhaps they wonder
Just what was all their haste about.

From Ulm to Metz, from Metz to Munich
Courage will see the war gets fed.
The war will burst out of its tunic
Given its daily shot of lead.
But lead alone won't really nourish:
War must have soldiers to subsist.
It's you it needs to make it flourish.
The war is hungry. So enlist!

With all its luck and all its danger
This war is dragging on a bit.
Another hundred years or longer:
The common man won't benefit.
Filthy his food, no soap to shave him
The regiment steals half his pay.
But still a miracle may save him:
Tomorrow is another day!
    The New Year's come. The watchmen shout.
    The thaw begins. The dead remain.
    Wherever life has not died out
    It staggers to its feet again.

118 SONG OF UNCONDITIONAL SURRENDER

Back when I was young, I was brought to realise
What a very special person I must be
(Not just any old cottager's daughter, what with my looks and
        my talents and my urge towards Higher Things)
And insisted that my soup must have no hairs in it.
No one makes a sucker out of me!

(All or nothing, only the best is good enough, each man for
        himself, nobody's telling *me* what to do.)
Then I heard a tit
Chirp: Wait a bit!
    And you'll be marching to the band
    In step, responsive to command
    And acting out your little dance:
    Now we advance.
    And now: parade, form square!
    Then men swear God's there –
    Not a bloody chance!

In no time at all anyone who looked could see
That I'd learned to take my medicine with good grace.
(Two kids on my hands and look at the price of bread, and the
        things they expect of you!)
When they finally came to feel that they were through with me
They'd got me grovelling on my face.
(Takes all sorts to make a world, you scratch my back and I'll
        scratch yours, no good banging your head against a brick
        wall.)
Then I heard that tit
Chirp: Wait a bit!
    And you'll be marching to the band
    In step, responsive to command
    And acting out your little dance:
    Now they advance.
    And now: parade, form square!
    Then men swear God's there –
    Not a bloody chance!

I've known people tried to storm the summits:
There's no star too bright, or seems too far away.
(Dogged does it, where there's a will there's a way, by hook or
        by crook.)
As each peak disclosed fresh peaks to come, it's
Strange how much a plain straw hat could weigh.

(You have to cut your coat according to your cloth.)
Then I hear the tit
Chirp: Wait a bit!
   And they'll be marching to the band
   In step, responsive to command
   And acting out their little dance.
   Now they advance
   And now: parade, form square!
   Then men swear God's there –
   Not a bloody chance!

119   SONG OF THE SOLDIER BEFORE THE INN

A drink, man, quick! It's a crime
The cavalry have no time
Fighting for King and Country.

Your breast, girl, quick! It's a crime
The cavalry have no time
Riding for King and Country.

Your bid, mate, quick! It's a crime
The cavalry have no time
Must follow the flag of our Country.

No sermon, now, Rev! It's a crime
The cavalry have no time
Dying for King and Country

120   SONG OF THE ROSE

The red garden rose we planted
Has fair and stately grown;
Our fondest hopes were granted.
Scarlet heavy-scented flowers
Beguiled our summer hours:
   Blessed those are who a garden own
   Where such a rose-tree flowers.

Though, through the pine woods wailing
The winter wind makes moan
Its rage is unavailing.
Long before the autumn ended
Our roof with tiles we mended:
   Blessed those are who a roof still own
   When such a wind comes wailing.

121 LULLABY

Hush-a-bye, Baby, and sleep for a while;
Other's brats whimper, but mine only smile:
Wet straw their pillows, but you lie on down
And silk soft as an angel's evening gown.
They get a dry crust, but you shall have cake
And warm milk to refresh you whenever you wake.
Hush-a-bye, Baby, sleep without care:
One baby lies in Poland, the other is who knows where.

122 ROLL-CALL OF THE VIRTUES AND THE VICES

An Oppression Evening was held recently at which, to a fanfare of trombones, a number of prominent personalities appeared as a demonstration of their solidarity with those in power.

Vindictiveness, with a get-up and hairstyle like those worn by Conscience, displayed her infallible memory. Small and crippled, she was greeted with thunderous applause.

An unfortunate entrance was made by *Brutality*. Looking distractedly around her, she lost her footing on the daïs, but made up for this by angrily stamping on the floor hard enough to make a hole in it.

She was followed by *Resentment*, who with frothing lips appealed to the ignorant to cast off the burdens of knowledge. 'Down with the know-alls!' was his cry; after which the know-nothings bore him from the hall on their worn shoulders.

Smarminess too put in an appearance and proved herself a mighty scrounger. On her way out she bowed to one or two fat swindlers whom she had helped to high positions.

An old favourite, the soubrette *Schadenfreude*, provided one of the brighter spots. Unhappily she suffered a minor accident by laughing till her ribs bust.

First to appear in Part Two of this competitive show was that well-known sportsman *Ambition*. He jumped so high in the air that he hurt his tiny head against one of the rafters. Both then and later, when a steward pinned a medal with a long pin straight into his flesh, his upper lip remained stiff.

Looking a little pale, possibly from stage fright, *Justice* introduced herself. She spoke of trivialities and promised to give a comprehensive lecture any day now.

That strapping young fellow *Curiosity* talked about how the regime had opened his eyes, likewise about the responsibility of hooked noses for bad public administration.

An appearance was put in by *Self-Sacrifice*, a tall stringy individual with an honest face and a large imitation pewter plate in his calloused hand. He was collecting pennies off the workers and repeating softly in a weary voice 'Remember the children'.

Order too came on the daïs, her spotless cap covering her hairless head. She awarded medical diplomas to the liars and surgical degrees to the murderers. Despite having been out all night thieving from backyard dustbins, she had not a speck of dust on her grey dress. A long and apparently endless queue of the robbed filed past her table as with arthritic hands she wrote each of them a receipt. Her sister *Economy* displayed a basket full of crusts which she had torn from the lips of patients in the hospitals.

With weals on his neck, and gasping for air as if being driven to death, *Hard Work* gave a free demonstration. In less time than it takes to blow your nose he machined a shell-case, while as an encore he brewed poison gas enough for two thousand families before you could say Jack Robinson.

All these famous persons, the children and grandchildren of *Cold* and *Hunger*, appeared before the people and unreservedly proclaimed themselves the servants of *Oppression*.

123 THE QUEEN'S LAMENT

As I bathed in Taurion's stream
In the morning early
From the olive trees appeared
Fifty foreign soldiers.
Saw and came and vanquished.

As weapon I'd a sponge
As a shield, clear water
Their breastplates protected me
For a fleeting moment.
Swiftly I was vanquished.

Frightened then, I looked about
Screaming for my maidens.
And the maids were frightened too
Screaming in the bushes.
All of them were ravished.

Nine songs from 'The Good Person of Szechwan'

124 SONG OF THE SMOKE

Once I believed intelligence would aid me –
I was an optimist when I was younger.
Now that I'm old I see it hasn't paid me:
How can intelligence compete with hunger?
    And so I said: Drop it!
    Like smoke twisting grey
    Into ever colder coldness, you'll
    Blow away.

I saw the conscientious man get nowhere

And so I chose the crooked path instead
But crookedness makes our sort get there slower.
There seems to be no way to get ahead.
  Likewise I say: Drop it!
  Like smoke twisting grey
  Into ever colder coldness, you'll
  Blow away.

The old, they say, find little fun in hoping.
Time's what they need, and time begins to press.
But for the young, they say, the gates are open.
They open, so they say, on nothingness.
  And I too say: Drop it!
  Like smoke twisting grey
  Into ever colder coldness, you'll
  Blow away.

125   THE WATER-SELLER'S SONG IN THE RAIN

I sell water. Who will taste it?
– Who would want to in this weather?
All my labour has been wasted
Fetching these few pints together.
I stand shouting Buy my water!
And nobody thinks it
Worth stopping and buying
Or greedily drinks it.
(Buy water, you devils!)

O to stop the leaky heaven
Hoard what stock I've got remaining:
Recently I dreamt that seven
Years went by without it raining.
How they'd all shout Give me water!
How they'd fight for my good graces

And I'd make their further treatment
Go by how I liked their faces.
(Stay thirsty, you devils!)

Wretched weeds, you're through with thirsting
Heaven must have heard you praying.
You can drink until you're bursting
Never bother about paying.
I'm left shouting Buy my water!
And nobody thinks it
Worth stopping and buying
Or greedily drinks it.
(Buy water, you devils!)

126 WHY ARE YOU SO UNPLEASANT?

To trample on one's fellows
Is surely exhausting? Veins in your temples
Stick out with the strenuousness of greed.
Loosely held forth
A hand gives and receives with the same suppleness. Yet
Greedily snatching it has got to strain. Oh
How tempting it is to be generous. How welcome
Friendliness can somehow feel. A kindly word
Escapes like a sigh of contentment.

127 SONG OF THE DEFENCELESSNESS
OF THE GOOD AND THE GODS

In our country
The capable man needs luck. Only
If he has mighty backers
Can he prove his capacity.
The good
Cannot help themselves and the gods are powerless.

So why can't the gods launch a great operation
With bombers and battleships, tanks and destroyers
And rescue the good by a ruthless invasion?
Then maybe the wicked would cease to annoy us.

The good
Cannot remain good for long in our country
Where cupboards are bare, housewives start to squabble.
Oh, the divine commandments
Are not much use against hunger.
  So why can't the gods share out what they've created
  Come down and distribute the bounties of nature
  And allow us, once hunger and thirst have been sated
  To mix with each other in friendship and pleasure?

In order to win one's midday meal
One needs the toughness which elsewhere builds empires.
Unless twelve others are trampled down
The unfortunate cannot be helped.
  So why can't the gods make a simple decision
  That goodness must conquer in spite of its weakness
  Then back up the good with an armoured division
  Command it to fire, and not tolerate meekness?

128 THE SONG OF GREEN CHEESE

A day will come, so the poor were informed
As they sat at their mothers' knees
When a child of low birth shall inherit the earth
And the moon shall be made of green cheese.
  When the moon is green cheese
  The poor shall inherit the earth.

Then goodness will be a thing to reward
And evil a mortal offence.

'Where there's merit there's money' won't sound quite so funny
There will really be no difference.
    When the moon is green cheese
    There won't be this difference.

Then the grass will look down on the blue sky below
And the pebbles will roll up the stream
And man is a king. Without doing a thing
He gorges on honey and cream.
    When the moon is green cheese
    The world flows with honey and cream.

Then I shall become a pilot again
And you'll get a deputy's seat.
You, man on the loose, will find you're some use
And you, Ma, can put up your feet.
    When the moon is green cheese
    The weary can put up their feet.

And as we have waited quite long enough
This new world has got to be born
Not at the last minute so there's nothing left in it
But at the first glimmer of dawn
    When the moon is green cheese
    The very first glimmer of dawn.

129 DON'T BE TOO HARD

A slight connivance, and one's powers are doubled.
Look how the cart-horse stops before a tuft of grass:
Wink one eye for an instant and the horse pulls better.
Show but a little patience in June, and the tree
By August is sagging with peaches. How
But for patience could we live together?
A brief postponement
Brings the most distant goal within reach.

130 ON SUICIDE

In such a country and at such a time
There should be fewer melancholy evenings
And lofty bridges over the rivers
While the hours that link the night to morning
And the winter season too each year, are full of danger.
For, having seen all this misery
People won't linger
But will decide at once
To fling their too heavy life away.

131 SONG OF THE EIGHTH ELEPHANT

Seven elephants worked for Major Chung
And an eighth one followed the others.
Seven were wild and the eighth was tame
And the eighth kept an eye on his brothers.
    Keep moving!
    Major Chung owns a wood
    See it's cleared before tonight.
    That's orders. Understood?

Seven elephants were clearing the wood
The eighth bore the Major in person
Number Eight merely checked that the work was correct
And spared himself any exertion.
    Dig harder!
    Major Chung owns a wood
    See it's cleared before tonight.
    That's orders. Understood?

Seven elephants got tired of their work
Of shoving and digging and felling
The Major was annoyed with the seven he employed
But rewarded the eighth one for telling.
   What's up now?
   Major Chung owns a wood
   See it's cleared before tonight.
   That's orders. Understood?

Seven elephants, not a tusk in their heads
While the eighth's were in excellent order.
So Eight used his wits, slashed the seven to bits
And the Major had never laughed louder.
   Dig away!
   Major Chung owns a wood
   See it's cleared before tonight.
   That's orders. Understood?

132 TRIO OF THE VANISHING GODS ON THEIR CLOUD

All too long on earth we lingered.
Swiftly droops the lovely day:
Shrewdly studied, closely fingered
Precious treasures melt away.

Now the golden flood is dying
While your shadows onward press
Time that we too started flying
Homeward to our nothingness.

VIII The American Years
1941–1947

(Hollywood in wartime. Writing of *Simone Machard*, *Schweik in the Second World War* and *The Caucasian Chalk Circle*. Adaptation of the *Duchess of Malfi* with H. R. Hays and W. H. Auden. Writing and production of second, American version of *Galileo* with Charles Laughton. Renewed contact with Eisler and Weill; first work with Dessau.)

Soon as the conqueror occupies your town
He must feel he's isolated, on his own.
Not one of you must ever permit him to come in:
He won't come as a guest, so treat him like vermin.
No place for him shall be laid, no meal prepared
Every stick of furniture must have disappeared.
Whatever can't be burned has to be hidden
Pour all your milk away, bury each crust of bread as bidden
Till he's screaming: Help me! Till he's known as: Devilry.
Till he's eating: ashes. Till he's living in: debris.
He must be given no mercy, no kind of aid
And your town must be a memory, from the map let it fade.
Let each prospect be blank, every track bare and savage
And provide no vestige of shelter, only dust and sewage.
Go forth now and ravage!

134 SIMONE'S SONG

As I went to Saint-Nazaire
I forgot my trousers.
All at once I heard a cry:
Where've you put your trousers?
I replied: at Saint-Nazaire
Skies are blue as ever
And the wheat's as tall as I
And the sky blue as ever.

Five songs from
'Schweik in the Second World War'

135   SONG OF THE NAZI SOLDIER'S WIFE

What did the mail bring the soldier's wife?
From the ancient city of Prague?
From Prague it brought her some high-heeled shoes.
Just a card with news and some high-heeled shoes
That was what she got from ancient Prague.

What did the mail bring the soldier's wife?
From Warsaw on Poland's plains?
From Warsaw it brought her a fine linen blouse
To wear in the house, a superb linen blouse.
That was what came from Poland's plains.

What did the mail bring the soldier's wife?
From Oslo's well-equipped stores?
From Oslo it brought her an elegant fur.
Just the thing for her, an elegant fur!
That was what she got from Oslo's stores.

What did the mail bring the soldier's wife?
From the port of Rotterdam?
From Rotterdam it brought her a hat.
And she looked good in that very Dutch-looking hat
Which was sent her from Rotterdam.

What did the mail bring the soldier's wife?
From Brussels in Belgium's fair land?
From Brussels it brought her some delicate laces.
Nothing ever replaces such delicate laces.
That is what she got from Belgium's fair land.

What did the mail bring the soldier's wife?
From the lights of gay Paree?
From Paris it brought her a lovely silk dress.
To her neighbour's distress, a lovely silk dress
That was what she got from gay Paree.

What did the mail bring the soldier's wife?
From the desert around Tobruk?
From around Tobruk it brought her a pendant.
A copper pendant that looked so resplendent
That was what it brought her from Tobruk.

What did the mail bring the soldier's wife?
From the Russian steppe-lands?
From Russia it brought her her widow's veil
So we end our tale with the widow's veil
Which she got from Russia's steppes.

136 SONG OF THE GENTLE BREEZE

Come here, my dearest, and make haste
No one dearer could I pick
But once your arm is round my waist
Don't try to be too quick.
   Learn from the plums in the autumn
   All golden on the trees.
   They fear the whirlwind's terrible strength
   And long for the gentle breeze.
   You can scarcely feel that gentle breeze
   It's like a whispering lullaby
   Which makes the plums drop off the trees
   Till on the ground they lie.

Oh, reaper, don't cut all the grass
But leave one blade to grow.
Don't drain the brimming wine-glass

Don't kiss me as you go.
 Learn from the plums in the autumn
 All golden on the trees.
 They fear the whirlwind's terrible strength
 And long for the gentle breeze.
 You can scarcely feel that gentle breeze
 It's like a whispering lullaby
 Which makes the plums drop off the trees
 Till on the ground they lie.

137   SONG OF THE 'CHALICE'

Come right in and take a seat
Join us at the table
Soup and Moldau fish to eat
Much as you are able.
 If you need a bite of bread
 And a roof above your head
 You're a man and that will do.
 The place of honour's here for you
 Given 80 Hellers.

We don't want to know your life
Everyone's invited.
Step inside and bring the wife
We shall be delighted.
 All you need's a friendly face
 Clever talk is out of place
 Eat your cheese and drink your beer
 And you'll find a welcome here
 So will 80 Hellers.

One day soon we shall begin
Looking at the weather
And we'll find the world's an inn
Where men come together.

All alike will come inside
Nobody will be denied
Here's a roof against the storm
Where the freezing can get warm
Even on 80 Hellers.

138 GERMAN MISERERE

One day our superiors said: Germany, awaken
The old town of Danzig has got to be taken.
They gave us tanks and bombers, and Poland was invaded.
In two weeks at the outside we had made it.
God preserve us.

One day our superiors said: Germany, awaken
Now Norway and France have got to be taken.
They gave us tanks and bombers, both countries were invaded.
Five weeks in 1940, and we'd made it.
God preserve us.

One day our superiors said: Germany, awaken
The Balkans and Russia have got to be taken.
The third year saw the Balkans and Russia both invaded.
We should have won, but something has delayed it.
God preserve us.

Wait till our superiors say: Germany, awaken
The depths of the ocean and the moon must be taken.
Over Russia's cold steppes they've left us to roam
And the fighting's tough and we don't know the way home.
God preserve us and bring us back home alive.

139 SONG OF THE MOLDAU

Deep down in the Moldau the pebbles are shifting
In Prague three dead emperors moulder away.
The top won't stay top, for the bottom is lifting.
The night has twelve hours and then comes the day.

But time can't be halted. The boundless ambition
Of those now in power is running its course.
Like bloodspattered cocks they will fight for position
But time can't be halted. Not even by force.

Deep down in the Moldau the pebbles are shifting
In Prague three dead emperors moulder away.
The top won't stay top, for the bottom is lifting.
The night has twelve hours, and then comes the day.

140 WHEN WE ENTERED FAIR MILAN

I wrote my love a letter
When we entered fair Milan:
Oh the war will soon be over
For the cook has lost his coppers
And the captain's lost his head
And we've shot away our lead.
   I never got an answer
   And the war went on five years
   But that wasn't so surprising
   So I drank instead, supposing:
   There she lies, in the embrace
   Of the man who took my place.

And we burnt the town around us
When we captured fair Milan
Till its palaces were gutted
And for seven days we looted
And we raped them old and young
For we knew they'd done us wrong.
   How could she go on waiting
   With the nights becoming lighter and the spring wind
      blowing fresh?
   Now it's time I found a lover
   He can't make me wait for ever –
   Women have such itching flesh.

But when we left the city
A second war began
Though the first was scarcely over
And I'll drink a thousand beakers
With a whore upon my knee
Till my love again I see.

Eleven songs from 'The Caucasian Chalk Circle'

141 GO CALMLY INTO BATTLE

Go calmly into battle, soldier
The bloody battle, the bitter battle
From which not everyone returns.
When you return I will be there.
I will be waiting for you under the green elm
I will be waiting for you under the bare elm
I will wait until the last soldier has returned
And even longer.
When you return from the battle
No boots will lie beside the door
The pillow beside mine will be empty
My mouth will be unkissed.
When you return, when you return
You will be able to say: all is as it was.

142 DANCE OF THE GRAND DUKE WITH HIS BOW

Oh, the green fields of Samara!
Oh, the bent backs of a warlike race!
O sun, o domination!

I am your prince. This bow they are bringing
Is elm tipped with bronze, strung with flexible sinew.
This arrow is mine, which I mean to send winging
To plunge itself deep, o my enemy, in you.

Oh, the green fields of Samara!
Oh, the bent backs of a warlike race!
O sun, o domination!

Off, off to the fight, bowstring taut. Aren't you frightened

To feel how much deeper the bronze will go worming
Its way through your flesh when that bowstring is tightened?
Fly, arrow, and cut up the enemy vermin!

So I tug, tug and tug at the bow that they made me.
How strong are my shoulders! A fraction more. Steady . . .
Why, it's broken! All lies! Elm and bronze have betrayed me.
Help, help! God have mercy: my soul is unready.

Oh, the cattle-stocked fields of Samara!
Oh, the bent backs of a warlike race!
Oh, the cutting up of the enemy!

143 FOUR GENERALS

Four generals set off for Iran
Four generals but not one man.
The first did not strike a blow
The second did not beat the foe
For the third the weather was not right
For the fourth the soldiers would not fight.
Four generals went forth to attack
Four generals turned back.

Sosso Robakidse marched to Iran
Sosso Robakidse was a man.
He struck a sturdy blow
He certainly beat the foe
For him the weather was good enough
For him the soldiers fought with love
Sosso Robakidse marched to Iran
Sosso Robakidse is our man.

144 SOLDIERS' SONG

1

O sadly one morning, one morning in May
I kissed my darling and rode far away.
Protect her, dear friends, until home from the wars
I come riding in triumph, alive on my horse.

2

When I lie in my grave and my sword turns to rust
My darling shall bring me a handful of dust.
For the feet that so gaily ran up to her door
And the arms that went round her shall please her no more.

145 A LITTLE SONG

Your father's a thief
Your mother's a whore:
All the nice people
Will love you therefore.

The son of the tiger
Brings the foals their feed
The snake-child milk
To mothers in need.

146 THE BATTLE BEGAN AT DAWN

So many words are said, so many words are left unsaid
The soldier has come. Whence he comes he doesn't say.
Hear what he thought but didn't say:

The battle began at dawn, grew bloody at noon.
The first fell before me, the second behind me, the third at my
    side.

I trod on the first, I abandoned the second, the captain sabred
    the third.
My one brother died by steel, my other brother died by smoke.
My neck was burnt by fire, my hands froze in my gloves, my
    toes in my socks.
For food I had aspen buds, for drink I had maple brew, for bed
    I had stones in water.

There was great yearning but there was no waiting.
The oath is broken. Why was not disclosed.
Hear what she thought, but didn't say:

While you fought in the battle, soldier
The bloody battle, the bitter battle
I found a child who was helpless
And hadn't the heart to do away with it.
I had to care for what otherwise would have come to harm
I had to bend down on the floor for breadcrumbs
I had to tear myself to pieces for what was not mine
But alien.
Someone must be the helper.
Because the little tree needs its water
The little lamb loses its way when the herdsman is away
And the bleating remains unheard.

147 THE 'IS THAT SO?' SONG

why must our sons bleed like cattle on st johns day?
why must our daughters weep like the willows at dawn by the
    shores of lake urmi?

the shah of shahs has to have a new province, oh woe!
the peasant has to sell his milch cow.
the roof of the world shall be conquered, oh woe!
the roofs of the hovels will rot.

our menfolk are driven to the earth's four corners,
that our masters may feast in their manors.
the soldier's slay each other
the warlords salute each other.
of the widow's tax each penny is bitten to test its soundness
but the swords break asunder.
the battle is lost
the helmets were paid for.
   is that so? is that so?
   yea, yea, yea, yea, yea, that is so.

the state bureaus are packed, the officials spill out into the
     street.
the rivers flow over the banks and lay waste the fields.
those who cannot let down their trousers unaided, rule empires
they cannot count up to four, but stuff down eight courses.
the land is peopled by the hungry, yet the cornfarmers can find
     no customers
the weavers go home from their looms in rags.
   is that so? is that so?
   yea, yea, yea, yea, yea, that is so.

that is why our sons have no more blood in their veins
our daughters no more tears left to shed
and only the willows shed tears towards dawn by the shores of
     lake urmi.

148 SONG OF CHAOS

Sister, hide your face; brother, take your knife, the times are out
     of joint.
The noblemen are full of complaints, the simple folk full of joy.
The city says: let us drive the strong ones out of our midst
Storm the government buildings, destroy the lists of the serfs.
Now the masters' noses are put to the grindstone. Those who
     never saw the day have emerged

The ebony chests of sacrifice are broken, the precious sesame
        wood is used for beds.
He who lacked bread now possesses barns; he who lived on the
        corn of charity, now measures it out himself.
Oh, oh, oh, oh.

Where are you, General? Please, please, please restore order.
The son of the nobleman can no longer be recognised; the child
        of the mistress becomes the son of her slave
The councillors are taking shelter in the barn; he who was
        barely allowed to sleep on the wall now lolls in bed.
He who once rowed a boat now owns ships; when their owner
        looks for them, they are no longer his.
Five men are sent out by their master. They say: go yourself,
        we have arrived.
Oh, oh, oh, oh.

149   THE LUCK OF THE POOR

The people say: the poor need luck
They won't get far by using their heads.
They won't grow fat by the work of their hands.
Therefore, it is said
God has devised for them games of chance
And the dog races. Likewise God
In his unremitting care for his poor folk
Sees to it that the tax inspectors sometimes slip.
For the poor need luck.

150   HE WHO WEARS THE SHOES OF GOLD

He who wears the shoes of gold
Tramples on the weak and old
Does evil all day long
And mocks at wrong.

O to carry as one's own
Heavy is the heart of stone.
The power to do ill
Wears out the will.

Hunger he will dread
Not those who go unfed:
Fear the fall of night
But not the light.

151 SONG OF AZDAK

1

Great houses turn to ashes
And blood runs down the street.
Rats come out of the sewers
And maggots out of the meat.
The thug and the blasphemer
Lounge by the altar-stone:
Now, now, now Azdak
Sits on the Judgement throne.

2

Beware of willing Judges,
For Truth is a black cat
In a windowless room at midnight,
And Justice a blind bat.
A third and shrugging party
Alone can right our wrong.
This, this, this, Azdak
Does for a mere song.

3

No more did the Lower Orders
Tremble in their shoes
At the bellows of their Betters

At *Come-Here*'s and *Listen You*'s.
His balances were crooked
But they shouted in the streets: –
'Good, good, good is Azdak
And the measure that he metes!'

4
He took from Wealthy Peter
To give to Penniless Paul
Sealed his illegal judgements
With a waxen tear, and all
The rag-tag-and-bobtail
Ran crying up and down: –
'Cheer, cheer, cheer for Azdak
The darling of the town!'

5
To love your next-door neighbour
Approach him with an axe
For prayers and saws and sermons
Are unconvincing facts.
What miracles of preaching
A good sharp blade can do:
So, so, so, so Azdak
Makes miracles come true.

6
To feed the starving people
He broke the laws like bread
There on the seat of justice
With the gallows over his head
For more than seven hundred
Days he calmed their wails
Well, well, well, did Azdak
Measure with false scales.

7

Two summers and two winters
A poor man judged the poor
And on the wreck of justice
He brought them safe to shore
For he spoke in the mob language
That the mob understands.
I, I, I, cried Azdak
Take bribes from empty hands.

152 GALILEO THE BIBLE-BUSTER

When the Almighty made the Universe
He made the Earth and next he made the Sun
Then round the Earth he bade the Sun to turn.
That's in the Bible – Genesis Book One
And since that time all beings here below
Were in obedient circles meant to go.
Around the Pope the Cardinals
Around the Cardinals the Bishops
Around the Bishops the secretaries
Around the secretaries the aldermen
Around the aldermen the craftsmen
Around the craftsmen the servants
Around the servants the dogs, the chickens and the beggars.
Up stood the learned Galileo
Glanced briefly at the sun
And said, Almighty God was wrong in Genesis Book One.
Now that is bold, my friends, this is no matter small:
Such heresies could spread at once like bad diseases
Change Holy Writ, forsooth, what will be left at all?
Why each of us would say and do just as he pleases
                                    as he pleases
                                    as he pleases.

Good people, what will come to pass
If Galileo's teaching spreads?
No altar boy will serve the mass
No servant girl will make the beds.
Now that is grave, my friends
This is no matter small
An independent spirit spreads like bad diseases.
For life is sweet, and man is weak and after all –
How good it is, just for a change, to do just as one pleases
                                        as one pleases
                                        as one pleases.

The carpenters take wood and build
Their houses, not the church's pews.
The members of the cobbler's guild
Now boldly walk the streets in shoes.
The tenant kicks the noble lord
Right off his land – like that!
The milk the wife once fed the priest
Now makes alas her children fat.

Now that is grave, my friends
This is no matter small:
An independent spirit spreads like bad diseases.
For life is sweet, and man is weak and after all –
How good it is, just for a change, to do just as one pleases
                                        as one pleases
                                        as one pleases.

The Duchess washes her chemise
The Emperor has to fetch his beer
His troops make love behind the trees
Commands they do not hear.

Now that he mentions it, I feel
That I myself could use a change
You know, for me you have appeal . . .
Maybe tonight we could arrange . . .

Now that is grave, my friends
This is no matter small:
An independent spirit spreads like bad diseases.
For life is sweet, and man is weak and after all –

No, no, no, no, no,
Stop, Galileo, stop!
An independent spirit spreads as do diseases!
People must keep their place
Some down and some on top!
Still it feels good, just for a change, to do just as one pleases!

Good creatures who have trouble here below
In serving cruel lords and gentle Jesus –
Who bids you turn the other cheek – just so:
While they get set to strike the second blow!
Obedience will never cure your woe:
Let each of us get set to do
And do just as he pleases!
                    as he pleases!

153 SONG OF FRATERNISATION

I remember I was just seventeen
When the foe invaded our land:
With a smile he laid aside his sabre
And with a smile he gave me his hand.
That May the days were bright
And starry every night.
The regiment stood on parade:
They gave their drums the usual thwack
They led us then behind a stack
Where they fraternised with us.

Our foes were strong and many
An army-cook was mine:
I hated my foe by daylight
But, O, I loved him by moonshine.
Now all the days are bright
And starry every night.
The regiment stands on parade:
They give their drums the usual thwack
Again, again, behind a stack
There they fraternise with us.

Such a love must come from Heaven
It was the will of Fate:
The others could never understand me
How I could love where I should hate.
Then came a rainy morn
A day of grief and scorn.
The regiment stood on parade:
The drums beat as they always do.
There stood my foe, my darling too:
Then they marched away from us.

154 THE NEW CANNON SONG

1
Fritz joined the Party and Karl the SA
And Albert was up for selection.
Then they were told they must put it all away
And they drove off in every direction.
   Müller from Prussia
   Requires White Russia
   Paris will meet Schmidt's needs.
   Moving from place to place
   Avoiding face to face
   Contact with foreign forces

Equipped with tanks or horses
Why, Meier from Berlin may shortly
End up in Leeds.

2

Müller found the desert too hot
And Schmidt didn't like the Atlantic.
Will they ever see home? What a problem they've got!
And it's making them perfectly frantic.
   To get from Russia
   Back home to Prussia –
   From Tunis to Landshut.
   Moving from place to place
   Once they come face to face
   With all those foreign forces
   Equipped with tanks or horses
   Their Leader cannot lead because he's
   Ditched them for good.

3

Müller was killed, and the Nazis didn't win
And the rats ran around in the rubble.
And yet today, in the ruins of Berlin
They're expecting a *third* lot of trouble.
   Cologne is dying
   Hamburg is crying
   And Dresden's past all hope.
   But once the USA
   Finds Russia's in the way
   With a bit of luck that ought ter
   Set off a new bout of slaughter
   And Meier, back in uniform, could
   Win the whole globe!

155 BALLAD OF THE GOOD LIVING OF HITLER'S HENCHMEN

That drug-crazed Reich Marshal, who killed and jested
We saw Europe ransacked by him for plunder
Then watched him sweat at Nuremberg, and no wonder –
His paunch dwarfed those by whom he'd been arrested.
And when they asked him what he'd done it for
The man replied: For Germany alone.
Is that what built him up to twenty stone?
Don't pull my leg, I've heard that one before.
No, why he was a Nazi was just this:
Only the rich can know what living is.

Then Schacht, the Doctor who cut out your money –
The sheer length of his neck still has me baffled –
As banker once he fed on milk and honey
As bankrupter he may escape the scaffold.
He knows he won't be tortured, anyway.
But ask Schacht, now he's finally been floored
Just why he joined the whole disgraceful fraud
He'll say ambition's what led him astray.
No question what pushed him to the abyss:
Only the rich can know what living is.

And Keitel, who left southern Russia smoking
And licked the Führer's boots clean with his spittle
For having built the Wehrmacht up a little –
Ask that tank general why, he'll think you're joking.
Sipping, he'll say he answered Duty's call.
Did Duty make his casualties so great?
No mention of his getting an estate:
That kind of thing we don't discuss at all.
He got one. 'How?' is a question we dismiss.
Only the rich can know what living is.

They've all got great ideas in untold numbers
And lay claim to the loftiest of wishes.
Not one mentions a taste for favourite dishes
But all of them find demons plague their slumbers.
Each of them saw himself as Lohengrin
Or Parsifal perhaps. How could they fail?
Behind Moscow they sought the Holy Grail
And just Valhalla's flat now, not Berlin.
They've solved their private problem, then, like this:
Only the rich can know what living is.

156   EPILOGUE TO 'THE DUCHESS OF MALFI'

May these deaths enacted here
Purge by pity and by fear
Till each chastened conscience be
From all fatal passions free.
Hidden hatreds, loves obscure
Fevers living could not cure
Pride and jealousy and lust
Ruined these to squandered dust.
Here their greatness ended: May
This portent teach us to survey
Our progression from our birth.
We are set, we grow, we turn to earth
Courts adieu and all delights
All bewitching appetites!
Sweetest breath and clearest eye
Like perfumes go out and die
Praise and conversation
Fall silent as we die alone.
Vain the ambition of kings
Who seek by trophies and dead things
To leave a living name behind
And weave but nets to catch the wind.

157 PROLOGUE TO THE AMERICAN 'GALILEO'

Respected public of the way called Broad –
Tonight we're asking you to step on board
Our world of curves and measurements, where you'll descry
The newborn physics in their infancy.
Here you will see the life of the great Galileo Galilei.
The law of falling bodies versus the *Gratias Dei*
Science's fight against the rulers, put on stage
At the beginning of the modern age.
Here you'll see science in its blooming youth
Also its first compromises with the truth.
The Good, so far, has not been turned to goods
But already there's something nasty in the woods
Which stops that truth from reaching the majority
And won't relieve, but aggravate their poverty.
We think such sights are relevant today
The modern age is quick to pass away
We hope you'll lend a charitable ear
To what we say, since otherwise we fear
If you won't learn from Galileo's experience
The Bomb will put in a personal appearance.

158 EPILOGUE OF THE SCIENTISTS

And the lamp his work ignited
We have tried to keep alight
Stooping low, and yet high-minded
Unrestrained, yet laced up tight.
Making moon and stars obey us
Grovelling at our rulers' feet
We sell our brains for what they'll pay us
To satisfy our bodies' need.
So, despised by those above us
Ridiculed by those below
We've found out the laws that move us

Keep this planet on the go.
Knowledge grows too large for nitwits
Servitude expands as well
Truth becomes so many titbits
Liberators give us hell.
Riding in new railway coaches
To the new ships on the waves
Who is it that now approaches?
Only slave-owners and slaves.
Only slaves and slave-owners
Leave the trains
Taking the new aeroplanes
Through the heavens' age-old blueness.
Till the last device arrives
Astronomic
White, atomic
Obliterating all our lives.

IX–X Reconstruction of a Thinking Theatre
1948–1956

(Writing and production of *Antigone*. Berlin production of *Mother Courage*, and formation of the Berliner Ensemble. Staging of *Puntila* in Zurich and Berlin. Death of Weill. Renewed work with Eisler and Dessau. Adaptations for the Berliner Ensemble, including *The Tutor* and *Trumpets and Drums*. Poems of reconstruction and last poems.)

Now
They placed the chair, the old one
Inscribed 'here shall sit
Only the good man, and for preference everybody'
With the prescribed motions
On its old spot. From the board with the masks on it
They tore down the torn masks.
Shouting in part, in part mumbling, they sang
The text and strove to keep it
Unsullied by feelings.
At the prescribed junctures their listeners
Applauded politely, to show
Themselves as initiates and moreover
In agreement.
And he meanwhile was waiting
For that point where the
Leading player has to sit down wrongly, and when they
Cat-called as indicated he saw
That they were honouring the rules, and
Left them.

160 BRIDGE VERSES FOR ANTIGONE

But Antigone went, King Oedipus' child, with her pitcher
Gathering dust to cover the body of dead Polyneikes
Which the wrathful tyrant had thrown to the dogs and the
       vultures.
To her, gathering dust, there appeared her sister Ismene.
Sadly the gatherer mourned the fate that had come to her
       brothers
Both of them killed in the war, the first as a hero, the second
Running away, then slain; but not by the foe: by his own side.
Now she could not persuade her dutiful sister to venture

On the forbidden trip to the cast-out corpse of her brother.
So in the dawning light the sisters quarrelled and parted.

Cheered by their seeming success in the long-drawn war for
      resources
Next the elders of Thebes placed victory wreaths on their
      foreheads
Made of the shining leaves of the green and poisonous laurel
Which can cloud the senses and render the footsteps unsteady.
Outside Creon's house they stood first thing in the morning.
So, coming back from the fray and leaving his army at Argos
There in the dawning light the tyrant found them all waiting.
And he leant on his sword and told them how, over in Argos
Vultures hopped from corpse to corpse; the elders applauded.
Swiftly they crowned his brow with laurel. Yet he would not
      give them
Up his sword; but grimly handed it to a retainer.

Railing at Oedipus' son, an example to frighten the people
Next the tyrant spoke of the need for the bloodiest purges
Cleansing his foes from Theban soil, when a runner reported
Terror had not instilled terror, for dust now covered the body.
Angrily cursing the sentry and all of those who were there, he
Tested the blade of his sword with his thumb to show that he
      meant it.
Pacing with downcast eyes the elders considered the mighty
Power of man, who has bent the sea to his keel, and the oxen
Too to his yoke and the horse to his bit, the while often
      emerging
Most his essential self as he bends other men to his purpose.

Next Antigone came, brought in for interrogation:
Why had she broken the law? She turned and looked at the
      elders.
When she saw they were shocked, she replied 'To set an
      example'.
Then she appealed to the elders' pity; the elders however

Turned to Creon instead. So Antigone told them 'The man who
Seeks for power drinks brackish water, and must go on
    drinking
Further. I am neither the first nor the last of his victims'.
But they turned their backs. And Antigone told them 'I warn
    you'.
'You would see us divided', the tyrant exclaimed. 'And, divided
Why, our city will fall to outsiders'. Coolly she answered
'That's what you rulers say again and again, and your subjects
Sacrifice all for you, then when their city's been weakened
And enslaved like this it is captured by the outsiders.
Men who bow their heads see earth, and earth shall receive
    them'.
'Insolence! Would you run down your homeland? You are an
    outcast'.
Then Antigone: 'But cast out from where? It is not home
For me where my head's been bowed. Oh, many are missing
From this city since you took over. Young men and older
Will they ever come back? You started with many, and only
You came home'. At that the tyrant had nothing to answer.

'Idiot', said the elders, 'but surely you know we're victorious?'
'She is my enemy', said the tyrant, 'it gives her no pleasure'.
'Better', Antigone said, 'than sit with you in your captured
Palaces now would it be to live in our home amid rubble.'
Coldly the elders stared, and ranged themselves with the tyrant.
Then from the house next came Ismene, her sister, and told
    them
'I was the one did the deed'. But Antigone told them 'She's
    lying'.
'Settle it', Creon said as he mopped his forehead, 'between you.'
But Antigone felt herself fainting, and she implored her
Sister to survive. 'It's enough', she said, 'if they kill me.'
Then said the tyrant 'When the festivities start in our city
Honouring Bacchus, she shall be buried alive in her coffin'.
And they led her away who had bowed her head to the ruler.

Promptly the elders handed his Bacchic mask to the tyrant
Chanting the choral song: 'You who cloak yourself ready for
    dancing
Stamp your foot not too hard on the ground, nor yet on the
    new grass
Those who provoked you, though, o victor, now let them praise
    you'.
To them then there came the younger son of the ruler
Hamon, Antigone's love, the chief on command of the
    spearmen
Speaking of discontent in the city about Polyneikes.
Slowly his father spoke of his secret preoccupations
Calling for ruthless force, but the son could not understand it.
So the father wooed him, ignoring the listening elders
Begging his obdurate son to forget her who'd disobeyed him.
But when his son stood firm Creon waved his mask to deride
    him
Flicking its raffia fringe in his face till the son, in reaction
Turned his back and went. The elders observed it and
    wondered.

Grimly the victor goes off to the feast
And the elders, appalled, hear music coming from the city: the
    Bacchic dance is parading.
This is also the hour when Oedipus' child in her chamber
Hearing Bacchus afar, prepares for her ultimate journey.
Now he summons his own who, always thirsting for pleasure
Give the peaceable god the joyful answer he called for.
Mighty the victory, then, and irrestistible Bacchus
As he nears each mourner and proffers the cup of oblivion.
Then she'll abandon the mourning robes which her sons' death
    made her
Sew, and hurry to join the orgy, seeking exhaustion.
When they came to the house to fetch Antigone, she now
Instantly collapsed in the arms of her kindly attendants.
Then the solemn elders reminded her how she had chosen
Deed and death for herself. She said 'Are you trying to mock me?'

And went on to bemoan her lot: her difficult youth and
Sombre parents whom she was now on her way to join, man-
        less
And that brother who'd dragged her down to the pit that he lay
        in.
Then the elders gave her the dish and the pitcher with wine and
Millet, gifts for the dead, and tried to console her by naming
Saints and heroes who'd died in a grand and dignified manner.
Earnestly saying she should accept what the gods had decided.
Then, overcome with wrath, she chided the elders for
        cowardice
And when she saw their weakness she found her own weakness
        had left her
'Chariots are what you expect', she cried, 'full of plunder! And
        chariots
Shall you see coming here to plunder our city! The living:
Those are the ones that I mourn.' And her wrath was stifled by
        sobbing.
And she looked around, saw Thebes as a lovable city
Roofs and hills and hedges, and solemnly bowed in its honour
Saying farewell. Then again she changed from pity to anger.
'You, my city, produced inhuman monsters, and that means
Dust and ashes for you.' To her maids: 'If anyone asks you
Where Antigone went, then say: To the grave, to find shelter.'

Turning away she went, and her step was light and determined.
After her gazed the elders unseeing, and chanted the chorus:
'She too formerly ate of the fresh-baked bread from the ovens
Deep in the shade of the rocks. Nor till her brother was
        murdered
Did she raise her voice so loudly in condemnation'.
But the warner cannot have got as far as the pit yet
When the festive city is seized by a terrible knowledge.
For, aroused by the rumours of strife in the house of the ruler
Enter the seer, the blind one. And, mocking, a figure that
        circles
Round about his path and rattles the mask with its raffia

Fringes above his head, pursuing him over the open
Square, and raising its foot in the dance's insolent measure
Pointing with scornful thumb to show up the old man's
      afflictions
Cheekily tapping the way with its stick for the tentative gait: it's
      Creon, drunk with his triumph. The elders look on in
      silence.

'Foolish old man, you don't seem to like festivities. Why have
You no wreath? Look at us!' And his voice was sharp with
      resentment.
'Must a blind man', said the seer, 'be followed by one even
      blinder?
Know that the gods dislike disputes and crimes against nature.
Ugly now loom the birds that have fed on Oedipus' offspring.'
Laughing, the ruler said 'Yes, your birds always fly as you want
      them
Following your slightest whim, a whim that is paid for in
      silver'.
'Don't offer that to me; what use is silver in wartime?'
Said the seer. 'But the war is over', the ruler responded.
'Is it over?' inquired the seer. 'For down at the harbour
Fish are still cured for the troops as though they were far from
      returning.
You are cruel. But why? What follies have you embarked on?'
Silent the tyrant stood and could not think how to answer.

Then the seer got up and left. And mumbling obscurely
Slowly the tyrant started to go. The elders observed it.
Fear by fear was addressed, they dared to ask him a question:
'What is the news of the war, Creon?' He replied to them 'Not
      good'.
Then they came up to him, and the mask of peace he was
      holding
Holding their own peace masks in their hands as they all
      approached him
And they argued about the war: was it their war or his war?

'You it was forced me to go to bring you back ore from the
    Argives.'
'But you told us we'd win.' 'I told you: sooner or later.'
And he prepared to leave. Once more the elders in anger
Gathered around their king and cried out 'Bring back our
    army!':
The army was cause for concern, but their own property more
    so.
Then he took the mask of peace, which he stuck in the soil
    there.
'Right, I will send for the army; my eldest shall bring it,
    Megareus.
Iron shall they have in their hands to smite ungrateful civilians.'

Still there hung in the air the menacing name of Megareus
When a runner arrived: 'Lord, stiffen your lip, for Megareus
Is no more and your army is beaten, the foe is approaching.'
Gasping, he spoke of the battle: the army, split by internal
Strife over Polyneikes' death, bore its spears with indifference
While the people of Argos like tigers fought for their
    homesteads.
'Tiger-like now they will come', said the runner. 'I am so happy
That I am here.' And he clutched his waist, and with fearful
    grimaces
Right before Creon's mask of peace he fell heavily earthwards.
At this Creon cried out, cried loudly out as a father.
Meanwhile the elders exclaimed 'A tiger-like foe is approaching
While victorious Thebes still dances. Summon the spearmen!'
And the elders tore off the victory wreaths from their foreheads
And they broke their Bacchic staffs and covered the body
Up with wreaths and masks, 'Woe to us!' loudly exclaiming.

Then the ruler remembered his next son, Hamon, the younger –
He who commanded the spearmen – and now to placate him
Hastened away forthwith to grant Antigone pardon.
But the elders regrouped, their brazen dishes resounding
Drumming to waken the town from its lethal victory junket.

Hollow the brazen alarm interrupted the dances to Bacchus
Till the triumphant strut gave way to a timorous scurry.
Threading her way through the crowds a childish messenger,
     youngest
Of those maids who had taken Antigone off, now addressed
     them:
'Bleeding to death lies Hamon, torn from life by his own hand!
When he saw Antigone there, saw how they had hanged her
Straight he fell on his sword, ignoring the pleas of his father'.
Led by Antigone's maids then came to the elders their awesome
Leader. And in his hands he carried a blood-spattered garment.

'Torn from life is Hamon. Torn from life are the Thebans.
Since I have failed, let them provide a meal for the vultures!'
And to the elders he showed the bloodstained cloak of the son
     who
Would not yield him the sword. And anxious now, and pathetic –
Never to learn, he who had led so many went stumbling
Off to the stricken city once more. But behind him the elders
Followed their leader still, this time to death and destruction.

161 SONG OF THE HOURS

In the first hour Jesus mild
Who had prayed since even
Was betrayed and led before
Pontius the heathen.

Pilate found him innocent
Free from fault and error
Therefore, having washed his hands
Sent him to King Herod.

In the third hour he was scourged
Stripped and clad in scarlet
And a plaited crown of thorns

Set upon his forehead.

Thus they dressed the Son of Man
So they could deride him
And they made him bear the cross
Where they crucified him.

In the sixth hour, naked now
To his cross they nailed him
And the people and the thieves
Mocked him and reviled him.

This is Jesus King of Jews
Cried they in derision
Till the sun withdrew its light
From that awful vision.

At the ninth hour Jesus wailed
Why hast thou me forsaken?
Soldiers brought him vinegar
Which he left untaken.

Then he yielded up the ghost
And the earth was shaken
Rended was the temple's veil
And the saints were wakened.

Soldiers broke the two thieves' legs
As the night descended
Thrust a spear in Jesus' side
When his life had ended.

Still they mocked, as from his wound
Flowed the blood and water
Thus blasphemed the Son of Man
With their cruel laughter.

Three songs for 'Mr Puntila and his man Matti'

162 PLUM SONG

In our village one fair morning
When the plums were ripe and blue
Came a gig as day was dawning
Bore a young man passing through.

As we picked the plums in baskets
He lay down beneath a tree
Fair his hair, and if you ask it's
Not much that he failed to see.

Once the plums were stoned and boiling
He joked condescending-wise
And thereafter, blandly smiling
Stuck his thumb in sundry pies.

Ere the plums were on the table
Up he jumped and off he ran.
Ever since we've been unable
To forget that fair young man.

163 THE BALLAD OF THE FORESTER AND THE COUNTESS

A countess there lived in the northern countree
And lovely and fair was she.
'Oh forester, see how my garter is loose
It is loose, it is loose.
Bend yourself down and tie it for me.'

'My lady, my lady, don't look at me so.
I work here because I must eat.

Your breasts they are white but the axe-edge is cold,
It is cold, it is cold.
Death is bitter, though loving is sweet.'

The forester fled that very same night.
He rode till he came to the sea.
'Oh boatman, oh take me away in your boat,
In your boat, in your boat.
Take me away far over the sea.'

A lady fox loved a rooster one day.
'Oh handsome, I must be your bride!'
The evening was pleasant but then came the dawn,
Came the dawn, came the dawn.
All of his feathers were spread far and wide.

164 PUNTILA SONG

I

Old Puntila went on a three-day blind
In the Tavasthus hotel.
He left an enormous tip behind
But the waiter said 'Go to hell!'.
O waiter, how can you insult him so?
Is life not gay and sweet?
The waiter replied 'How am I to know?
I've been far too long on my feet'.

2

The landowner's daughter, Eva P.
A novel once did read.
She marked the page where it told her she
Belonged to a higher breed.
She turned to the chauffeur all the same
With a curious kind of stare:

'Come sport with me, Mr What's-its-name
I'm told you've a man in there.'

3
Old Puntila met an early bird
As he strolled in the morning dew:
'O milkmaid with the milk-white breasts
Where are you going to?
You're going up to milk my cows
Before cockcrow, I see.
But I don't only want to get you roused
But to take you to bed with me'.

4
The bath hut on the Puntila farm
Is the place for a bit of fun
Where a servant may go to take a bath
When the lady's having one.
Old Puntila said 'I'm giving my child
To be a diplomatist's wife.
He won't mind her being a shade defiled
If his debts are paid for life'.

5
The landowner's daughter wandered in
To the kitchen at half-past nine:
'O chauffeur, I find you so masculine
Come bring your fishing line'.
'Yes, miss', the chauffeur replies to her
'I can see that you're ripe for bed
But can't you see that I prefer
To read the paper instead?'

6
The league of Puntila's would-be brides
Arrived at the nuptial feast.
Old Puntila swore he would have their hides

And roared like a wounded beast.
But when did a sheep get a woollen skirt
Since shearing first began?
'I'll sleep with you all, but you're only dirt
In the house of a gentleman'.

7
The women from Kurgela jeered, it's said
When they saw how they'd been foiled
But their shoes and stockings were worn to a shred
And their Sunday outing was spoiled.
And any woman who still believes
That a rich man will honour her claim
Can be thankful to lose no more than her shoes
And has only herself to blame.

8
Old Puntila thumped on the table, piled
With glorious wedding cake:
'How could I ever betroth my child
To that slab of frozen hake?'
He wanted his servant to have her instead
But the servant wanted to try her
Then said the servant: 'I'm not having her
She's not what I require'.

165 EIGHTEENTH-CENTURY SONG

Oh silent winter snow
That cloaks the earth below.
Men sit and idly gaze
Upon the snow-clad days.
And in the barn the silent cows
Hark to the silence as they drowse.

Six Songs from 'Trumpets and Drums'

166 MELINDA'S SONG

Chloe in the forest glade.
Achilles from behind a tree
Stepped, 'Oh could you, pretty maid
Favour me?'
    Fearfully the maiden gazed
    Hid her features in the meadow grass.
    Said the hero, mournful and amazed
    'Don't you care then for my gold cuirass?'

As Achilles turned to go
Birds fell silent in the brake.
Listening to the brook's bright flow
Chloe spake.
    Said the maid: 'It's easy to resist
    Lion, stag, and strutting peacock, too.
    Golden armour leaves me unimpressed
    But I have noticed that your eyes are blue'.

167 VICTORIA'S SONG

At certain times in life we're driven
Head over heels to make a painful choice
Whether to fate and passion we should give in
Or let ourselves be guided by reason's prudent voice.
    But the bosom swells with emotion
    And the mind hasn't got much to say
    The sail fills with wind on the ocean
    And the ship doesn't ask long: Which way?

Sister, what metal are you made of?
Where is your modesty and where your pride?
There's hardly any plight or peril you're afraid of
Once love has caught you up in its tumultuous tide.
    The doe runs after the stag
    And the lioness follows her lord
    And to be with her lover a maid
    Will go to the ends of the world.

168 WHEN I LEAVE YOU

When I leave you for the war, dear
Leave you standing on the shore, dear
On the queen's great ship as out of port we sail
Find another sweetheart, Minny
For this ship goes to Virginny
And when I'm gone, my love, my love for you will pale . . .

I'll be cheering with the others
For our husbands, sweethearts, brothers
When the queen's great ship goes sailing with the tide.
Jimmy dear, you must believe me
Memories of you will grieve me
When I'm walking with another at my side.

169 ARMY SONG

Seventeen reservists from Z Battery
Stand eyeing the women of Gaa
The each reservist pushes
One of them into the bushes
Where they take a close look at the evening star.
    And that will be the only star
    She'll see in Gaa
    It stays there for an hour or two, then au revoir.
    Aha.

In the morning you won't find Z Battery
They ride off at first light
But on leaving each reservist
Has a fig to give his dearest
– Which makes a pound of figs, if I am right.
    That fig will be the only thi-
    ng she'll get to see
    A fig is all she ever gets, apparently.
    Dear me.

170 SONG OF THE EXCEPTION

Everybody paid – more or less
When the king was in distress
Armies cost a lot each day
All paid up without delay
All except for E. N. Smith.

But the king got very tough
Didn't think they gave enough
Plucked them out of bed and alehouse
Packed them all off to the jailhouse
All except for E. N. Smith.

171 RECRUIT'S SONG

Come on, Johnny, pack your gear.
In Virginia you won't hear
Children's screams or woman's plea
Over the hills and over the sea.

Good King George is older now
Care and worry crease his brow
His empire's gone for a cup of tea
Over the hills and over the sea.

Sweetheart, if I'm left to die
Happiness will have passed us by
While good King George reigns immovably
Over the hills and over the sea.

Editorial notes

KEY TO MAJOR WORKS AND THEIR CONSTITUENT SONGS

Since I have tried to arrange the songs and poems in chronological order rather than strictly according to the works where they occur, the following gives some idea how those works are made up (including reference to discarded items). At the same time it shows what has been selected from each play or other work represented. Their titles are arranged in chronological order (so far as this is clear). The composers named are those most identified with the relevant works; complete reference to all settings being clearly out of the question.

1918–1922. **Baal.** Songs mostly to tunes by Brecht. Five of them (nos. 3–5, 7 and 9) were included in the *Devotions*, 'The drowned girl' (no. 9) and 'Death in the woods' (no. 4) being subsequently set independently by Kurt Weill. The 1926 Berlin production, directed by Brecht for a single club performance, was of a revised version bearing the title **Life story of a man called Baal.** According to Oskar Homolka, who played the title part, it included the poem 'Remembering Maria A'. (*Poems 1913–1956*, p. 35). Brecht himself sang the 'Hymn' (no. 5) on a darkened stage.

1919–1922. **Drums in the Night.** The only song is 'Legend of the dead soldier' (no. 2) to Brecht's own tune. This was varied later by Ernst Busch and subsequently adapted and orchestrated by various composers.

1919. **The Wedding.** Later renamed *The Petit-Bourgeois Wedding*. Contains the 'Ballad of chastity in a major key' (no. 8) to a tune by Brecht.

1921–1922. **In the Jungle.** Later revised as **Jungle** (Berlin 1923) and **In the Jungle of Cities** (Darmstadt 1927). In the original version, as used for the Munich première in May 1923, John Garga and the sailor Manky sang Kipling's 'There were three men that buried a fourth'. One script has them also singing lines from the 'Ballad of the girl and the soldier' (no. 18), later replaced by 'Fifteen men on a dead man's chest' from *Treasure Island*. The play also contains many unacknowledged quotations from Rimbaud. No specific music has been identified.

1923–1924. **Life of Edward the Second.** The play, an adaptation of Marlowe, is largely in blank verse. The Ballad-Singer's one song ('Eddy's tart has a beard on his chest') has a tune by Brecht. Mortimer, beside the monologue which we print (no. 12), has a song 'The women of England in widows' weeds'.

1924–1926. **Man equals Man.** Prior to the double première (Darmstadt and Düsseldorf, September 1926) the only song (no. 20) was to a tune which Brecht and Elisabeth Hauptmann had supposedly derived from *Madam Butter-*

fly, while Begbick was given three daughters who acted as a small jazz group. This tune was adapted by Meisel, Piscator's musical director, for the 1927 broadcast that so impressed Weill (and led to his meeting Brecht), and also for the 1928 Berlin production by Erich Engel, which used Meisel's 1927 settings of the 'Song of Widow Begbick's drinking truck' (no. 21) and the refrain of the 'Cannon song' (no. 19). For the second Berlin production, directed by Brecht himself at the Staatstheater in 1931, the play was extensively revised; Weill wrote the incidental music, including a 'Nachtmusik' and a 'Schlachtmusik', and set the newly-written 'Song of the flow of things' (no. 35). This music is now lost, having supposedly been confiscated by the Nazis. Some new music was written by Dessau after the Second World War, when the French director Jean-Marie Serreau staged the play in 1954.

1927–1929. **Mahagonny.** Following their first contact in spring 1927, Brecht and Weill agreed to write an opera on the Mahagonny theme, which had already inspired the former's 'Mahagonny Songs' to his own and/or Hauptmann's concocted tunes. Some of the related poems (like nos. 17 and 24) were never used in the larger project, but the eventual libretto **Rise and Fall of the City of Mahagonny** was a montage made up of the 'Songs', earlier poems like 'Lucifer's evening song' (no. 1) and 'Tahiti' (no. 11), the two English-language 'Songs' contributed by Hauptmann (nos. 25 and 26), the 'Poem on a dead man' (27), two 'city-dweller' poems (nos. 30 and 34) and a number of texts written specially for it (29, 31–33, 38, 53). Before Weill could start work on the music, however, he was asked to write a 'short opera' for the 1927 Baden-Baden Festival, which was to be centred on such small-scale works. Accordingly he and Brecht made the **Mahagonny Songspiel** or **Little Mahagonny** consisting of the four (nos. 13, 15, 25 and 26) 'Songs' printed that year in the *Devotions*, plus no. 14, a finale and five short orchestral interludes. Work on the opera was only completed during 1929, following *The Threepenny Opera*, whose commissioning and startling success neither man had allowed for. There was thus some thematic and artistic overlap between these two works, the 1928 version of *Man equals Man*, and the poems of the 'Reader for those who live in cities' on which Brecht had been working in 1926 and 1927. With Caspar Neher as a third partner, the overall structural principle that emerged was Brecht's montage-like concept of the 'separation of the elements'.

1928. **The Threepenny Opera** started as an adaptation of Elisabeth Hauptmann's translation of Gay's *The Beggar's Opera*, with which E. J. Aufricht, a new impresario, wanted to open his tenure of the Theater am Schiffbauerdamm on 31 August (his birthday). The work was done at speed, Brecht writing most of the songs that year (aside from the 'Cannon Song' no. 19, Peachum's opening song, which was taken from the original, and 'Pirate Jenny' no. 39 which had been set a year before by the cabaret composer F. S. Bruinier, who died that summer). Many of the 1928 songs were based on a German translation of Villon by 'K. L. Ammer' (Karl Klammer), who later squeezed a two and a half per cent royalty out of Hauptmann, in unfair lieu of Brecht.

Subsequently there was some reshuffling of numbers during the work's year-long run, and later Brecht added new items first for the film treatment in 1930 (nos. 72–74), then for the *Threepenny Novel* in 1934 (no. 101), and finally for a post-war version in 1949 (154, 155) which Weill was reluctant to accept.

1928–1929. Weill was commissioned to write a work specially for radio, perhaps because this new genre was to be the focus of the 1929 Baden-Baden Festival. His answer was the **Berlin Requiem**, broadcast by Radio Frankfurt on 22 May and consisting once again of a fluctuating montage of different poems by Brecht. Weill seems to have picked these with a view to commemorating the unhappy events of 1919, and at one time included 'Red Rosa' (no. 52). This song and his setting of 'At Potsdam "Unter den Eichen"' (*Poems 1913–1956*, p. 156) as a 'workers' chorus' met with opposition from some of the other stations (including Berlin radio itself) who had been expected to broadcast it. Nos. 4, 9 and 27 were also among the songs set, though 9, 'The Drowned Girl' from *Baal*, was the only one of the three to be finally included.

For the festival proper, which followed in July, Weill and Brecht wrote their first truly didactic piece, then called **Flight of the Lindberghs** and later renamed by Brecht **The Ocean Flight.** It was described as a 'Radio Play', published as such in the April number of *Uhu* (Berlin), added to by Brecht and Hindemith, and broadcast from the festival performance. From this we print no. 62. The actual term 'Lehrstück' however was reserved for a companion text which Brecht gave Hindemith to set under that title and later called the 'Badener Lehrstück' or **Baden-Baden cantata of acceptance** (no. 63 is from this). Subsequently Weill reset Hindemith's numbers for the first piece, while from autumn 1930 onwards Brecht refused to let the latter's music for the second be performed.

1929. **Happy End**, again commissioned by Aufricht for the Schiffbauerdamm, was intended to be the *TPO* mixture as before. Hauptmann wrote the dialogue, on an idea by Brecht for a Chicago gangster play. Brecht supplied the songs, Weill the music, Neher the sets. However, the times were changing; the play was too lightweight, and Brecht had become too involved with the 'Lehrstück' form and its possibilities, to overhaul it as he had done its precursor. As a result it had a very brief run and was quickly forgotten apart from its songs. Of these, nos. 54–61 appear to have been written specifically for it, though the most famous, 'Surabaya Johnny' (no. 37), had been conceived some two years earlier on the basis of a Kipling original and set as a cabaret song by Bruinier. Nos. 55 and 61, along with new material (such as nos. 84, 85), were soon afterwards used for the much more political **Saint Joan of the Stockyards**. This long unstaged work was not provided with any music in Brecht's lifetime.

At the end of the 1920s Brecht also had a number of play projects which he was unable to finish, and some of them contained memorable writing. We have included items from several of these. The most important was **The Bread-shop**, which dealt with Berlin life during the economic crisis of 1929–33, when unemployment was rocketing. From this come nos. 67–70. 'The horror of being poor' (no. 36) is from an earlier attempt at a similar theme, **The rich man and the poor man**, which dates from before Brecht became a convinced communist in 1929. **Downfall of the egoist Johann Fatzer** likewise is set in Germany of the 1920s, though it began turning into a 'Lehrstück' after both Piscator and Aufricht had failed to stage it; no. 71 is from the accompanying 'commentary'. Nos. 65 and 66 come from **Nothing comes from Nothing**, which was under consideration by Piscator at the same time as the *Fatzer* play. The splendid Anne Smith poem (no. 28) was from the earlier **Man from Manhattan**, a piece of 'Amerikanismus' which got swallowed up in the *Mahagonny* complex. In none of these cases however did Brecht ever get as far as recruiting a composer, and the same applies to the 'Lehrstück' **The Exception and the Rule** (nos. 64 and 83), which was completed but not performed till the 1950s, possibly for that very reason.

1929–1930. Through the communist actor-singer Ernst Busch, Brecht met Hanns Eisler, who had been working with the 'Red Megaphone' agitprop group since autumn 1927, setting texts by such Left poets as Erich Weinert and Robert Gilbert ('David Weber'). For Hindemith's 1930 festival, which was to shift from Baden-Baden to Berlin, Brecht now planned two linked didactic works derived from the Noh play *Taniko*: a 'school play' *Der Jasager* with Weill, and its updated and politicised counterpart in close collaboration with Eisler. This second was **The Decision** (known in the US as **The Measures Taken**), which was rejected by the festival committee and performed by three Communist choirs in Berlin at the end of that year. Here (in nos. 75–82) there was no montage or re-use of old material, though the songs soon became used separately for agitational purposes. A Bach-like cantata form was used as a very powerful dramatic medium, with the chorus as a kind of investigating committee judging the story acted out by one singer and three actors. (Brecht later barred this work from performance because of political opposition from right and left alike, and consequently never revised it, though he felt at the end of his life that its technique could serve as a model for the future.)

1931–1932. The second major work in collaboration with Eisler was a dramatisation in didactic, highly economical and portable form of Gorky's 1905 novel **The Mother**. Here again the songs (nos. 88–99) were written as part of the play, although the acting and dialogue were more important than in *The Decision*. At first only nine were composed, including items spoken to music, but with the 1935 New York production, which both Brecht and Eisler attended and criticised (see no. 109), the number increased, and the music was further extended, first by a cantata version which Eisler made for Vienna in 1949 and then by Brecht's more conventionally theatrical production of 1951 with the Berliner Ensemble. Other ventures with Eisler just before Hitler's take-over in 1933 were some political cabaret numbers, the communist film **Kuhle Wampe** (no. 86) and a sketch (no. 87) for a Christmas revue at the end of 1932.

1933–1937. Though they continued to collaborate on agitational songs (like no. 108, which would be reused for *The Days of the Commune* two decades later) the main Brecht-Eisler project of the first years of their exile was **The Round Heads and the Pointed Heads**, which developed from a commission to make an adaptation of *Measure for Measure*. Here, as in the case of *Happy End*, the songs (nos. 100, 103–106 and 110–111) are stronger than the play. This had its première in Danish at a small Copenhagen theatre, and has never had a definitive German production. With Weill, who emigrated first to France, then in 1936 to the United States, Brecht wrote the sung ballet **The Seven Deadly Sins** in 1933 (no. 102); with Piscator's former dramaturg Leo Lania he worked in London on the **Oilfield** project (no. 107), which however came to nothing. Of the various plans which he and Eisler had discussed in Moscow in 1935, the most fruitful appears to have been that for short plays about life in Nazi Germany, which led to the writing of the first **Fear and Misery of the Third Reich** scenes in the summer of 1937. Only a handful of these however had been completed by the time of Eisler's final departure for the United States at the end of that year, so that the long 'German march-past' poem (no. 114) that gave them their overall structure was not set by him. Paul Dessau, who had not yet come to know Brecht, set part of it for the Paris première in 1938, but his music was not subsequently used and it was Eisler who set the interludes for the new wartime (**Private Life of the Master Race**) framework for the New York production of 1945.

1939. **Mother Courage** was written in Sweden within weeks of the outbreak of war. Its songs originally included 'The Ballad of the Waterwheel' (no. 106), a revised version of 'Surabaya Johnny' (no. 37), the 'Solomon Song' (no. 44) from *The Threepenny Opera* – these three apparently to be sung in their Eisler and Weill settings. The 'Mother Courage's song' (no. 117) was from the first to be set to the 'L'Etendard de la Pitié' melody which Brecht had adopted some twenty years earlier for 'Ballad of the Pirates' (*Poems* p. 18). The Finnish composer Simon Parmet, who had initially undertaken to compose or arrange music for the play, was replaced for the première by the Zurich Schau-spielhaus's musical director Paul Burkhard (1911–1977).

It is not clear exactly when the 'Ballad of the Waterwheel' was dropped and 'Surabaya Johnny' took the new form of 'Fraternisation song' (no. 153), but in California in 1946 (where he was now in contact with Brecht) Paul Dessau assumed the task of writing homogeneous settings for the majority of the songs as we have them (nos. 117–121), finishing with the addition of the 'Song of the Hours' (no. 161) in 1948–49.

1939. Within days of completing *Mother Courage* Brecht went on to write the radio play **The Trial of Lucullus** (see no. 123) for the composer Hilding Rosenberg to set for Stockholm radio. This came to nothing when the radio authorities became nervous of the play's anti-war message and its likely reception by their neighbours in Nazi Germany. In the US however the script was translated by Hoffman Hays, who had been working with Eisler, then composed by Roger Sessions and performed at Berkeley in 1947. Brecht evidently took exception to this, despite the power of the score, and barred further performances. Dessau, whom Brecht asked to approach Stravinsky in California with a view to making an opera version, eventually started writing the opera himself, with controversial results in 1951 when the East German State Opera was prevented from staging it publicly until it had been revised.

1939–1941. **The Good Person of Szechwan**, which had been in Brecht's mind even before he went into exile, was written and completed in Scandinavia. Here again the songs appear to have been mainly written for the play (nos. 125–132), aside from the 'Song of the smoke' (no. 124) which derives from an early cabaret song (no. 10). One of them (no. 130) was set as a separate song by Eisler in California; the rest were composed by Dessau following his work on *Mother Courage*. Brecht had however hoped to interest Weill in the play once he himself got to America in 1941, and accordingly in 1943 he wrote a shortened and tightened-up version of it, which Weill might use for a semi-opera. Nothing came of this, for Brecht had no wish to be a mere librettist, while Weill seems to have wanted the kind of 'book and lyrics' which he had used so successfully for musicals like *Lady in the Dark* (1941). The music for the play's première, which like that of *Mother Courage* took place in wartime Zurich, was by the local composer H. G. Früh (1903–1945).

1938–1956. The original version of **Galileo Galilei** had its première in Zurich about seven months after *The Good Person of Szechwan*. It had been written in Denmark in 1938 (when it included no. 115) but there were apparently no songs in Leonard Steckel's production. In 1944 Brecht began work in Santa Monica on an English version in collaboration with Charles Laughton, and with various helpers wrote the Ballad-Singer's long song (no. 152) and the verses which introduce each scene. For the eventual Hollywood production by Joseph Losey and Brecht in July 1946 (with Laughton in the title part) Eisler wrote settings for these words, which were translated back for the final German **Life of Galileo** after Brecht's return to Europe in 1947. The prologue and epilogue for the New York production of the Laughton version were evidently not used, since Brecht wrote these in German and they were only translated for our edition of the play (nos. 157–158).

1942–1946. In the United States Brecht wrote **The Visions of Simone Machard** in 1942 with Lion Feuchtwanger (nos. 133 and 134), and Eisler began writing the music, though he soon gave up, only resuming in 1946. This, he told Hans Bunge, was because Brecht wanted him to give higher priority to the music for **Schweik in the Second World War** (1943), which Weill had originally been planning to write (with Lenya singing Mrs Kopecka) but abandoned because of a clash with Piscator's *Schweik* plans and a consequent uncertainty about the rights. Eisler had already composed at least two of the numbers – 113 and 138 – independently, though most of the rest (including nos. 136, 137, 139 and the quasi-operatic 'scenes in the higher regions' featuring Hitler) were completed much later. The only one of Brecht's American projects to reach Broadway, aside from the Laughton *Galileo*, was an adaptation of **The Duchess of Malfi** for Elisabeth Bergner, on which he worked with Hays and W. H. Auden (nos. 140 and 156). But this was a failure and most, if not all, of Brecht's contribution was cut by the director George Rylands.

1944. **The Caucasian Chalk Circle** was a hybrid of two different stories: the Chinese tale of the chalk circle and the disputed child, and a short story which Brecht had written about a rumbustious judge in his own home town of Augsburg. He also envisaged a mixture of two types of song: an Asian type of narrative singing by a traditional bard or ballad-singer who tells the story in poetic language, and songs by the individual characters (the majority of our nos. 141 to 151). Eisler considered the task impossible and turned it down, and since the intended Broadway production starring Luise Rainer soon fell through, Brecht was in no hurry to find another composer before his return to Europe. There he tried to interest the Austrian Gottfried von Einem, with a view to production at the Salzburg Festival and in Vienna; then subsequently approached Carl Orff and Boris Blacher before turning to Dessau around 1952. Over the following two years Dessau tried to give him what he wanted, by making use of Azerbaidjani (Caucasian) folk tunes and exotic instrumentation, till in October 1954 Brecht could direct the Berliner Ensemble in the play's full-scale German première, with Ernst Busch doubling the parts of the ballad-singer and the judge. Despite this production's success Brecht was not happy with the music, and would have preferred something simpler.

1948–1950. Dessau also wrote the music for the Ensemble's 1949 production of **Mr Puntila and his Man Matti** (a play originally written in Finland in 1940/41), when Brecht first added the inter-scene narrative verses of the 'Puntila Song' and one or two other small items (see nos. 162–164). He did the same for the company's adaptations of **The Tutor** by Goethe's contemporary Lenz (see no. 165) and of Molière's *Dom Juan*, making use of eighteenth-century models. For the 1948 Swiss **Antigone** production which prepared Brecht, Helene Weigel and Caspar Neher for their assault on the Berlin theatre there was no music: the whole play was in verse apart from the prologue, and the hexameter 'bridge verses' (no. 160) had a special rôle in both production and rehearsal.

1955. For the Berliner Ensemble adaptation and production of Farquhar's *The Recruiting Officer* as **Trumpets and Drums** only months before his death, Brecht turned to Rudolf Wagner-Régeny, a composer now resident in the GDR who had written operas with Neher under the Third Reich. The model for this play's use of songs (see our nos. 166–171) was to be *The Threepenny Opera*. But once again the songs seem to have been written specially for the occasion, even though no. 169 might be thought to hark back to Brecht's Kipling phase. With Wagner-Régeny Brecht did as he used to do with Dessau (but did not do with Eisler); that is to say he would sing melodies and beat out rhythms to show the composer what he wanted.

1. Brecht's own tunes
   – to the *Mahagonny* and *Baal* songs are printed in his *Hauspostille*, Berlin, 1927, also in some later reprints and Eric Bentley's English-language version *Manual of Piety*, New York, 1966. This last adds Brecht's tune for the 'Legend of the Dead Soldier' from the first edition of *Trommeln in der Nacht*. All are melodies only.

2. Paul Dessau
   Die Verurteilung des Lukullus, Oper in 12 Szenen. Piano score, Henschel, E. Berlin, 1961.
   Lieder aus 'Der gute Mensch von Sezuan'. E. Berlin, 1952. Five of these songs are also in –
   Lieder und Gesänge. Henschel, E. Berlin, 1957, new edition 1962. (Fifty-two songs for voice and pf., further including twelve from *The Caucasian Chalk Circle*, ten from the *Lucullus* opera and four written for *Man equals Man*.)
   Eight songs from the incidental music to *Herr Puntila und sein Knecht Matti* are in Brecht's *Versuche 10* (Suhrkamp, Frankfurt).

3. Hanns Eisler
   Die Massnahme, Lehrstück, op. 20. Piano score. Universal-Edition, Vienna and Leipzig, 1931. Out of print. Some songs are included in vols I and II of Eisler's –
   Lieder und Kantaten. Breitkopf und Härtel, Leipzig, 1956–66, which also contain items from *The Mother*, *The Round Heads and the Pointed Heads* etc. There are ten volumes in all. The boys' choruses from *Galileo* are in vol. IV, *Simone Machard* items in vol. V, and *Fear and Misery* and *Days of the Commune* items in vol. VI. However, this series is in course of being superseded by the East German Academy's new Collected Works (*Gesammelte Werke*), published by Deutscher Verlag für Musik, Leipzig, (1976–).
   Neun Balladen aus 'Die Mutter', for voices and four instruments. Deutscher Verlag für Musik, Leipzig, 1977. These are from the 1931 version of the play.
   Die Mutter. Kantate für Mezzo-Sopran, Bariton und zwei Klaviere. Deutscher Verlag für Musik, Leipzig, 1977 is a much later concert arrangement.
   Brecht/Eisler: *Lieder Gedichte Chöre*, Editions du Carrefour, Paris, 1934, contains three songs from *The Mother*.
   The *Brecht-Eisler Songbook* contains a selection of songs with German texts and translations by Eric Bentley.

4. Paul Hindemith

Lehrstück (the Badener Lehrstück). Piano score, Schott, Mainz, 1929. New edition with English text by Geoffrey Skelton, 1974.

Lindberghflug. Hindemith's *Sämtliche Werke*, Band I, 6 (Schott, Mainz, 1982) includes the original version of this collaborative work by Hindemith and Kurt Weill, of which the six numbers composed by the former were later re-composed by Weill.

5. Rudolf Wagner-Régeny

Pauken und Trompeten (Bühnenmusik). Piano score. Peters, Leipzig, 1980.

6. Kurt Weill

Aufstieg und Fall der Stadt Mahagonny. Opera (UE 9851), Universal-Edition, Vienna and Leipzig, 1929 and 1964. Revised edition 1969.

Das Berliner Requiem. Kleine Kantate. Edited by David Drew (UE 9786), Universal-Edition, Vienna, 1967.

Der Jasager. School Opera. Piano score (UE 8206). Universal-Edition, Vienna and Leipzig, 1930. New Edition with English text by J. M. Potts, 1969.

Der Lindberghflug. Radio Lehrstück. Piano score. Universal-Edition, Vienna and Leipzig, 1930. For first, collaborative version see under Hindemith above.

Die Dreigroschenoper (The Threepenny Opera). A play with music. Piano score (UE 8851). Universal-Edition, Vienna and Leipzig, 1928 and subsequent reprints.

Die Sieben Todsünden (The Seven Deadly Sins). Ballet mit Gesang in acht Teilen. Piano score. Schott, Mainz, 1960. With English translation by W. H. Auden and Chester Kallman, 1972.

Happy End. Comedy with music in 3 Acts, by Dorothy Lane (pseudonym for Elisabeth Hauptmann). Piano score with English translation by Michael Geliot. Universal-Edition, Vienna, 1950 (UE 11685). Adaptation by Michael Feingold (UE 17243), 1981. (These omit 'hosanna Rockefeller'.)

Mahagonny. Piano score, reconstructed by David Drew. Universal-Edition, Vienna, 1963.

7. Miscellaneous.

The *Großes Brecht-Liederbuch* edited in three volumes by Fritz Hennenberg and co-published by Suhrkamp, Frankfurt, and Henschel, E. Berlin contains a large selection of songs set by the above composers and also by Brecht's first musical collaborator F. S. Bruinier, who lapsed into relative obscurity after his early death in 1928. The piano accompaniments are somewhat simplified.

Publications by Universal-Edition, Vienna, listed above are distributed in the United States by European-American Music Inc., New York. Publications by Breitkopf and Härtel and Deutscher Verlag für Müsik (Leipzig) are distributed in the UK by Schott.

The following notes give the German title(s) of each poem and page references to the one-volume *Die Gedichte von Bertolt Brecht in einem Band* published by Suhrkamp, Frankfurt, 1981, whose pagination is the same as that of the three volumes of poems in the 1967 collected works (GW) or, from p. 1085 on, the same publisher's *Gedichte und Lieder aus Stücken und Prosatexten*. These are mostly followed by page references to the nine-volume *Gedichte* (Ged.) which preceded GW in the early 1960s. Some poems not in GW are marked 'adN', because they are in the 'Supplement 2' *Gedichte aus dem Nachlass* published by the same publishers in 1982. Some, marked 'St', are only to be found in the 'plays' volumes (vols. 1 to 9) of GW. There are also references to Fritz Hennenberg's three-volume *Das grosse Brecht-Liederbuch* (GBL), co-published by Suhrkamp and the East Berlin Henschel-Verlag in 1984, where a number of songs are published with musical settings, mainly by Brecht himself, Weill, Eisler and Dessau.

♭ indicates that the translation fits one or more of the musical settings favoured by Brecht.

In addition our notes assign the poems to the main collections in which Brecht published them. These were:

> *Bertolt Brechts Hauspostille* (*Devotions for the Home*) 1927, preceded by a virtually identical *Taschenpostille* (*Pocket Devotions*) in 1926. We refer to these jointly as the *Devotions*.
> *Lieder Gedichte Chöre* (*Songs Poems Choruses*) with Hanns Eisler, 1934.
> *Svendborger Gedichte* (*Svendborg Poems*), 1938.

Between them these three books contained 27 songs from his plays. Some others were included in his occasional *Versuche* booklets between 1930 and 1936. His earliest collection of eight *Songs to the Guitar by Bert Brecht and his Friends* (1918) was not published. A mixed selection published in East Germany in 1951 was edited by Wieland Herzfelde under the title *100 Gedichte* (*100 Poems*); it included some previously unpublished items.

More detailed notes then follow, giving the poem's context in the play or prose work where it occurs, as well as some textual variants and other details. Generally the conventions used (e.g. 'BBA' for the Bertolt Brecht Archive in East Berlin) are as in *Poems 1913–1956*. Dates in brackets are those supplied by the BBA and the German editors. Relevant books published since then include, beside the Brecht *Letters* (English edition in course of preparation), Elisabeth Hauptmann's *Julia ohne Romeo* (Aufbau, E. Berlin, 1977) which contains *Happy End*; the Eisler-Bunge conversations *Reden Sie mehr über Brecht* (Rogner &

Bernhard, Munich, 1971); Albrecht Dümling's *Lasst euch nicht verführen. Brecht und die Musik* (Kindler, Munich, 1985); David Drew's *Kurt Weill: A Handbook* (Faber, London, 1987), and the 1100-page *Musik bei Brecht* by Joachim Lucchesi and Ronald K. Shull (Henschel, E. Berlin and Suhrkamp, Frankfurt, 1988).

1.♭ *Lucifer's evening song.* Gegen Verführung. 260. Ged. 1, 143. In *Devotions* 1922–67.

(*c.*1917). Called 'Lucifer's evening song' on the two earliest scripts, and included in *Devotions* as 'concluding chapter'. In the 1922 scheme it was headed 'Letzte Warnung', or 'Final warning'. Subsequently set by Weill as part of *Rise and Fall of the City of Mahagonny*, when the hero Paul (or Johann) Ackermann (sometimes called Jim Mahoney) sings it before the electric chair in scene 11, with full chorus. Also included in Rudolf Wagner-Régeny's opera *Persische Episode*, on a libretto by Caspar Neher (this setting is in GBL 116). There is an early tune in a handbook belonging to Brecht's brother Walter, who reproduced it in his recollections (Insel, Frankfurt, 1984).

2.♭ *Legend of the dead soldier.* Legende vom toten Soldaten. 256. Ged. 1, 136. GBL 7, 8. In *Devotions* 1926–67 and *Songs Poems Choruses* 1934.

(1918). First printed as an appendix to *Drums in the Night*, with directions that it should be sung by Glubb at the beginning of Act 4. Brecht's tune is given in the *Devotions*, which states that the poem is dedicated to the memory of Christian Grumbeis, born at Aichach on 11 April 1897 and killed on the Russian front in spring 1918: (there is no evidence that he was a real person). Brecht used to perform it himself, and may have included it in his one Berlin cabaret appearance – with Trude Hesterberg's 'Wilde Bühne' in December 1921. It was also in Ernst Busch's cabaret repertoire in the 1920s; he varied Brecht's melody in alternate verses. Eisler's arrangement is in vol. 1 of his *Ges. Werke*. There is an unpublished setting for men's chorus by Weill, performed in Berlin under Karl Rankl on 26 December 1929.

In the German Brecht originally referred to the war's 'fifth' spring, a mistake which he only corrected in the 1940s when H. R. Hays translated the poem for *Selected Poems*. This is the poem which Brecht's publishers Kiepenheuer refused to accept for the *Devotions* around 1924–25, with the result that Brecht took that book away from them. It is also supposed to have brought about Brecht's inclusion in a Nazi blacklist in Munich in 1923. There may be some link with George Grosz's drawing of doctors passing a skeleton as 'KV' or medically fit, which appeared in *Die Pleite*, Berlin, in April 1919.

3.♭ *Ballad of the adventurers.* Ballade von den Abenteurern. 217. Ged. 1, 79. In *Devotions* 1922–67.

(1917). Sung by Baal in scene 18 (last café scene) of *Baal*. In the earliest (1918) version of that play only the first and last stanzas are given, introduced by Baal announcing 'I propose to sing: the Adventurers!' In the 1919 version he sings stanzas 1, 2 and 4. Evidently 3 was added later. Brecht's tune is given in the *Devotions*.

4. *Death in the woods.* Vom Tod im Walde *or* Der Tod im Wald. 1088, Ged. 2. 180. In *Devotions* from 1922, but omitted from *Devotions* section in GW.

(1918?) Read by Baal to Ekart in scene 17 of the play, where it was included from 1918 version on. Omitted from 1926 version. There is no known tune by Brecht. However, in 1927, it was set as an independent piece for bass voice and ten wind instruments by Kurt Weill and performed at a Berlin Philharmonic concert on 23 November that year.

Our text is that used in the GW version of *Baal*, where there were no geographical clues. Nor were there in the 1918 and 1919 versions, though clearly Brecht was revising the poem all the time. For the *Devotions*, (whose text was used by Weill), it was somewhat Americanised; thus the first two lines became 'And a man died in the Hathoury woods / Where the Mississippi roared round him' while lines 4 and 5 of the fourth stanza went 'Freezing when Hathoury's branches spread / As they smoked in silent irritation'. Stanzas 5–7 were different, roughly thus:

> You're behaving like a surly bear!
> Be a gentleman! You're suicidal!
> What has got into you there?
> Weak with greed, he fixed them with a stare:
> Let me live! And eat! Take breath! Be idle!
> Ride off in your wind without a care!
>
> That was what no friend could understand.
> Thrice they called him 'gentleman', said 'please!'
> Thrice the fourth man mocked such terms as these:
> Earth stretched out to hold his naked hand
> As he lay cancerous among black trees.
>
> Swallowed by the woods then, he decayed.
> Soaked with dew they dug him in for ever
> Before midday in the grassy shade
> (Numb with shock, they stood there, cold with hate)
> By the lowest leafage covered over.

This poem is like an elaboration of Kipling's 'There were three friends that buried the fourth' from *The Light that Failed*, which Brecht adapted more than once to his own ends. At the same time Klaus Schuhmann points out how directly it relates to the earlier 'Song of the Fort Donald railroad gang', with its rising waters and screaming forest (*Poems 1913–1956*, p. 3). Like 'Fort Donald', 'Hathoury' appears to be an invented name; it is not to be found in *The Times Atlas*.

5.♭ *Hymn of Baal the Great*. Der Choral vom grossen Baal. 249 and 1085. Ged. 1, 125, GBL 9. In *Devotions* 1922–1967.

(1918). Theme song of *Baal* in all versions. Put at the start in all but the 1918 version, and sung by Baal to what the 1926 version called 'his own invention, the tin-stringed banjo'. Tune by Brecht is given in his *Devotions*. He used to sing it himself around 1919, and for the 1926 production he sang it on a darkened stage. Münsterer sees it as embodying 'the quintessence of his philosophy' in his Augsburg days.

The number of verses varies from version to version. That in the 1926 play has seven, omitting our verses 3, 5, 6, 8 and 9. That in the *Devotions* omits 3, 5 and 6. That in the 1918 and 1919 scripts has not got the last verse, but includes all the others with seven more. These are as follows:

After verse 4:
> As Baal lurches his way across our planet
> That's one beast well sheltered by the sky.
> Sky is blue. His bed has steel to span it
> Where that lusty girl the world can lie.

After verse 7:
> Whether God exists or God does not
> Won't trouble Baal so long as there's a Baal
> Baal however worries quite a lot
> If there's ale to drink or lack of ale.

After verse 9:
> If you're slack there'll be no fun for you!
> What one wants, says Baal, one has to do.
> So do a shit, says Baal, it's worrying
> But it's worse not to do anything.

After verse 10:
> Strength's required, for pleasure makes you weak
> If things go wrong don't turn the other cheek
> He'll stay ever young, through thick and thin
> Who each evening does himself in.
>
> And suppose Baal breaks something in half
> That's to find out what it's got inside
> Too bad perhaps, but it's good for a laugh.
> Might be his star; but Baal just lets it ride.
>
> Might have dirt on it, but it's still Baal's
> With all that's on it lying where it falls.
> He loves his star, and knows that it is his.
> Because Baal knows it's the only star there is.

6. *Baal's song*. Baals Lied. adN. 40. G B L 4.

(1918). Sung by Baal in the cabaret scene of the 1918 version of the play. Included in *Songs to the Guitar* with a tune and a handwritten note: 'With Lud[wig Prestel] by the Lech on the night of 7 vii 18'. The Lech is the river at Augsburg.

7.b *Orge's song*. Orges Gesang. 1087. Ged. 2, 178. In *Devotions* 1922–38.

(1918?). Sung by Baal in scene 3, of the 1919, 1922 and definitive versions of the play. Brecht's tune is given in the *Devotions*. Orge was Brecht's nickname for his Augsburg friend Georg Pfanzelt. The 'grass mound' echoes the title of a late 19th century sentimental song.

8.♭ *Ballad of chastity in a major key.* Keuschheitsballade in Dur. 1244. Ged. 9, 8. In *Songs to the Guitar by Bert Brecht and his Friends.*

(1918?). Sung by the bridegroom's Friend in *A Respectable Wedding* (*Plays 1* Methuen edition, p. 284). Also mentioned in plan for an unwritten play *Die Bälge* ('Brats'), 1920. Brecht's tune is in *Songs to the Guitar.*

9.♭ *The drowned girl.* Vom ertrunkenen Mädchen. 252. Ged. 1, 131, GBL 35. In *Devotions* 1922–67.

(c. 1920). Published in *Die Weltbühne* (Berlin) 30 November 1922. Read by Baal to Ekart in scene 15 of the 1922 (and definitive) *Baal* and in scene 8 of the 1926 *Life Story of a Man called Baal.* Earliest typescript makes the girl 'murdered' (*erschlagen*) rather than drowned. Set by Kurt Weill for male trio and small orchestra as part of the *Berlin Requiem*, 1928. It has been compared to Rimbaud's and Georg Heym's 'Ophelia' poems, but relates in the play to the death of Johanna, the young girl whom Baal has seduced.

10. *The song from the opium den.* Der Gesang aus der Opiumhöhle. 90. Ged. 2, 48.

(c.1920). Brecht's typescript subtitles this 'Canon'. He appears to have submitted it to Trude Hesterberg for her 'Wilde Bühne' Berlin cabaret in 1921/22. Reworked in January 1941 by Brecht and Margarete Steffin to make the 'Song of the Smoke' in *The Good Person of Szechwan* (see no. 124), which was later set by Paul Dessau.

11. *Tahiti.* Tahiti. 105. Ged. 2. 40.

(c.1921). Was included in the 'Hong Kong' scene of the 1925 version of *Man equals Man.* Verses 1–3 occur in modified form in scene 16 of *Rise and Fall of the City of Mahagonny*, when Ackermann, Jenny and Bill (or Heinrich) pretend to sail off on the billiard table. They follow this with a verse of 'Stormy the night and the waves roll high', better known as the nineteenth-century ballad 'Asleep on the Deep' (English version by Arthur C. Lamb). Weill's setting however is new. Further references to 'Tahiti' will be found in scenes 1 and 10 of *In the Jungle of Cities.* Gedde and Topp have not been identified.

12. *When Paris ate the bread of Menelaus.* St 212.

Spoken by Mortimer in scene 9 of *The Life of Edward the Second* (after Marlowe) by Brecht and Lion Feuchtwanger, which the former directed for the Munich Kammerspiele in spring 1924. Oskar Homolka played this part.

13.♭ *Mahagonny Song no. 1.* Mahagonnygesang Nr. 1. 243. Ged. 1, 115 GBL 12. In *Devotions* 1926–67.

Date uncertain. No typescript known prior to publication. Constitutes scene 4 of *Rise and Fall of the City of Mahagonny*, where it is sung before the curtain by Ackermann and his three friends. Also included in the 1927 'Songspiel' version. Brecht's tune given in *Devotions* and GBL was transcribed by F. S. Bruinier and taken over and modified by Weill.

14.♭ *Mahagonny Song no. 2.* Mahagonnygesang Nr. 2. 1130. Ged. 2, 202. GBL 13. In *Devotions* 1926–38.

Date uncertain. No surviving typescript known prior to publication. Sung by the four friends at the start of scene 16 of *Rise and Fall of the City of Mahagonny* and also included in the 1927 'Songspiel' version. Brecht's tune is given in *Devotions* but Weill made an entirely new setting.

15.♭ *Mahagonny Song no. 3*. Mahagonnygesang Nr. 3. 244. Ged. 1, 117. GBL 14. In *Devotions* 1925–67.

(Early 20s). Sung by Trinity Moses, with refrain by Jenny and male quartet, in scene 19 of *Rise and Fall of the City of Mahagonny*. Also included in 1927 'Songspiel' version. Brecht's two earliest typescripts give it no number. One of them consists seemingly of jottings, thus:

> LIFE IS HARD SAID THE MEN OF MAHAGONNY
> HE WILL HAVE EATEN HIS GRASS
> THAT IS ALL THEY SAID life isn't much but it's everything
> GREY IS THE EVENING BUT BLACK IS THE NIGHT.

Brecht's tune, given in *Devotions* and GBL, was not made use of by Weill.

16.(♭) *Mahagonny Song no. 4*. Mahagonnygesang Nr. 4. 136. Ged. 2,204.

(Early 20s). The refrain of this song occurs in *Rise and Fall of the City of Mahagonny*, where Trinity Moses and Willy (Fatty) sing it in the middle of the short scene 3. No tune by Brecht is known.

17. *Mahagonny Song no. 5* [mis-numbered 4]. Mahagonnygesang Nr. 4. adN. 168.

Omitted from previous collections presumably on grounds of decency. Brecht's TS is in a folder with other early poems and fragments. There is nothing to explain why there should be two number 4s. No tune by Brecht known.

18.♭ *Ballad of the girl and the soldier*. Ballade vom Weib und dem Soldaten. 239. Ged. 1, 106 GBL 19. In *Devotions* 1922–67, mostly under the title 'Ballad of the soldier'.

Sung by Eilif in scene 2 of *Mother Courage*, 1939; setting by Dessau, 1946. Cited in first version of *In the Jungle of Cities*. First set as an independent song by F. S. Bruinier (20 November 1925); then by Eisler (op. 39), for the 1928 production of Lion Feuchtwanger's play *Kalkutta 4 Mai* (Eisler's first Brecht setting). In *Hundred Poems* it was subtitled 'after Kipling', being in fact an elaboration of the verse at the end of Kipling's story 'Love-o-Women' in *Many Inventions* which in turn appears to derive from the music-hall song of 'My Great and Only' in *Abaft the Funnel*. See pp. 48–50 of J. Willett: *Brecht in Context* (1983).

W. H. Auden translated it under the title 'Song of the Goodwife and the Invaders' for the National Theatre's 1965 *Mother Courage* production by William Gaskill.

19.♭ *Song of the three soldiers*. Lied der drei Soldaten. 127, 1099. Ged. 2, 215. GBL 24. In *Devotions 1926–67*.

In 1928 this Kipling pastiche was incorporated in *The Threepenny Opera* as 'The cannon song' and sung (to Weill's setting) by Macheath and Brown at the former's wedding party in scene 2. In the earlier (*Devotions*) version the soldiers' names were George, John and Freddy; there were other slight variations, and the refrain was lacking. This refrain first appeared with two other poems written in 1924–25 'Ach, Jimmy, kümmre dich nicht um den Hut' and 'Der tote Kolonialsoldat' (adN. 165 and 173 respectively). The former of these is thought to have been intended for *Man equals Man* and set by Edmund Meisel; indeed the refrain was published in the programme for the 1928 Berlin production of that play under the title 'Cannon Song'. It also occurred in the 1931 script but was cut in performance. The M S of 'The dead colonial soldier' includes a tune. For Brecht's new post-World War II version of the song, see no. 154 below.

20.♭ *The 'man equals man' song*. Der 'Mann-ist-Mann' Song. 138. Ged. 2, 184. GBL 15.

(1925). Printed as an appendix to the 1926 version of *Man equals Man* together with a tune by Brecht, but omitted from subsequent versions, though Paul Dessau arranged it for a production by Jean-Marie Serreau in 1951. In 1926 it was to be sung on the first appearance of the four (Kipling-style) soldiers in scene 2: see stage direction 'They have drunk whisky and are singing the "Man equals Man" song.' Then sung again in the scene with the dummy elephant, when the five verses are split among 'numbers' 1–4 and 6. For the 1927 Berlin broadcast it seems that the tune was arranged by Edmund Meisel, Piscator's musical director, and sung (according to Fritz Hennenberg) by Brecht himself. An earlier version has the soldiers finally marching off 'singing "it's a long way to Tipperary"', after a famous British army favourite of World War I.

21.♭ *The song of Widow Begbick's drinking truck*. Song von Witwe Begbicks Trinksalon. 1089. GBL 51.

Sung by the soldiers at the beginning of scene 4 of *Man equals Man* (all versions). Set by Kurt Weill for the 1931 production, but the music has been lost and a new setting was composed by Dessau in 1956 and subsequently included in his *Lieder und Gesänge*. My translation of the refrain, which was made originally for the Brecht-Kipling programme *Never the Twain*, substitutes phrases from Kipling's poem 'The Service Man' for Brecht's 'From Delhi to Kamatkura / Supposing you had missed someone / He was sitting in Widow Begbick's tank'; the rest of it is from Brecht.

22.♭ *What a bit of all right in Uganda!* Ach, wie war es lustig in Uganda! 1093.

Final chorus of the four soldiers in *The Elephant Calf*, 1926. This song was not in the 1925 version of *Man equals Man*, when virtually the entire *Elephant Calf* was incorporated as the penultimate scene. It then ended 'to the singing of yes we have no bananas'.

23. *The chewing-gum song*. Der Kaugummi-Song. adN. 182.

Evidently intended for the stage (though not explicitly for either version of *Mahagonny*), since the title is followed by the direction '*Two men and two women standing in front of Beechnut posters and chewing Beechnut to the music.*' No musical setting is known. Beechnut, a well-known make of gum, is also mentioned in 'Late lamented fame of the giant city of New York' (*c.* 1930. *Poems 1913–1956*, p. 169, middle of stanza 8).

24.♭ *The 'Johnny-doesn't-want-to-be-human' song.* Der Johnnywillkeinmenschsein-Song. 1128. Ged. 2, 208.

Verse 2 is not included in *Rise and Fall of the City of Mahagonny*, whose hero Ackermann sings the song to his friends in scene 8. Setting by Weill. A tune is sketched out on one of Brecht's T Ss. These add a chorus after 'Why the hell has nothing happened at all?'.

> Oh, Johnny, keep your hair on, do.
> That's how it is in Mandalay.
> Johnny would like to eat his hat.
> But why would you like to eat your hat?
> Don't be so bloody proud, Johnny
> You know it's not allowed, Johnny.
> You've gone too far, old chap
> I tell you, it's just a trap.
> You're forcing us to beat you
> How can you expect us to treat you
> As human?

In the opera this is sung and divided up between the three friends, and leads to Ackermann's final 'I don't want to be human'.

25.♭ *Alabama song* 1127. Ged. 2, 206. In *Devotions* 1926–38.

Written before November 1925. Originally written in English on Brecht's behalf by Elisabeth Hauptmann, who marked the photostat in the Brecht-Archive 'English by Hauptmann'. Included in the *Mahagonny* 'Songspiel' and in the full opera, where it is sung by Jenny and a six-girl chorus before the curtain as scene 2. Brecht's tune is printed in *Devotions*. F. S. Bruinier wrote a setting for voice and piano dated 20 November 1925 and entitled 'The Moon of Alabama. English song'. Weill's article 'On the gestic character of music' (in his *Ausgewählte Schriften*, Suhrkamp-Verlag, 1975, pp. 43–4) reproduces Brecht's melody for the refrain, comparing it with his own setting to show how the 'gestic' quality and, to some extent, the rhythm have been preserved in the latter. Actually the refrains correspond less closely than do their two respective settings of the verse.

The earliest typescript includes a fourth verse, as follows. Words italicised represent a variation that ran through all four verses before they were revised to read as now:

> *O lead* us the way to the next chewing-gum
> *Be quick and ask not* why
> *O we* must *have* the next chewing-gum
> For if we don't *have* the next chewing-gum
> *We must die, we must die.*

In the last verse too, the original phrase was 'the next *best* dollar'. Verse 2 was omitted in Weill's piano score of the opera. It was reinstated in *Versuche 2* (1930), where 'pretty girl' was changed to 'pretty boy', in accordance with

Brecht's typed libretto, presumably as being more appropriate to the sex of the singers.

26.♭ *Benares song*. 247. Ged. 1, 120. In *Devotions* 1926–38.

Written in 1926, according to Elisabeth Hauptmann. Original text in English, marked by her on the photostat in the Brecht Archive 'by Hauptmann, Brecht's handwriting'. Their tune, which they devised by crossing 'There's a tavern in the town' with 'One fine day' from *Madame Butterfly* is appended to *Devotions*. The song was then set by Weill and taken into the *Mahagonny* 'Songspiel', but not included in the opera libretto or any of the published versions of Brecht's text. It was however included in the 1929 piano score, to be sung before the curtain as no. 19 (see *Collected Plays* vol. 2 iii, pp. 117–8 for the text, both with and without the modifications made by Auden and Chester Kallman). Then it was cut for the Leipzig première.

The original manuscript reads

in stanza 1, 1.5 'Is here no telephone?'
 1.9 'Where the sun is shining'

in stanza 2, 1.1–2 'There is no money in this land.
 There is no girl to shake with hands.'

in stanza 3, 1.1–2 'There is no great fun on this star
 There is no door that is a cha-jar.'
 1.8 'Worse of all, Benares'.

The *Devotions* follow these readings with minor corrections.

27.♭ *Poem on a dead man*. Gedicht über einen Toten. 1133.

(*c.* 1925). Though not figuring in Brecht's libretto script, this poem was set by Weill to become the finale of *Rise and Fall of the City of Mahagonny*, where it follows Ackermann's death and accompanies the concluding demonstrations and counter-demonstrations. At first it formed part of the *Berlin Requiem*, 1929, but was later taken out. The title is written on the T S in Elisabeth Hauptmann's handwriting.

28. *Anne Smith relates the conquest of America*. Anne Smith erzählt die Eroberung Amerikas. adN. 171.

Included in material for the unfinished opera *Man from Manhattan*, or *Sodom and Gomorrah*, on which Brecht began work in 1924. This project, though not a poem, was later swallowed up in *Mahagonny*.

29.♭ *Deep in Alaska's snow-covered forests*. Tief in Alaska's weissverschneiten Wäldern. St 520.

Sung by Ackermann at the beginning of scene 9 of *Rise and Fall of the City of Mahagonny*.

30. *On the cities*. Über die Städte. 215. Ged. 1, 73. Added to *Devotions* in the 1950s.

(1925?). Sung by chorus of men in scene 3 of *Rise and Fall of the City of*

Mahagonny. Published in *Simplizissimus* 5 September 1927. One TS is on the back of a draft dated 1925. 'On the cities (2)' was written about 1926 and included in the 'Poems belonging to the Reader for Those who live in Cities'; See *Poems 1913–1956*, p. 142.

31.♭ *Mahagonny theme song.* Erstens, vergiss nicht. St 532.

Sung by the chorus of men, following the diversion of the threatened hurricane and the discovery of the new principle 'Du darfst es' – 'You may (do) it', rendered in 'Blasphemie' (no. 34) as 'Just do it'.

32.♭ *Wonderful is the first approach of evening.* Wunderbar ist das Heraufkommen des Abends. St 518.

Sung by Ackermann and his three friends in scene 8 of *Rise and Fall of the City of Mahagonny*, leading into the 'Johnny-doesn't-want-to-be-human' song (no. 24.)

33.♭ *A damnable day will dawn.* Wenn der Himmel hell wird. St 548.

Sung by Ackermann as scene 17 of *Rise and Fall of the City of Mahagonny*. It is night and he is in chains.

34.♭ *Blasphemy.* Blasphemie. St 526. Ged. 1, 179.

Sung by Ackermann in scene 11 of *Rise and Fall of the City of Mahagonny*. The title of the poem comes from a TS which allocates it to the *Reader for Those who live in Cities* (1926–27), with which it was published as no. 7 of the 'Poems belonging' in Ged. 1. The link between the *Reader* poems and the opera is also to be seen in the next poem of the same group (*Poems 1913–1956*, p. 144), with its reference to hurricanes in 'Miami and all Florida'.

35.♭ *Song of the flow of things.* Das Lied vom Fluss der Dinge. 1090.

Sung by the Widow Begbick in *Man equals Man* in 1931, 1937 and final versions: the first four lines occurring at the end of scene 4 and the rest spaced out in scene 9 (the six-part transformation scene). Here it replaced the earlier 'Man equals man' song (no. 20 above). Weill set it to music for the 1931 production, starting with a 'kleine Nachtmusik' for the first four lines. This setting has been lost except for one MS page, and in 1956 was replaced by Paul Dessau's, which confines itself to the first four lines (*Lieder und Gesänge*, p. 87) and the refrain (*Lieder und Gesänge*, p. 88), the remainder being spoken. The main body of the poem, apart from the refrain, closely resembles the 'women's' poems in the *Reader for Those who live in Cities*, and has no reference to the events or characters of the play. The theme, as Antony Tatlow has pointed out (*The Mask of Evil*, p. 456) recalls Heraclitus's 'Upon those who step into the same river different and ever different waters flow down'.

In the earliest (surviving) version, which is inserted in Helene Weigel's copy of the 1931 script – she played Begbick – stanza 2 finishes not with the refrain but with a repetition of the first four lines. Stanza 3 follows virtually as now when Begbick has announced the packing-up of her canteen (in episode 11), but after 'My name was finished' comes the refrain, and she continues:

I have become disorderly and I began to drink
And started drinking in the morning and went on drinking in the morning
Then there was a battle on the Orange River

And I walked drunk across this field up to the enemy
And I lifted my skirts and I said
More than one bad word.
Then that was the name I had from Transvaal to Rangoon.
Like linen [and so on to the end of the refrain].

Those seven lines were subsequently deleted. Another subsequently omitted passage comes at the start of the final stanza, as follows:

I was in many places, and observed carefully and saw
Many people persist in wickedness
They turned into criminals and idiots and had
To be killed! then I said
Do not count on anything, neither good nor bad.
However often [etc., as in opening four lines]
I also spoke to many people [as now, to the end].

36. *The horror of being poor*. Das Entsetzen, arm zu sein. 156. Ged. 2, 183.
(c. 1926). From a projected play *The Rich Man and the Poor Man*.

37.♭ *The Song of Surabaya Johnny*. Das Lied vom Surabaya-Johnny. 325. Ged. 2, 242. GBL 17, 33.
(1927). Was set by F. S. Bruinier in spring 1927 for cabaret performances by Lore Braun and Kate Kühl. Brecht himself worked on it with the latter when she was appearing at a Berlin music hall called Bendows Bunte Bühne. In Lion Feuchtwanger's play *Kalkutta 4 Mai*, which that author had revised with Brecht's help and published in 1927, Lady Marjorie Hike is discovered (Act 2, scene 1) *'carefully practising the Song of Surabaya-Jhonny [sic] to a kind of banjo'*, in order to sing and dance it to her friend Warren Hastings. She complains that this song is

damned difficult. I heard it on the coffee plantations in Ceylon, and it's my ambition to perform it the way that unspeakable crowd of run-down clerks and hardened drinkers did while watching the moon coming up over the young plants.

The song's actual text is not included in Feuchtwanger's play as published, and it seems to have been omitted from the Berlin production of 12 June 1928 (for which Eisler wrote the music). Around that time Tucholsky asked Kate Kühl if he could borrow her copy of her text; he thought the poem 'marvellously done' and wanted to publish it in *Die Weltbühne*. Brecht however held it back for a further year before putting it into Act 3 of *Happy End*, for which Kurt Weill made a new setting.

Once again the song's origins lie in a poem by Kipling: this time in 'Mary, pity women!' which Brecht and Elisabeth Hauptmann translated (GW 1055) and originally meant to include in *The Threepenny Opera*. However, only the refrain ('Nice while it lasted' etc.) appeared in the final script, where Weill set it as 'Polly's song', to be sung at the end of scene 4. The remainder then became resituated in an imagined India, though its gest of impassioned accusation and abandonment still reflects Kipling's conversation with a barmaid in a London pub. Of the Kipling phrases in the refrain 'Ah Gawd, I love you so' translates Brecht's German; while 'done the worst that you know' and 'where can I 'ide or go?' correspond more freely to his 'why are you so crude?' and 'why am I not happy?'

38.♭ *Jenny's song.* [Denn wie man sich bettet]. 1132. Ged. 2, 209. G B L 37.

(1927/28) Sung by Jenny in scene 16 of *Rise and Fall of the City of Mahagonny* and bearing the title 'Lied der Jenny' in Weill's script, which dates from before 1929. An early text starting 'As I put on my wedding dress' (Als ich mein Brautkleid anzog) was included in the first version of *The Threepenny Opera* and labelled 'From Mahagonny'. Brecht's handwritten draft includes a tune. There is also a fragment dated c. 1927 by the Brecht Archive which goes very roughly:

'but if you want to know what I think, gentlemen:

> Well, you gents, that's nothing new to me.
> I tell you it's all my eye
> Yes, love and good health and virtue
> And that half-baked reward in the sky.
> Oh 'heaven's' such a lovely word to speak
> It calls for a good kick up the bum
> The question is who eats whom.
> That's the only information to seek.
> So best set out to take things as they come
> You should eat while you've still got room.'

The first typescript of the opera libretto (held by Universal-Edition) adds a third stanza as follows:

> 3
> I can't go with you in future, Jimmy
> Yes Jimmy, it's sad for me
> You'll still be my favourite person
> But I'm wasting my chances, you see.
> I must use the little time that's left me
> Jimmy
> If I'm not to lose hold of it
> I'm only going to be young this once –
> That's too short
> I tell you, Jimmy
> That I'm shit.
> Oh, Jimmy you know what my mother told me
> She thought me a shocking case (etc.)

39. *Pirate Jenny.* Die Seeräuber-Jenny oder Träume eines Küchenmädchens. 1097. Ged. 2, 213. G B L 23.

Sung by Polly (*not* Jenny) at her wedding in scene 2 of *The Threepenny Opera*.

Also included under the title 'Dreams of a Kitchen-maid' (Träume eines Küchenmädchens) as an epigraph to chapter X of *The Threepenny Novel*. Christopher Isherwood's translation was made for *A Penny for the Poor* (1937) the title under which the novel was published in England. A musical setting by F. S. Bruinier is dated 8.3.27, roughly a year before *The Threepenny Opera* was first mooted. This suggests that the song was originally independent of the play, and may help explain the confusion of names which has led so many actresses, starting with Lotte Lenya in Pabst's film version of the play, to wrench it out of its dramatic context. On the two earliest typescripts, parenthetical remarks (presumably to be spoken) have been added after each verse and before the refrain. They are

> (i) 'And the laughter is great'.
> (ii) 'Far from it, they're still laughing'.
> (iii) 'And the laugh will stop'.
> (iv) 'And the laughter will stop'.

Weill's setting has some similarity to Bruinier's. For a version which fits it see our edition of the play.

40. *Barbara song*. Der Barbara-Song. 1102. Ged. 2, 217. GBL 16, 25. Also called 'Die Ballade (or 'Der Song') vom Nein und Ja'.

Written by spring 1927, when Bruinier transcribed Brecht's parodistic tune for the refrain. Weill made a related version which was to be sung the following year by Polly Peachum in scene 3 of *The Threepenny Opera* and introduced by a projected title saying 'By means of a little song Polly informs her parents of her marriage to the bandit Macheath'. At the première however it was shifted to follow the 'Ballad of immoral earnings' in scene 7. Later included in the *Threepenny Novel*, where it introduces Book One and is called 'Polly Peachum's song'. The origin of the title 'Barbara song', which dates from 1928, is not clear. Brecht had published a short story called 'Barbara' the previous year, but it was only later that he and Helene Weigel gave the name to their daughter.

41.♭ *Ballad of good living*. Die Ballade vom angenehmen Leben. 1109. Ged. 2, 227. GBL 28.

Sung by Macheath in scene 6 of *The Threepenny Opera*. Published in *Das Stichwort*, September 1928 as being 'After Villon'. This is an amended version of K. L. Ammer's translation of the Villon ballade 'Il n'est trésor que de vivre à son aise'. See no. 155 for revised post-war version. A folder of typescript 'song texts for *Threepenny Opera* gramophone records' includes a variant second stanza:

> The Bishop of Saint John may love his neighbours
> And yet he'll say he loves his bottle better.
> He earns his living as a smooth confessor
> Where I earn mine by herculean labours.
> All of us grab as much as we dare take
> And if you say you don't, you're kidding me
> Not even Art's prepared to work for free:
> Hats off to those who admit they're on the make.

He that takes most deserves the highest bliss
You must live well to know what living is.

Two further stanzas introduce Book Three of the *Threepenny Novel*, but do not occur in any version of the play.

42.♮ *Ballad of immoral earnings*. Die Zuhälterballade. 1107. Ged. 2, 225. GBL 27.
   Sung by Macheath and Jenny in scene 7 of *The Threepenny Opera* (1928). Also known as the 'Tango-Ballade'. Adapted from K. L. Ammer's translation of 'Ballade de Villon et de la grosse Margot'. According to Eisler, the third stanza was cut at the première because the singer refused to sing it.

43.♮ *Ballad in which Macheath begs forgiveness of all men*. Ballade in der Macheath jedermann Abbitte leistet. 1122. Ged. 2, 236.
   Also called 'Memorial inscription'. Sung by Macheath in scene 9 of *The Threepenny Opera*.
   First two stanzas adapted from K. L. Ammer's translation of the 'Epitaphe en forme de Ballade' which was made by Villon for himself and his companions when expecting to be hanged. The third and fourth from the 'Ballade par laquelle Villon crye mercy à chascun'. A revised version made in 1948 substitutes new stanzas 3 and 4:

The men who break into your houses
Because they've got no place to sleep in
The slanderer who's full of grouses
And likes to curse instead of weeping;
That woman stealing your bread ration
She's like your mother as two pins –
They act in such a feeble fashion.
I pray you to forgive their sins.

Show greater pity for *their* troubles
And less for those who, in high places
Led you to war – and worse disgraces –
And made you sleep on bloodstained cobbles.
They forced you into rape and robb'ry.
And now they're pleading 'Please forgive' –
So choke their mouths with the fine debris
Of the fair cities where you lived.

And those who claim the whole thing's over
And those who pardon every sin
Are asking for a great iron crowbar
To smash their ugly faces in.

44.♮ *Solomon song*. Salomon-Song. 1119. Ged. 2, 233.
   Sung by Jenny before the curtain at the end of scene 7 of *The Threepenny Opera* (1928). Written for Lenya during rehearsals, but omitted at première. Freely based on K. L. Ammer's translation of Villon's 'Double Ballade from the Grand

Testament', from which the last line of each stanza is taken: 'bien est eureux qui riens n'y a'. Stanza 4 first appeared in the Malik edition of the plays in 1937. A later version of the song was included in *Mother Courage* (1939) and sung by Mother Courage and the Cook in scene 9; setting by Dessau, 1946. This consisted of stanzas 1 and 3, followed by three new stanzas, as under:

> You heard of honest Socrates
> The man who never lied:
> They weren't so grateful as you'd think
> The rulers just arranged to have him tried
> And handed him the poisoned drink.
> How honest was the people's noble son!
> The world however couldn't wait
> And quickly saw what followed on.
> It's honesty that brought him to that state.
> How fortunate the man with none!
>
> Saint Martin couldn't bear to see
> His fellows in distress.
> He met a poor man in the snow
> And shared his cloak with him, and so
> Both of them promptly froze to death.
> His place in Heaven was surely won.
> The world however couldn't wait
> And quickly saw what followed on.
> Unselfishness had brought him to that state.
> How fortunate the man with none!
>
> Here you can see respectable folk
> Keeping to God's own laws.
> So far He hasn't taken heed.
> You who sit safe and warm indoors
> Help to relieve our bitter need!
> How virtuously we had begun!
> The world however couldn't wait
> And quickly saw what followed on.
> It's fear of God has brought us to this state.
> How fortunate the man with none!

Interspersed between the stanzas in this version are prose passages spoken by the Cook.

45.♭ *Ballad of sexual obsession*. Die Ballade von der sexuellen Hörigkeit. 1106. Ged. 2, 233. GBL 26.

Sung by Mrs Peachum in *The Threepenny Opera* (1928). The first two stanzas form the Interlude before scene 5, with stanza 3 following in scene 7. In the original Berlin production it had to be cut because the singer Rosa Valetti thought it too obscene; consequently it was omitted from Weill's piano score. (The phrase 'up and doing' for Brecht's 'liegt wieder oben' was the idea of Hans Hess.)

46.♭ *Appeal from the grave*. Ruf aus der Gruft. 1121.

Sung by Macheath in scene 9 of *The Threepenny Opera*. The 1928 stage script gives it the title 'Epistle to his friends'. Based on the 'Epistle en forme de ballade à ses amis' in Villon's *Codicille*, with its refrain 'le lesserez là, le povre Villon?'

47.♭ *Second Threepenny finale*. Zweites Dreigroschen-Finale. 1116. Ged. 2, 229.

(1928). In the published text this is sung by Macheath (verse 1), Jenny (verse 2) and chorus at end of scene 6 of *The Threepenny Opera*. In Weill's score the soloist was Mrs Peachum.

48.♭ *Love song*. Liebeslied. St 438.

(1928) Sung by Polly and Macheath at the end of scene 2 following their wedding.

49.♭ *Song of the inadequacy of human endeavour*. Das Lied von der Unzulänglichkeit menschlichen Strebens. 1118. Ged. 2, 231. GBL 29.

Sung by Peachum in scene 7 of *The Threepenny Opera* (1928). The first three verses recur as an epigraph to chapter IX of the *Threepenny Novel* (1934). Early typescripts have 'Planens' rather than 'Strebens' in the title, referring to the shortcomings of human planning. Weill's MS calls it 'Beggars' March'. In Pabst's film it was sung by the Ballad-Singer.

50.♭ *The crimes of Mac the Knife*. Die Moritat vom Mackie Messer. 1093. Ged. 2, 211. GBL 22.

(1928). Sung by a ballad-singer as a prelude to *The Threepenny Opera*. According to the impresario E. J. Aufricht's memoirs it was a last-minute addition during the rehearsals, designed to counter the prettifying effect of a blue scarf the actor wished to wear. Brecht meant thereby to establish Macheath from the outset as a dangerous and nasty character.

The 'Moritat' was a traditional form of ballad narrating events, often of a horrifying nature, sung to hurdy-gurdy accompaniment in a public place, particularly fairs, and often with pictorial illustrations. The word is sometimes thought to derive from 'Mordthat' – a murderous deed. Brecht has the two servant girls in scene 4 of *Schweik in the Second World War* sing a late eighteenth century example 'with much feeling'.

An early version omits verses 2, 3 and 7. Three new verses written for the conclusion of Pabst's *Threepenny Opera* film (1931) go:

> So we reach our happy ending.
> Rich and poor can now embrace.
> Once the cash is not a problem
> Happy endings do take place.
>
> Don't you fish in troubled waters
> Said the heiress to the whore.
> Now they share luxurious quarters
> Sponging on the starving poor.

Some in light and some in darkness.
That's the kind of world we mean.
Those you see are in the light part.
Those in darkness don't get seen.

In 1934 Brecht used them as an epigraph to Book 2 of his *Threepenny Novel*. Then in 1948 he wrote a new two-verse ending aimed at the post-war 'denazification' process in West Germany:

Now the sharks are disappearing
And we're all amazed to hear
Every time a shark's indicted
That the shark had no idea.

And he simply can't remember
And his cover can't be blown
Since a shark is not a shark if
No one else can prove he's one.

According to the Finnish composer Simon Parmet, Weill's tune is based on a Russian folk melody that had appealed to Brecht.

51.♭ *Chorale.* Schlusschoral. 1125–6.

(1928). Final chorus of *The Threepenny Opera*. In 1948 Brecht wrote a new version in two stanzas:

Don't punish small-scale crime too harshly. Never
Will it withstand the frost, for it is cold.
Think of the darkness and the bitter weather
Which in this vale of sorrows we behold.

But let us fight the arch-criminals together
Track down those men, before their scent is cold
Who made the darkness and the bitter weather
And caused the fearful sorrows we behold.

52.♭ *Red Rosa.* (Grabschrift 1919). 429. Ged. 3, 20. In *Songs Poems Choruses*.

This modified version of the published poem was made for setting as part of Weill's *Berlin Requiem*, which was composed in 1928 and first performed the following year, ten years after Rosa Luxemburg's death in Berlin at the hands of right-wing *Freikorps* irregulars. An earlier, politically less significant text called 'Marterl' was printed in Weill's *Song Album*, and now figures in the piano score of the Requiem. It starts 'Here lies the virgin Johanna Beck' and is thought to have been written about 1925.

53.♭ *The lovers.* Die Liebenden. St 535. Included in *100 Poems*, 1950.

Also known as the 'Crane Duet' and sung by Ackermann and Jenny in scene 14 of *Rise and Fall of the City of Mahagonny*. It was added after Weill had completed the first version of the score, and appears in the 1929 piano reduction.

According to Ernst Bloch (the philosopher) Brecht wrote it in a single night to add an element of 'high art' to the brothel scene, which had been threatened with censorship.

54.♮ *In those golden days of childhood*. In der Jugend goldenem Schimmer.

One of the short parodistic Salvationist or sentimental songs figuring in act 1 of *Happy End* (1929) by Brecht and Hauptmann.

55.♮ *God's little lieutenant*. Der kleine Leutnant des lieben Gottes *or* Kampflied der schwarzen Strohhüten. 1145.

This may be at least partly by Elisabeth Hauptmann. Originally included in *Happy End* (1929), where it was set to music by Weill and sung by Lilian Holiday on her first entrance as a Salvationist in Act 1, then again at the end of the play. Its setting by Weill includes a few notes of the 'Internationale'. Subsequently put into *St Joan of the Stockyards* for the Black Straw Hats to sing in scenes 2d (verse 2) and 5 (verse 1). There is also a setting for this by Paul Dessau.

56.♮ *Bilbao song*. Der Bilbao-Song. 319. Ged. 2,239. GBL 30.

Sung by Bill Cracker, owner of the Chicago establishment 'Bill's Ballroom', as the opening song of *Happy End*. Included with adaptation as 'The Bide-a-Wee' in Marc Blitzstein's version of *The Threepenny Opera*. There was also a 'Song of the Bilbao men' due to be included in the first (1925) version of *Man equals Man*, but it may well have borne no relation to the present song. It seems very possible that Brecht thought Bilbao was in the United States.

57.♮ *The sailors' song*. Der Matrosen-Song. Also known as 'Was die Herren Matrosen sagen'. 321. Ged. 2, 244. GBL 31.

Sung by Lilian Holiday the Salvationist in Act 1 of *Happy End*, in the hope of ingratiating herself with Bill Cracker and his gang. Brecht later considered taking the song into *Saint Joan of the Stockyards* along with other items from the earlier play.

58.♮ *The song of Mandalay*. Der Song von Mandelay. 324. Ged. 9, 21. GBL 32.

(1929) Sung by the transvestite gangster Sam Worlitzer in Act 3 of *Happy End*, on being told that he looks like a brothel madam. The text's misspelt geography derives vaguely from Kipling's poem 'Mandalay'; hence it was included in the Brecht-Kipling show *Never the Twain* (1970) for which the present translation was made. A related text based on the same refrain is sung by Begbick and the Men in scene 14 of *Rise and Fall of the City of Mahagonny* and leads into the Crane Duet (no.53 above). It is here translated from Weill's piano score:

> After removing your gum
> First give your hands a good scrubbing.
> Let her take her time
> And drop the odd kindly word.
>
> Quick, fellows, hey!
> Let us sing the song of Mandalay:
> Love is a thing to be kept within limits.

> Best make it quick, for we're counting the minutes
> And the moon won't shine forever on you, Mandalay.
> Best make it quicker, till the yellow moon goes under.

The first stanza is cited at the head of Brecht's report of 4 Feb 1927 on a competition held by the *Literarische Welt*. Other drafts may go back as early as 1923: two contain sketches for a tune, and the name of the 'house' (the *Puff*, a slang word for brothel) varies from 'mother julie's' to 'Widow Begbick's' – this last in a version included in a 1929 script of *Man equals Man*. The earliest, under the title 'Mandalay joy house', relates the whole concept firmly to the first 'Mahagonny songs', as follows:

1. at mamma's
   a woman cost 5 dollars/yes, that was mahagonny
         what a man when it comes to love
   we queued up half the night from 6 o'clock
   with a newspaper and our stale crust
         shot through the half-open teakwood door
   we shot and we now and again sang
         johnny be quicker for the green
         moon's going under.

2. at mamma's . . .
   it was strictly first come first served
   yes that was mahagonny yes that was mahagonny
   today we're fucking away with revolvers in our flippers
   up against the half-open teakwood door
   where they kept on singing
         johnny be quicker for the green
         moon's going under.

3. at mamma's . . .
   every man learnt savoir vivre
   yes that was mahagonny
   that was where a man got a lifelong
   knowledge of love
   and in due course a woman got something too
         for even without teakwood he hears
         an old song and shooting and:

(Presumably the two-line refrain then follows.)

59.♭ *Song of the tough nut*. Song von der harten Nuss. GBL 34. Not in GW.
   Sung by Bill Cracker in Act 3 of *Happy End* as a response to 'Surabaya Johnny'. It appears to have been an addition at rehearsal stage, since the song is not in BBA 994, the stage script. In Paris five years later Weill used his tune as part of the incidental music to Jacques Deval's play *Marie Galante*.

60.♭ *Ballad of the Lily of Hell*. Ballade von der Höllenlilli. 327. Ged. 9, 23.

(1929) Sung by 'The Fly' (The Lady in Grey) in Act 3 of *Happy End*, 1929. It has been suggested, none too plausibly, that the title refers to Lilli Prien, a local Spartacist, whose husband Brecht briefly sheltered when Augsburg was taken over by the White forces in April 1919. The song was certainly written some ten years after the event.

61.♭ *Hosanna Rockefeller.* Hosianna Rockerfeller. St 783–4.

(1929). Not included in the stage script of *Happy End*, but sung at the end of the Brecht-Engel production in 1929 in front of stained glass windows representing the saintly figures of the great millionaires. Weill's setting for chorus is available from Universal-Edition. The three verses recur in the last scene of *St Joan of the Stockyards*, where they are followed by a refrain sung by full chorus to drown Joan's closing speech.

62. *Ideology.* Ideologie. Also called 'Bekämpfung des Primitiven' (Struggle against what is primitive). 1134. Ged. 2, 249.

Sung by the Airman as section 8 of the radio cantata *Lindbergh's Flight.* (1929, later renamed *The Ocean Flight*) and published in *Versuche 1*, 1930. It looks as if this section must have been added during the cantata's fourth revision. It was not included in the original Weill-Hindemith setting of the former year.

63. *Do men help each other?* Untersuchung, ob der Mensch den Menschen hilft. 1138. Ged. 2, 253.

Start of scene 3 of the *Badener Lehrstück vom Einverständnis*, where the leader of the chorus presents first a sequence of photographs showing man's inhumanity to man, then a knockabout sketch in which two clowns saw up a third. The composer was Hindemith.

64. *The song of the lawcourts.* Lied von den Gerichten. 1154. Ged. 3, 212.

Sung by the cast of *The Exception and the Rule* in scene 8 of that play, while they are changing the set for the court scene which follows. Brecht never found a composer for this Chinese-based Lehrstück, till in 1948 Dessau wrote the music for a production by Jean-Marie Serreau, some eighteen years after the text had been written.

65. *The 'Nothing comes from nothing' song.* Der Aus-nichts-wird-nichts-Song. 1258.

Described as 'Song and chorus' and written about 1929–30 when Brecht was working on the unfinished play from which it takes its name. No musical setting is known.

66. *Again and again in renewed conflicts.* [Immer wieder in erneuerten Kämpfen.] 1260. Ged. 9, 10.

(*c.* 1931). Another fragment from the *Nothing comes from Nothing* project. No music known.

67. *The unemployed.* [Ihr, die Ihr eben.] 1253. Ged. 9, 27.

Opening chorus of the Als (= *A*rbeits/*os*en, or unemployed) from the unfinished *The Breadshop* (1929–30).

68. *Round for the unemployed.* Rundgesang der Als. 1253.

Also from the *Breadshop* material. Compare the round 'A dog went into the kitchen' in *Drums in the Night*, *Plays I* pp. 105–6.

69. *The way downwards*. Der Weg nach unten. 1255. Ged. 9, 29.
From the *Breadshop* material.

70. *But even below us*. Aber auch unter uns gibt es noch Ebenen. 1254. Ged. 9, 30.
From the *Breadshop* material.

71. *Hold tight and sink*. Fatzer, Komm. 1247. Ged. 2, 194.
First of the 'choruses' appended to the incomplete *Fatzer* material. The German title is clearly an abbreviation for 'Fatzer Kommentar', which would identify it as part of the commentary accompanying that unfinished play. It was published separately in *Versuche 1*, 1930.

72.♭ *The whitewash song*. Das Lied von der Tünche. 1168. Ged. 3, 234. In *Hundred Poems*.
(1930). Also called 'Song von der Tünche' and 'Tünchnerlied'. First appeared as a song for the police in 'The Bruise', Brecht's treatment for Pabst's *Threepenny Opera* film; but was not used. Put into *The Round Heads and the Pointed Heads*, where it serves in Eisler's setting as a choral interlude before scene 3. Subsequently taken into the Berliner Ensemble production of *Arturo Ui* (1959) as an interlude sung by the Goebbels figure, Givola. The setting for this was by Hans-Dieter Hosalla.

The link between this song and Brecht's mental picture of Adolf Hitler, whom he (like many others) imagined once to have been a 'house-painter', may have been a coincidence. (See 'Hitler Chorale I' in *Poems 1913–1956*, p. 208 and 'Das Lied vom Anstreicher Hitler' in *Songs Poems Choruses*, GW 441: both written in 1933 according to the BBA). If not, then this would have been Brecht's first anti-Nazi poem by some years. Either way the satire is political.

73. *Song of the Commissioner of Police*. Lied des Polizeichefs. 338. Ged. 9, 17.
(1930). From 'The Bruise', Brecht's film treatment for *The Threepenny Opera* in *Versuche 3*, 1931 (p. 233 of 1959 re-edition). The first verse is an epigraph to the *Threepenny Novel*, for which Isherwood made this translation.

74. *Song to inaugurate the National Deposit Bank*. Gründungssong der National Deposit Bank. 339. Ged. 9, 18.
(1930). From 'The Bruise,' *Versuche 3*, p. 236. Intended to be sung by Macheath's gang, who are seen in the film as newly fledged bank directors.

75.♭ *Praise of the USSR*. Lob der UdSSR. 1140. Ged. 3, 214.
Sung by the Control Chorus at the end of scene I of *The Decision* (1930). An early TS has 'honour' rather than the 'hope of the exploited' in line 5, 'fame' rather than 'knowledge' quietly welcoming those present, and the 'history' of the world rather than its 'future' as the object of concern in the last line.

76.♭ *Praise of illegal activity*. Lob der illegalen Arbeit. 1140. Ged. 3, 70. Included in *Songs Poems Choruses*.
Sung by the Control Chorus in scene 2 of *The Decision*. An early script omits the last four lines.

77.♭ *Song of the rice-barge hauliers*. Gesang der Reiskahnschlepper. 1141. Ged. 3, 215.

Sung by the coolies (solo and chorus) in scene 3 of *The Decision*. In the early scripts the verse order varies slightly. Included in *A Hundred Poems* 1950.

78.♭ *Strike song*. Streiklied. 1143. Ged. 3, 217.

Sung by the Control Chorus and the Young Comrade in scene 4 of *The Decision*. It replaced an earlier 'Song of the cotton-spinners'.

79.♭ *Supply and demand*. Also called 'The merchant's song' or 'Song of merchandise'. (Angebot und Nachfrage, Lied des Händlers, or Song von der Ware). 1144. Ged. 3, 219.

Sung by the Merchant (i.e. one of the Agitators) in scene 5 of *The Decision*. In an early recording Brecht takes the part of the Young Comrade, interpolating the questions that follow the sixth line of each verse. Eisler's setting omitted verse 2.

80.♭ *Alter the world, it needs it*. Ändere die Welt, sie braucht es. 1144. Ged. 3, 219.

Sung by the Control Chorus at the end of scene 5 of *The Decision*. The printed text ends with four lines that Eisler did not set:

> Tell us more.
> For some time we have listened to you not
> As if judging you, but as
> Men who must learn.

Instead Eisler concluded with a fortissimo 'Who are you?' In Brecht's first version of the play this was followed by the injunction:

> Striking, disappear from the newly cleaned room!
> For you were the last of the dirt
> You must get rid of.

81.♭ *Praise of the Party*. Lob der Partei. 464–5. Ged. 3, 68–9. In *Songs Poems Choruses* and *100 Poems*.

This is a combination of two poems. In scene 6 of the play ('The Betrayal') sections 1 and 2 are spoken, the first four lines being given to the Young Comrade and the rest to the other three Agitators. They sometimes bear the separate title 'But who is the Party' ('Wer aber ist die Partei?'). The last section is then sung under the title 'Praise of the Party' by the chorus.

82.♭ *We are the scum of the earth*. Wir sind der Abschaum der Welt. St 659.

Sung by the chorus at the end of scene 7 of *The Decision*.

83. *The sick man dies and the strong man fights*. Der kranke Mann stirbt und der starke Mann ficht. 1154.

(1930) Sung by the Merchant in scenes 3 (stanza 1) and 6 (stanza 2) of *The Exception and the Rule* (1929–30). Though a version to be sung by John Garga and Manky was in early texts of *In the Jungle*, there was no musical setting till 1948, when Dessau wrote one at Brecht's request for a travelling production by

J-M. Serreau. Once again, like 'Death in the woods' (no. 4) this poem originates in Kipling's 'There were three friends that buried the fourth', whose key line is 'The strong man fights but the sick man dies', an antithesis here reversed by Brecht.

84. *The voices.* Der Auftrag. 1149. Ged. 3, 206.

Spoken by Joan's five 'voices' in scene 9j of *St Joan of the Stockyards.* The play was written in 1930/31 with the collaboration of Elisabeth Hauptmann and Emil Burri, using material from *Happy End.* No production could be mounted before the fall of the Weimar Republic, apart from a Berlin radio broadcast on 11 April 1932.

85. *The snow's blowing this way.* Der Schnee beginnt zu treiben. 1149. Ged. 3, 205.

(1929). These words appear as the lights go down on scene 9g of the same play. In 1942 Eisler set them for voice and piano under the title 'Winterspruch'.

86.♭ *The spring.* Das Frühjahr kommt. 367. Ged. 3, 220.

(1931). Written for *Kuhle Wampe*, the collective film by Brecht, Eisler, Ottwalt and Dudow which had its première in Moscow in May 1932. The song was half-sung off screen by Helene Weigel while lovers were seen in a wood. It was composed with her vocal abilities in mind.

87.♭ *A horse makes a statement.* Ein Pferd gibt Auskunft. adN. 262. Ged. 6, 102. Also known as 'O Falladah, die du hangest!'.

Adapted from Brecht's early poem 'Falada, Falada' (*Poems 1913–1956*, p. 33) and set to music by Eisler to make a sketch for a 1932 Christmas revue by Friedrich Holländer called *Es war einmal* . . . This was to have included sketches by Erich Kästner, Ernst Toller and other writers, but appears not to have been performed.

88.♭ *As the raven.* Wie die Krähe. 640. Ged. 3, 63. Also called 'An die Frauen' (To the women) and (for the 1935 New York production) 'The Song of the Question'.

Sung to Vlassova by the chorus of revolutionary workers to conclude scene 1 of *The Mother* (1932). Dümling says Eisler's setting was originally a fugue, with rhythmically spoken words. It was recomposed for the 1949 cantata version.

89.♭ *Praise of Communism.* Lob des Kommunismus. 463. Ged. 3, 67. In *Songs Poems Choruses.*

(1931). Sung by Vlassova to the group of neighbours in scene 6b of *The Mother.* No. 2 of Eisler's *Neun Balladen aus dem Lehrstück Die Mutter*, op.25. Also in the cantata version. Minor variants include the title, which Eisler often preferred to give as 'Praise of Socialism', and the 'problem/solution,' antithesis two lines from the end. Here Brecht's earliest 1931 draft had 'problem/solution' amended to 'confusion/clarity'. Later versions read 'chaos/order' as in the collected plays.

90.♭ *Praise of learning.* Lob des Lernens. 462. Ged. 3, 66. GBL 38. In *Songs Poems Choruses.*

(1931). Eisler's MS calls it 'Praise of knowledge' [*Wissenschaft*]. Sung by the Revolutionary Workers to Pelegea Vlassova and other adults as they learn to read in scene 6(c) of *The Mother*. No. 3 of Eisler's *Neun Balladen*. Also included in the cantata version. The meaning of the line 'You must be ready to take over' and the original 'Du musst die Führung übernehmen' ('you must take over the lead') was debated during Brecht's hearing by the Un-American Activities Committee in 1947.

91.♭ *Praise of the revolutionary*. Lob des Revolutionärs. 466. Ged. 3, 72. In *Songs Poems Choruses*.

(1931). Sung (nominally 'recited') by Vlassova to Ivan Vesovchikov in scene 6(d) of *The Mother*, with reference to her arrested son Pavel. No. 4 of Eisler's *Neun Balladen*, but apparently cut at the première and in the 1949 production. Is also in the cantata version and his *Lenin Requiem*. Brecht's first version omits lines 4–6. Instead it had four other lines which he deleted, going:

> Whoever fights for communism
> Runs great risks
> But all the oppressed
> Need him.

92.♭ *To be sung in prison*. [Sie haben Gesetzbücher und Verordnungen.] 1157. GBL 39. Called 'A Song for Prison' in the 1935 New York production.

Sung by Pavel in prison following his mother's visit in scene 7 of *The Mother*. No. 5 of Eisler's *Neun Balladen*. We have taken Eisler's title. Brecht sometimes called it 'Song for all who want to lose heart' ('Lied für alle, die verzagen wollen'). It was at one point to have been included in *Songs Poems Choruses*.

93.♭ *Praise of the third thing*. Lob der dritten Sache. 1159.

(1931) Sung by Vlassova at the end of scene 9, after her son Pavel has escaped from prison and passed through for the last time. Included in the cantata version.

94.♭ *Report on the death of a comrade*. Bericht über den Tod eines Genossen. 466. Ged. 3, 71. In *Songs Poems Choruses*. Also called 'Grabrede' and (in the 1935 New York production) 'The Death of a Comrade'.

(1931). Sung by the chorus of Revolutionary Workers to Vlassova in scene 10 of *The Mother* as a report on the execution of her son. No. 8 of Eisler's *Neun Balladen*. Also in 1949 cantata version. A file of related material in the Eisler Archive contains a 'Song of the mother on the heroic death of the coward Vesovchikov' – i.e., not her son – dating from 1931 and possibly displaced by this. Published in Ged. 2, 171 but not in GW, it goes

> So what was he like
> He was as always
> When he went up to the wall
> He could die.
> Nor did he compare it with others
> Nor himself with others either, but
> Set himself, menaced, to change swiftly into
> Unmenaceable dust. And all that

Happened later he performed as if
Pre-agreed, as though fulfilling
A contract. And extinguished were
All his inner wishes. From any kind of movement
He strictly abstained. His inner self
Caved in, then disappeared. Like a blank sheet
He evaded everything
But description.

There is a short four-part 'Cantata on the Death of a Comrade' by Eisler for voice and piano dating from 1935. Its words however are taken from the work of Ignazio Silone, a writer admired by both men.

95.♭ *Get up, the Party's under threat*! Steh auf, die Partei ist in Gefahr! 1159.

Sung to Vlassova on her sickbed by the chorus of Revolutionary Workers in scene 9 of *The Mother*. No. 9 of Eisler's *Neun Balladen*. Also in cantata version. In the course of the song Vlassova gets up, dresses unsteadily and leaves. An early, shorter script belonging to Eisler shows that he substituted the call 'Get up' for Brecht's original 'Raise yourself', it bears handwritten amendments by both men.

96. *Song of the only way*. Das Lied vom Ausweg. 461. Ged. 3, 65. In *Songs Poems Choruses* as 'The song of the soup'.

(1931). Not in the original *Neun Balladen*. In cantata version. Sung in scene 2 of *The Mother* by Masha in answer to Vlassova. Cut before the 1932 première and restored in 1935.

97. *Song of the patches and the coat*. Lied vom Flicken und vom Rock. St 839. Called 'The Whole Loaf' in the 1935 New York production.

(1931). Sung by the factory workers in scene 3 of *The Mother*, as they press for a strike. Initially called 'Condemnation of reformism', this title however was deleted, possibly by Eisler, who first appears to have set the song for the New York production of the play. Included in the cantata version.

98. *But he was very much frightened*. Sehr aber erschrak er. St 884.

Recited by Vlassova in scene 10 of *The Mother* following her son Pavel's death.

99.♭ *Praise of dialectics*. Lob der Dialektik (or 'Wer noch lebt, sage nicht niemals'). 1160. Ged. 3, 7. Called 'Dialectics' in the New York production. In *Songs Poems Choruses* and *100 Poems*.

Recited by Vlassova at the end of scene 14, the last scene of *The Mother*, on the eve of the 1917 Revolution. Set to music for the 1935 production. The version in *Songs Poems Choruses* starts as a poem whose first seven lines are not included in the play. They were clearly written after 1932 and go:

Today injustice strides around with a confident step.
The oppressors are getting ready for a thousand years.
Power assures us 'It will all stay as it is'
No voice is heard but the voice of the rulers

And in the markets Exploitation proclaims 'This is only the start.'
But among the oppressed many are now saying:
'What we want is never going to work'.

In the 1949 cantata version it is musically extended.

100.♭ *Chorus of landed gentry.* Rundgesang der Pachtherren. 1180. GBL 42.

(1932). Sung by the satisfied landlords at the end of *The Round Heads and the Pointed Heads* (1936). Was in Brecht's unperformed adaptation of *Measure for Measure* from which this play derives. Also called 'The Perhaps Song' (Das Vielleicht-Lied).

101. *War song.* Kriegslied. 1126. Ged. 9, 17.

(1934) Introduces chapter 2 of Book 1 of the *Threepenny Novel*. This was originally published in English in 1937 as *A Penny for the Poor* in a translation by Desmond Vesey, for whom Isherwood made his verse translations.

102.♭ *Sister, from birth.* Schwester, wir sind alle frei geboren. St 2870. Ged. 3, 151.

Sung by Anna 2 in 'Envy', the final section of the Brecht-Weill ballet *The Seven Deadly Sins* (1933). It is introduced by ten lines of unrhymed verse. Auden's translation was made for the original choreographer Georges Balanchine's New York production in 1958.

103.♭ *Song of the stimulating impact of cash.* Lied von der belebenden Wirkung des Geldes. 1174. Ged. 3, 237. GBL 41.

(1934). Original title 'nervus rerum'. Sung by the Judge at the start of scene 7 of *The Round Heads and the Pointed Heads*. Eisler's settings for this play were ready in August 1934. In his conversations with Hans Bunge (*Fragen Sie mehr über Brecht*, 1972) he describes his singing this song and the 'Ballad of the waterwheel' at Brecht's request to the well-to-do Stefan Zweig in London in July 1936, some four months before the play's Copenhagen première.

In one of Brecht's early typescripts of the play (BBA 263) the last refrain is changed, seemingly to lessen the irony, ending 'And the law becomes a different law'.

104.♭ *Ballad of the button.* Die Ballade vom Knopfwurf. 1169. Ged. 3, 235.

(1934). Sung by Mrs Cornamontis the brothel madam at the end of scene 4 of *The Round Heads and the Pointed Heads* (first court scene) in reply to a landlord's suggestion that poor men sometimes win their case against the rich.

105.♭ *The What-you-have-you-hold song.* Das Was-man-hat-hat-man Song. 1171.

(1934). Sung by Callas, a tenant farmer who has just recovered two horses from his landlord in scene 6 (Mrs Cornamontis's café) of *The Round Heads and the Pointed Heads* and again in scene 7 when a new judgement takes the horses away from him once more.

In one script (BBA 257) Callas rounds off the second of these with a further verse:

> The man said: That's too thick
> Became a bolshevik

Went out and coolly snatched it.
Now he eats himself sick
And treats the rest as ratshit.

106.♭ *Ballad of the waterwheel*. Ballade vom Wasserrad. 1175. Ged. 3, 239. GBL 40.

(1934). Published in *Unsere Zeit* (Paris), 1 May 1934. Sung by Callas's daughter the prostitute Nanna at the end of scene 8 of *The Round Heads and the Pointed Heads*. Brecht's several drafts for this song suggest that writing it was not easy. Some give the gist in prose, broken by the occasional verse phrase which found its way into the final text. Thus:

Oh, we had many masters
Often they changed above our heads
Then we had others
But we never saw no one.

Or again:

1

in the schoolbooks we read
that the great of this earth go up like comets
and go down like comets too
for us who've had to feed the great
it has always been a matter of indifference.

2

and the schoolbooks say that they differ vastly
indeed our masters have included lions and pigs
for us who had to feed them both
we didn't need other masters but none.

In GW the refrain is the same all through. Our version of the final refrain is from the Eisler setting, which is dated 27 July 1934. There is also a draft when the water ends up 'full and unrestrained', sweeping the whole wheel away.

Around 1939 Brecht wished at one point to include the song in scene 8 of *Mother Courage*.

107. *Once again man's handiwork crumbles*. Wieder zerfallen die Werke von Menschenhand. 530. Ged. 9, 38.

(1934). Written for an unfinished play by Brecht and Leo Lania called *The Oilfield* and based on the latter's *Konjunktur* (or 'Boom') which Piscator staged in 1928. At that time Lania was one of Piscator's principal dramaturgs, along with Brecht and others. Later he worked on the script of the *Threepenny Opera* film and was again involved in film projects with Brecht when they met in London in 1934. After 1949 he edited an American magazine called *United Nations World*.

108.♭ *All of us or none*. Keiner oder alle. 649. Ged. 4, 33. In *Svendborg Poems*.

(1934). A late 'Kampflied' written in London at the same time as the 'United Front' song and probably for the same Comintern patrons. Set by Eisler in December 1934, published for the International Brigades in 1937, and later included in *The Days of the Commune*, where it is sung by an unspecified voice or voices at the end of scene 11. Notes in the margin of one of Brecht's drafts suggest that he may have had the start of the Communist Manifesto in mind when planning the song, which he did partly in prose (as for the Waterwheel, above). The original refrain 'Keiner oder alle' evidently had its pendant 'Alles oder nichts' added as an afterthought (note that the translation reverses the order of these two phrases). One version of it goes:

> All of us or none!
> Go on battling till you free them
> One and all, and let us see them
> Standing in the morning sun.

109.♭ *Letter to the New York workers' company 'Theatre Union' about the play 'The Mother'.*
Brief an das Arbeitertheater 'Theatre Union' in New York, das Stück 'Die Mutter' betreffend. 1160. Ged. 9, 109.

(1935). The poem as it now stands reflects Brecht's (and Eisler's) disagreements with the company over its adaptation and production of *The Mother*. The first, naturalistic version of Paul Peters's adaptation was sent to Brecht in Denmark in the late summer of 1935, and it seems that this 'letter' may have been finished before Brecht arrived in New York, which was some five weeks before the première. The drafts show the first three sections very much as now, and it is notable that they deal entirely with the play as Brecht had envisaged and seen it in 1931–1932. He seems to have begun section 4 without actually criticising the adaptation, thus:

> Comrades, I see you
> Reading the short play with concern.
> Will the world understand it? I hear you asking.
> Will they renounce the familiar opiate, the spiritual
>   participation
> In other people's anger . . .

and so on to the end, omitting the word 'unbounded' in the last line. Then comes another draft of the section which includes his critique of the adaptation more or less as now down to 'Will the workers understand you?', then goes on:

> They underrated [the audience] as you've done, concerned not to follow
>   it, rather to
> Show it the way, swiftly show it the way with long strides
> Trusting its power unconditionally. If you dilute the actor's
>   phrases
> With moods, how is the
> Audience to lay those often-heard phrases
> On the balance? [. . .] it is not as approximations
> Among many others, that the statements must

Emerge. Nor like drunkards who
(Since they can no longer stand on their own legs)
Mutually drag each other forward till they all fall down.
That's no way to lead. Not by creating some general feeling
Which quickly disperses in the cold light of day
But by putting your knowledge and experience on the table, comrades.
The form may seem new to you, but why be
Frightened of what's new? Is it hard to bring off?
To the man who's exploited, continually deceived
Life itself is a perpetual experiment
An uncertain business which is nowhere taught.
If I speak to you thus
Like a teacher, it is not mere presumption but
Because I myself find it very hard to shoulder
The daily lessons and transmit them further. You must forgive
My impatience: It's a matter of
Wrong or not wrong, striding forwards or staying behind
Not just of me and you. Remember that, comrades.
That's what I wanted to tell you.

110.♭ *Nanna's song*. Nannas lied. 1166. Ged. 3, 231. In *A Hundred Poems*.

(1936). First draft titled 'Lied der Hure' (Blues). Sometimes called 'Lied eines Freudenmädchens'. The first version gives her only 'seven summers'. It is sung by Nanna Callas in Eisler's setting in scene 2 of *The Round Heads and the Pointed Heads*. The last line of the chorus is a quotation from Villon. Another setting was written by Weill as a Christmas present for Lotte Lenya in America in 1939.

111.♭ *Madam's song*. Kuppellied (or Lied der Kupplerin). 1177. Ged. 3, 233.

(*c*. 1936). Sung by Mrs Cornamontis to Isabella, who has come to the brothel for instruction in love-making. Nanna will take her place for money, because 'cash makes you randy'. Eisler's setting makes ironic use of the most famous chromatic progression from Wagner's *Tristan and Isolde*. Later Dessau too made a setting which he added to his *Good Person of Szechwan* score.

A rejected verse of the first draft goes:

Some I saw were frigid and exhausted.
Till a shudder suddenly passed through
They were frantic if he spurned them
And were frantic if he took them too.
It was love. Was that what made her swoon?
Sure, his cheque book did, but not the moon.
Anything he did was right.
He felt love had reached high noon.
She felt blazingly alight.
Both experienced that great passion
Which you can't recapture quite.
And the spur? Cash makes you randy

As I've learnt night after night.

112. *Ballad of knowledge.* Ballade vom Wissen. 1233. Ged. 7, 143.

(1936/37). A song akin to those in *The Round Heads and the Pointed Heads* and written around the same time, but not used, published or set to music till at the end of his life Brecht put it into his unfinished last play *Turandot.* There it is sung in instalments in scene 8 by four of the Tuis, or inverted intellectuals.

113.♭ *Sheep march.* Kälbermarsch. 1219. In *A Hundred Poems.*

(1936). Also called 'Ballade von den erwachten Kälbern' and (by Dessau) 'Horstdüssel-lied', a reference to the refrain's parodying of the Nazi 'Horst-Wessel Song' ('Düssel' means 'idiot'). We have changed Brecht's 'calves' to sheep, who in English are more associated with such behaviour. Set by Eisler early in 1943 as one of *Vier Lieder für Kurzwellensendung nach Deutschland,* and included in *Schweik in the Second World War,* where Schweik in scene 7 sings it to his companions in a military prison. The earliest version starts with the first line of the Nazi song:

> Make clear the streets, here come the brown battalions!
> How can the sheep tell where those streets may lead?
> Once there were seven sheep, now there are millions.
> And, decked with flags, they won't appear to bleed.

Eisler's setting of the refrain uses the Nazi tune but twists it off course with his last notes. Dessau's setting (1943) also parodies the Nazi hymn.

114. *The German march-past.* Die Deutsche Heerschau. St 1075 et seq.

The unrhymed introductory section and the first three stanzas form the prelude to *Fear and Misery of the Third Reich* (1935–38), while the rest of this processional poem (cf. 'The anachronistic procession' in *Poems 1913–1956*) is made up of the one or two stanzas prefixed to each of the play's twenty-four scenes. For those introducing other, previously unpublished scenes see volume 4 iii of the collection *Plays* in our edition. There are furthermore stanzas, or hints of stanzas, introducing Goering ('a fat clown in 7 uniforms'), Himmler, Todt and those health experts who recommend the nutritional value of wood. No known scenes correspond.

The notion of stringing the scenes together on a long poem evidently originated when Slatan Dudow in Paris decided to perform some of them under the title *99 %.* Paul Dessau then set them to music and appears to have sung them, but his settings are unpublished and have never been revived.

115. *Mary, Mary sat her down.* Maria sass auf einem Stein. 1186.

Children's song, to a traditional German tune. Sung in the last scene of the 1938 version of *Galileo.* It was dropped from Brecht and Laughton's Hollywood version, but restored in the final German text.

116. *My audience.* Mein Zuschauer. 792. Ged. 9, 71.

This is the only one of the 'Messingkauf Poems' written between 1930–1950 which appears to be an integral part of the *Messingkauf Dialogues* proper (1939–40), where it comes in the 'Fragments from the Fourth Night'. See the note in *Poems 1913–1956*, pp. 503–5.

117.♭ *Mother Courage's song*. Mutter Courages Lied. 1187. Ged. 5, 171. GBL 44.

Theme song of *Mother Courage and her children* (1939), written by Brecht to a tune called 'L'Étendard de la pitié' which he had used for the 'Ballad of the Pirates' in 1918. Simon Parmet wrote a setting in Finland in 1940/41, but it was not used for the original Zurich production of 1941, though the theatre's composer Paul Burkhard used the prescribed tune. Dessau made the now accepted arrangement of this in Hollywood in 1946.

The first two stanzas and their refrains are sung on Courage's entrance with the cart in scene 1; the two central quatrains in scene 7 ('Mother Courage at the peak of her business career'); the next stanza ('From Ulm to Metz' etc.) at the end of scene 8, when she has teamed up with the Cook; while the last is an offstage chorus which concludes the play. There is also a discarded quatrain by Brecht which goes:

> From Stuttgart we moved on to Hagen
> As we pursued our tireless course.
> In Stuttgart we gave up our waggon
> In Hagen we gave up our horse.

In the text originally set by Dessau the second stanza ran:

> This county has been razed to stubble.
> Yours is the fame. But where's the bread?
> Let Mother Courage solve that trouble
> And feed your men before they're dead.
> Bombardments on an empty belly
> Are not a diet to keep them well.
> But feed them up to face the mêlée
> And they will follow you to hell.

118.♭ *Song of unconditional surrender*. Lied von der grossen Kapitulation. 1192. Ged. 5, 178 GBL 45.

Sung and partly spoken by Mother Courage in scene 4 to the Young Soldier as they sit waiting to make their official complaints, then lose heart and change their minds. Also called 'Song of waiting' (Lied des Abwartens). Set by Dessau in 1946. The spoken (i.e. bracketed) passages were all additions to the original 1939 script.

119. *Song of the soldier before the inn*. Reiterlied, or [Soldatenlied]. 1193. Ged. 5, 180.

Sung by a soldier outside Mother Courage's canteen tent in scene 6 of the play. It was an addition on the 1939 script. Set by Dessau in 1946–9. Auden's version for William Gaskill's 1965 National Theatre production, which we have chosen to use, is in his *City Without Walls*.

120. *Song of the rose*. [Lied von der Bleibe.] 1196. Ged. 5, 183.

Sung by a voice off, this is heard by Mother Courage and Kattrin in scene 10 as they pass a peasant cottage. They pause, then move on. Setting by Dessau, 1946, later arranged for women's chorus (1954). We print the Auden version.

121. *Lullaby.* [Wiegenlied.] 1196. Ged. 5, 184.

Sung by Mother Courage over the dead body of her daughter in the last scene of the play. Set by Dessau 1946–49 to a melody supposedly provided by Helene Weigel. We print the Auden translation.

122. *Roll-call of the virtues and the vices.* Appell der Laster und Tugenden. Pr 1457. In the Steffin collection.

(*c.* 1939). One of the group of 'Visions' written around the start of the Second World War. See note in *Poems 1913–1956* pp. 511–12 and the five similar prose-poems printed in that book. This one was taken into the posthumously published *Flüchtlingsgespräche* (Conversations between Exiles) which Brecht wrote between 1940–1944. 'Soubrette' is an old theatrical term for actresses specialising in pert maidservant parts.

123. *The Queen's lament.* [Als ich einst in Taurion ging.] St 1464.

Spoken by the Queen in scene 9 ('The Trial') of the radio play *The Trial of Lucullus* (1939) which Brecht and Dessau subsequently made into an opera (1949) and were persuaded to revise and rename in 1951. The translation follows the original rhythms but does not necessarily fit either Dessau's setting or that by Roger Sessions which preceded it.

124. *Song of the smoke.* Lied vom Rauch. 1199. Ged. 5, 191. GBL 47.

Sung by the Grandfather, Husband and Niece from the family of eight in scene 1 of *The Good Person of Szechwan.* Originally called 'Song of the impoverished family' (Lied der Verarmten Familie). A reworking of the 'Song from the opium den' (no. 10): see the note on this. Set to music by Dessau in 1947–8.

125. *The water-seller's song in the rain.* Lied des Wasserverkäufers in Regen. 1200. Ged. 5, 193.

Sung by Wang the water-seller in scene 3 of *The Good Person of Szechwan* (1940). Set to music by Dessau in 1947–8.

126. *Why are you so unpleasant?* [Den Mitmenschen zu treten]. St 1570.

In scene 7 of *The Good Person of Szechwan* (1940). Shen Teh addresses the question in our title to Mrs Shin, then speaks the poem to the audience.

127. *Song of the defencelessness of the good and the gods.* Das Lied von der Wehrlosigkeit der Götter und Guten. 1202. Ged. 5, 194.

'Interlude before the curtain', following scene 4 of *The Good Person of Szechwan* (1940). Set by Dessau in 1947. Sung and mimed by Shen Teh as she changes into her tough bad cousin Shui Ta. This interlude was cut in the script of the Zurich première in 1943. Compare Lilian Holiday's similarly militant call for mobilisation 'all to get a bowl of soup to make the poor man's supper' in the *Happy End* song 'God's little lieutenant', (no. 55).

128. *The song of green cheese.* Das Lied von Sankt Nimmerleinstag. 1204. Ged. 5, 198. GBL 48.

Sung by Yang Sun the pilot in scene 6 (the wedding scene) of *The Good Person of Szechwan* (1940). 'Sankt Nimmerleinstag' is literally 'Saint Never's Day'. Setting by Dessau, 1947–8.

129. *Don't be too hard*. Ein wenig Nachsicht und die Kräfte verdoppeln sich. 1199. Also called 'Lied von der Nachsicht'.

(1940). In scene 1 of *The Good Person of Szechwan* Shen Teh tells the Carpenter 'Don't be too hard, Mr Lin To. I can't meet all your demands at once'; then speaks this poem to the audience.

130.♭ *On suicide*. Über den Selbstmord (or 'Angesichts des Elends'). St 1524. Ged. 5, 192. GBL 77.

(1940). Included in one of Brecht's rough plans for 'Poems in Exile'; given to Eisler in 1942, and set under this title for voice and piano as part of the latter's 'Hollywood Songbook'. Added at an uncertain date to the first script of *The Good Person of Szechwan* for Shen Teh to speak to the audience in scene 3.

131. *Song of the eighth elephant*. Lied vom achten Elefanten. 1205. Ged. 5, 200. GBL 49.

Sung by Yang Sun in scene 8 (the factory scene) of *The Good Person of Szechwan*. Added to the first script in January 1941 and set by Dessau in 1947–8. Note by Brecht in *Letters* no.797. It seems possible that there was a private allusion in this Kiplingesque song to the carved elephants which Brecht used to give Margarete Steffin, his collaborator on the play.

132. *Trio of the vanishing gods on their cloud*. Terzett der entschwindenden Götter auf der Wolke. St 1606.

(1941). Sung by the three gods at the end of *The Good Person of Szechwan*. Added to the first script in January 1941. Consciously intended by Brecht to be 'beautiful', so he said on reading the original, not very beautiful version of this translation (which was accordingly rewritten).

133.♭ *The angel speaks*. [Wenn der Eroberer kommt in eure Stadt.] 1214. Ged. 6, 168.

(1942). Sung to Simone by The Angel at the end of scene 2 of *The Visions of Simone Machard* (1942–3). Set to music by Eisler in 1955.

134.♭ *Simone's song*. [Liedchen.] 1213. Ged. 6, 167.

Sung by Simone as she imagines herself to be marching off to Orléans in the first dream scene of *The Visions of Simone Machard*. Early versions have other place names – Rocamer, Saint-Omer, even Saint-Tropez with a query – instead of the more euphonious Saint-Nazaire. Set by Eisler, probably in 1955.

135.♭ *Song of the Nazi soldier's wife*. Das Lied vom Weib des Nazisoldaten. 1215. GBL 43. In *A Hundred Poems*.

(1942). First published in *Freies Deutschland*, Mexico City, no. 5, on March 1942. Originally called by its first line 'Und was bekam des Soldaten Weib?' Set by Weill in 1943 for a 'Voice of America' broadcast, where it was sung by Lenya; then again in 1950 by Dessau, and by Eisler at an undetermined date. Put into *Schweik in the Second World War* where it is sung to her customers by Mrs Kopecka the publican in scene 1. A setting by Mischa Spoliansky was broadcast by BBC German Service about 1943.

According to Brecht's *Arbeitsjournal* entry for 9 May 1942, Eisler originally complained of the song's critical attitude to the private soldier, saying that he too had sent salami home to his mother from Italy in 1917. Brecht comments 'what I must have had in mind was: and what did the mail bring the SA-man's wife? that's what it will have to be called'. However, the SA were not part of the invading German army, and it was only much later that the title confined the criticism to those soldiers who were specifically Nazis. Among other, lesser changes Brecht discarded a verse (which is in the Weill setting) referring to a colourful Rumanian blouse from Bucarest; this may have been because the Rumanians were the Nazis' allies. Rotterdam at one point was to have been Amsterdam. In another version, Warsaw was omitted.

136.♭ *Song of the gentle breeze.* Das Lied vom kleinen Wind. 1216. Ged. 6, 169. Sung by Mrs Kopecka (a role originally written for Lotte Lenya) in scene 3 of *Schweik in the Second World War.* Set by Eisler in 1955.

137.♭ *Song of the 'Chalice'.* Das Lied vom 'Kelch'. 1220. Ged. 6, 172.

(*c.* 1942). Sung by Mrs Kopecka 'in honour of Mr Baloun' as seen in a vision by Private Schweik in scene 8 (the Russian steppes in winter) of *Schweik in the Second World War.* Settings by Eisler, 1956 and Dessau *c.* 1948. An early draft reckons prices in *Kreutzer* (the old Austro-Hungarian coinage) instead of *Heller* and gives two lines of melody in Brecht's notation.

138.♭ *German Miserere.* Deutsches Miserere. 1222.

(1943). In *Poems in Exile,* 1944. Sung in scene 8 of *Schweik in the Second World War* by the crew of an armoured troop-carrier. This setting by Eisler, 1943. Another setting for solo voice and piano by Dessau is dated the same year and dedicated to Paul Robeson. There appears to be an allusion in the title to Brecht's recurrent concept of the 'German Misère'.

139.♭ *Song of the Moldau.* Das Lied von der Moldau. 1218.

(1943). Sung by Mrs Kopecka at the end of scene 6 of *Schweik in the Second World War,* repeating the first stanza again after the second; then as a finale by a 'chorus of all the actors, who take off their masks and come right downstage' – this time without any repetition. According to Elisabeth Hauptmann (speaking to Herbert Knust) it is based on Maurice Magre's song 'Au fond de la Seine', which Weill had set for Lys Gauty in 1934. (Michael Morley cites the words: 'Au fond de la Seine il y a de l'or, des bateaux rouillés, des bijoux, des armes . . . et puis des cailloux et des bêtes grises'.) The first four notes of Eisler's setting however derive from Smetana's tone-poem *Vltava* (this being the Czech name for the river in Prague which Germans call 'Moldau').

In his *Materialien* volume on the play (Suhrkamp, Frankfurt, 1974) Knust prints eleven of Brecht's various attempts at the song, which evidently gave him difficulty and was the last part of the play to be finished in the autumn of 1943. A first prose outline goes:

> I
>
> on the banks of the river moldau stands the city of prague
> its lofty buildings and its low ones
> are reflected in the river moldau's water

2
a tradition says the moldau's waters
come from the tears that the people has laughed and wept

3
the city of prague has stood for 1000 years
the moldau's bed has never been empty

4
but they say that when there is too much weeping in the city of
prague the moldau will overflow its banks

5
and carry off
the slave drivers in the offices
the slave drivers in the churches
the slave drivers in the lawcourts

Eisler, unlike Brecht, knew Prague well, and it is worth recalling that this city was also the setting for *Hangmen also Die*, the film on which both men had worked for Fritz Lang a year earlier.

140. *When we entered fair Milan*. Als wir kamen vor Milano. 879. Ged. 6, 187.

(*c.* 1943). Sung offstage by a soldier at the beginning of Act 2 of Webster's *The Duchess of Malfi* as adapted by Brecht, who later considered putting it in the Berliner Ensemble's production of *Mother Courage*. No setting is known. In the German (which makes some notable use of English word order) there are five verses, of which 2 and 4 are indented as here, but printed as though they were refrains. Only the first and last are in the English text on which H. R. Hays and W. H. Auden successively worked as translators of Brecht's new material.

Though this partial translation appeared in a script copyrighted in Hays's name only, and though Hays told me that he had made it, it looks like Auden's work. This would date it around the time when Auden came into the project and Hays walked out: i.e. about December 1943. (The central section, from 'I never got' to 'itching flesh' was translated by me.)

For the Broadway production of the play in September 1946, which credited Auden on the programme but reverted to Webster's text, Benjamin Britten composed music which has so far not been traced.

141. *Go calmly into battle*. Geh du ruhig in die Schlacht, Soldat. 1223. Ged. 6, 174.

Also known as 'Ich werde warten auf dich'. Half spoken, half sung by Grusha in scene 2 (the Prologue being counted as scene 1) of *The Caucasian Chalk Circle*, 1944. Set to music by Paul Dessau, 1953–4. A reaction to Nathalie René's translation of 'Wait for me', a war poem by Konstantin Simonov, which Brecht found in *Moscow News* and stuck in his *Working Journal* for 25 November 1942.

During 1944 Christopher Isherwood had been asked by Brecht to translate the play, and on his refusal Brecht turned to Auden, who suggested bringing in his friends the Sterns. It was he however who translated the verses, which he revised in 1959 for publication by Methuen. The original project for a Broadway production starring Luise Rainer fell through.

142. *Dance of the Grand Duke with his bow.* Bogentanz des Grossfürsten. adN. 270.

A pencilled note by Elisabeth Hauptmann says this poem was discarded from *The Caucasian Chalk Circle*. It was not among the material set by Dessau.

143. *Four generals.* [Vier Generäle zogen]. 1224. Ged. 6, 175. GBL 54.

(1944). One of Grusha's 'Lieder auf der Wanderung'. Sung by her at the beginning of scene 3 of *The Caucasian Chalk Circle*, as she sets off for the Northern Mountains. Set by Dessau in 1953–4. It has been suggested that Sosso Robakidze denotes Joseph Stalin, whose armies had defeated the Germans at Stalingrad some months earlier. (Robakidse is said to be the name of a Georgian writer). There also appears to be some connection with the Spanish Civil War song 'los cuatro generales'.

144. *Soldiers' song* [Zieh ins Feld ich traurig meiner Strassen] 1226. Ged. 6, 178.

(1944). Sung by the two Ironshirts as they trudge after Grusha in scene 3 of *The Caucasian Chalk Circle*, and freely translated by Auden. According to Rudolf Vapénik, Brecht had made use of a literal German version of a Moravian folk song which is among the Slovak folk songs collected by Bartók. The song was set by Dessau in 1953–4.

145. *A little song.* [Dein Vater ist ein Räuber]. 1225. Ged. 6, 177

(1944). Sung by Grusha to the child Michel at the end of scene 3 of *The Caucasian Chalk Circle*. Two settings by Dessau in 1953–4.

146. *The battle began at dawn.* [Die Schlacht fing an im Morgengrauen.] 1227. Ged. 6, 180.

Sung by the Singer at the end of scene 4 of *The Caucasian Chalk Circle* where Simon returns from the war and meets Grusha again. Two settings by Dessau in 1953–4. Said to be derived from an Esthonian epic which Hella Wuolijoki had translated and shown Brecht. The 'Hear what he [or she] thought but didn't say' in the third line of each stanza was not in the earliest script.

147. *The 'is that so?' song.* [Warum bluten unsere Söhne nicht mehr?] Also called 'Lied vom Krieg'. 1227. Ged. 6, 181.

(1944). Sung by Azdak to the Ironshirts early in scene 5 as a song brought back from Persia by his grandfather. The refrain 'yea, yea, yea,' etc. is supplied by Shauva the policeman. The present text is typed in English without capital letters: an anonymous translation probably made in consultation with Brecht. Spacing as in the original.

148. *Song of chaos.* Lied vom Chaos. 1230. Ged. 6, 185.

Sung by Azdak to Shauva (who interposes the 'oh, oh's) at the end of scene 5, when he has heard of the Governor's return. The song derives from an ancient Egyptian poem cited at length by Brecht in his 'Five difficulties in writing the truth', which was first published in 1939 (GW zLK 234). His 'The peasant's address to his ox', similarly based on an Egyptian poem of 1400 BC, appears to have been written in 1938 and is in *Poems 1913–1956*, p. 313.

149. *The luck of the poor.* [Im Volk heisst es: der Arme braucht Glück]. adN. 371.

(1944). Song cut from the earliest script of *The Caucasian Chalk Circle*, where it comes near the beginning of scene 6 ('The Chalk Circle'). Set by Dessau in 1960 as an addition to the 48 numbers which he composed six years earlier.

150. *He who wears the shoes of gold.* Ginge es in goldnen Schuhen. 1230.

Sung by the Singer in scene 6 of *The Caucasian Chalk Circle* as an interpretation of Grusha's thoughts, shortly before the actual performance of the test. Set by Dessau in 1953–4.

151. *Song of Azdak.* Lied vom Azdak. 1228. GBL 55.

Also called 'Ballade vom Azdak'. Sung by the Singer and/or his musicians to introduce episodes in scene 5 ('Story of the Judge') of *The Caucasian Chalk Circle* following Azdak's appointment as Judge. Stanzas 3 and 4 were added in 1954. In the Berliner Ensemble's stage version the sixth stanza is omitted.

152.♭ *Galileo the Bible-buster.* [Als der Allmächtige sprach sein grosses Werde]. Also called 'The terrible teachings and opinions of Court Physicist Galileo Galilei'. 1184.

Sung by the Ballad-Singer and his wife in the crucial scene 10 of *Life of Galileo* to show the subversiveness of Galileo's physics. The song was written in English – it is not clear exactly by whom, but Abe Burrows of *Guys and Dolls* fame was among those involved – on the basis of the German version included in the first (1938) script. Apparently omitted from the original Zurich production, that earlier version is translated in the notes to the play in our edition. This is the text set by Eisler for the Hollywood production in July 1947. As a result, when Brecht in the 1950s began preparing a new and final text, he had to make fresh German versions of this (and also the interscene songs) which would fit the Eisler music. The pre-1943 song vanished from sight and the final version is an expansion of this one.

153. *Song of fraternisation.* Lied vom Fraternisieren. 1189.

(c. 1946). Originally called 'Lied der Soldatenhure' ('Song of the soldiers' whore'). Sung by Yvette the camp whore in scene 3 of *Mother Courage*. Set by Dessau (1946?) and added as an amendment to the 1946 script of the play. Before then she was initially required to sing Weill's 'Surabaya Johnny' (no. 37 above) at this point, then its text was amended so as to make Johnny a Dutchman called 'Pipe-and-Drum Henny', who wanted to take her to Utrecht rather than Burma. Some of the resulting farrago rubbed off on the new song. The concept of 'fraternisation' – notably between the occupation forces and German women – was much discussed after the German surrender of 1945. (This is Auden's translation.)

154.♭ *The new Cannon song.* Der neue Kanonen-Song. 1100.

(1946). When peace came in 1945 Brecht at first was none too keen to see *The Threepenny Opera* revived. Told that September of a rumour that the Russians had stopped a Berlin production – allegedly because of the Second Act Finale's all-too-topical line 'food is the first thing, morals follow on' – he noted in his Journal that he would not himself have licensed it, since 'in the absence of any revolutionary movement the "message" becomes plain anarchism'. In 1946 however, when he was starting to prepare his return to Europe, he evidently had second thoughts.

The rewriting of the 'Cannon song' (no. 19 above) was a first step towards what he later described to Weill as a juridically 'new version' of the play, which he hoped would tour West Germany with Hans Albers as Macheath, incidentally by-passing Bloch-Erben, his former Berlin agents. By December 1948 the Munich Kammerspiele had accepted the text; Brecht was back in Germany, had seen Albers, a successful film actor under the Nazis, and got his old friend Jakob Geis to supervise operations. On 27 April 1949 the première took place. However, Weill took exception to the changes and to the theatre's handling of his music, the new songs were dropped and the planned tour never materialised. The 'new version', so Brecht wrote to Weill that January, really only involved 'temporary changes, to be valid for the present time only (and not to be published)'. They would be published as an appendix in *Stücke 3* in 1955.

155.♭ *Ballad of the good living of Hitler's henchmen*. Die Ballade vom angenehmen Leben der Hitlersatrapen. 1111.

(1946). Second of the new *Threepenny Opera* songs written for the 1949 production in Munich and published in *Stücke 3*, 1955. The remaining changes, made to the 'Mac the Knife' song, the 'Ballad in which Macheath begs forgiveness' and the final 'Chorale' were too slight to constitute distinctively 'new versions' and are outlined in our notes to the original songs (nos. 39–51). At the same time there were temporary changes in the dialogue, notably as affecting the beggars, whose mutilations Brecht now played down, out of consideration for the war wounded and their relatives.

Goering, Schacht and Keitel were all tried and condemned by the International War Crimes Tribunal at Nuremberg in autumn 1946. Schacht was Hitler's main financial adviser from 1933 on. Keitel was head of the Wehrmacht, or combined Armed Forces. Brecht alludes to his supposed liking for French brandy, as also to Goering's drug-taking.

156. *Epilogue to 'The Duchess of Malfi'*. No published German text.

Written by Auden with some use of passages from Webster's *The Devil's Law-Case*.

157. *Prologue to the American 'Galileo'*. Prolog zur Amerikanischen Aufführung. 936. Ged. 9, 69.

Written presumably for the New York production of 7 December 1947 (a transfer to Broadway of the Los Angeles production starring Laughton).

158. *Epilogue of the scientists*. Epilog der Wissenschaftler. 937. Ged. 9, 70.

Also from the American *Galileo*. The first atomic bomb had been dropped on Hiroshima on 6 August 1945.

159. *The thinking man's vision of the time after him*. Gesicht des Denkenden von der Zeit nach ihm. 1249.

Dated *c.* 1930 by BBA and thought by the editors of GW to relate to the *Fatzer* play among whose fragments it was found. Like the *Aus nichts wird nichts* project, this featured. 'Mr Keuner, the thinking man', a favourite mouthpiece of Brecht's. However, the poem seems to relate to the *Antigone* production at Chur in 1948 – which was a virtual tryout of the Brecht-Neher collaboration and of Weigel's long neglected acting abilities before the return to Berlin – and is stylistically akin to other theatre poems of the 1940s.

160. *Bridge verses for Antigone.* Antigone-Legende. In W. Hecht (ed.): *Materialien zur 'Antigone'*, Suhrkamp, 1967.

(1948). These hexameters were interspersed like captions among Ruth Berlau's photographs of Brecht's and Neher's production in the album *Antigone-Modell 1948*. Brecht originally wrote them for the benefit of the Swiss provincial actors in the small theatre at Chur who were working with him (and with his Antigone, Helene Weigel) for the first time, and brought them along in instalments to the rehearsals. The idea, according to the theatre's director Hans Curjel, was 'to draw the actor from the neutral zone into the field of action' – this being the way the stage was divided. Weigel apart, the actors were 'baffled' by this 'paedagogical experiment', and few people appreciated what must in every sense have been a classic production. At the same time the poem reflects Brecht's work on the long, unfinished Lucretian 'didactic poem on human nature' which incorporates a hexameter version of the *Communist Manifesto* and fills GW pp. 895–930.

161. *Song of the Hours.* Horenlied. Also called 'Stundenlied'. 1190.

(1948). Sung in scene 3 of *Mother Courage* by the Chaplain after the arrest of Swiss Cheese. Not in the early scripts, but appears in that for the 1949 Deutsches Theater production, where the Chaplain was to have sung it before the curtain; however, it was cut, and only reintroduced in 1951. It is based on a protestant hymn by Michael Weisse (d. 1534).

Set by Dessau, 1948–9. There is also a setting, independently of the play, by Gottfried von Einem, who in spring 1949 asked Brecht for a suitable text. This was first performed by the Hamburg radio orchestra on 1 March 1959, under Hans Schmidt-Isserstedt.

162.♭ *Plum song.* [Das Pflaumenlied.] 1208.

(1948). Sung by Sly Grog Emma in scene 3 of *Puntila* while Puntila is combing the village for alcohol and flirting with the women in the dawn light. Appended to the fair-copy 1940 script, then included in the text for the Zurich première of June 1948. There are notes for a melody based on Brecht's recollections of 'When it's springtime in the Rockies' by Robert Sauer (1927). Set by Dessau in 1949.

163. *Ballad of the forester and the countess.* [Ballade vom Förster und von der Gräfin.] 1209. GBL 50. GW St 1694.

(1948). Sung offstage by Red Surkkala at the end of scene 9 (the betrothal party) of *Puntila*. In the first (1941) version of the play its place was taken by a song with a similar theme, 'Der Wolf ist zum Huhn gekommen'.

Dessau's setting (1949) of the Ballad is 'based on the tune of an old Scottish ballad'. This has been identified as 'Henry Martin'.

164.♭ *Puntila song*. Das Puntila-Lied. 1209.

(1949). Sung by Sly Grog Emma (a role created by Therese Giehse) between the scenes of *Puntila* in the Berliner Ensemble production of November 1949, for which Brecht wrote it. Each verse introduces an episode in the play, the 'Notturno' or open-air pissing scene (10) being omitted and scenes 7 and 8 run together. Setting by Dessau (1949) in *Versuche 10* (1950).

165. *Eighteenth-century song*. [O stille Winterzeit.] 1239.

(1949). Sung by Mrs von Berg at the happy ending of scene 16 of the Berliner Ensemble adaptation of *The Tutor* by Lenz. Set by Dessau (1950) but cut during rehearsals of Brecht's and Neher's production that spring.

166. *Melinda's song*. [Lied der Melinda.] 1241. GBL 56.

(1955). Also known as 'Melinda's Lied' or 'Melinda's song to the harp'. Sung by Melinda Moorhill at the start of scene 3 of *Trumpets and Drums*, Brecht's (and Elisabeth Hauptmann's) Berliner Ensemble adaptation of Farquhar's *The Recruiting Officer*. Setting by Rudolf Wagner-Régeny (1955).

167. *Victoria's song*. Lied der Victoria. 1241.

(1955). Also known as 'Viktoria's Lied'. Sung by Victoria Balance, the inadvertent transvestite, in an interlude before the curtain at the end of scene 6 of *Trumpets and Drums*.

168. *When I leave you*. [Wenn ich von dir gehen werde.] 1242.

(1955). Also known as 'Abschiedslied'. Sung by Thomas Appletree, a rustic recruit, and his girl Maggie in scene 8 ('By the Severn') of *Trumpets and Drums*. Set by Wagner-Régeny. 'Minny' was Maggie's name in an earlier script.

169. *Army song*. Lied der Kompanie. 1242. GBL 57.

(1955). Sung by Captain Plume to Victoria in scene 11 (gaol). Setting by Wagner-Régeny. Omitted from the duplicated Berliner Ensemble script. What seems like a first attempt in Brecht's handwriting consists of two lines:

> seven lofty fellows of the infantry
> stood eyeing the women of [?Char]

Subsequent drafts start with 'Dshaa' as the place, then finally settle on 'Gaa', a possible corruption of 'Goa'. The parting gift in line 4 of the second stanza was initially an apple, then becomes a date. Since in German the date has a sexual double meaning normally lacking in English we have substituted the more ambiguous fig.

170. *Song of the exception*. Lied von der Ausnahme. 1243.

(1955). Sung by the imprisoned Miner in an interlude at the end of scene 11 of *Trumpets and Drums*. Set by Wagner-Régeny. Brecht has 'I. N. Smith', but the German 'I' is pronounced 'E'.

171. *Recruits' song*. Rekrutenlied. 1244.

(1955). Sung by the recruits as they march off at the end of *Trumpets and Drums*. Set by Wagner-Régeny. 'Cheer up, boys', says a draft. 'You'll be fighting one against ten'.

INDEX OF THE TITLES IN ENGLISH AND GERMAN

Note. These include alternative titles in some cases, and also some German first lines where the proper titles are not widely known. For further information see the corresponding note.

	GW and pocket vol. page	Ged. Vol. and page	GBL No.	Music by
I THE AUGSBURG YEARS 1913–1920				
1. Lucifer's evening song. (c.1920)	260	1,143		Weill
2. Legend of the dead solder (1918)	256	1,136	7	Brecht
Five Songs from *Baal*:				
3. Ballad of the adventurers (1917)	217	1,79		Brecht
4. Death in the woods (?1918)	1088	2,180		Weill
5. Hymn of Baal the Great (1918)	1085	1,125	9	Brecht
6. Baal's song (1918)	adN. 40		4	Brecht
7. Orge's song (?1918)	1087	2,178		Brecht
8. Ballad of chastity in a major key (?1918)	1244	9,8		Brecht
9. The drowned girl (c.1920)	252	1,131	35	Weill
II THE MAHAGONNY MYTH 1920–1925				
10. The song from the opium den (c.1920)	90	2,48		
11. Tahiti (c.1921)	105	2,40		
12. When Paris ate the bread of Menelaus	St 212			
Mahagonny Songs 1 to 5:				
13. Mahagonny song no. 1	243	1,115	12	Brecht/Weill
14. Mahagonny song no. 2	1130	2,202	13	Brecht/Weill
15. Mahagonny song no. 3 (early 1920s)	244	1,117	14	Brecht/Weill
16. Mahagonny song no. 4 (early 1920s)	136	2,204		
17. Mahagonny song no.[5]	adN.168			
18. Ballad of the girl and the soldier	239	1,106	19	Brecht/Bruinier /Eisler/Dessau
19. Cannon song	1099	2,215	24	Weill
Three songs from *Man equals Man*:				
20. The 'Man equals man' song	138	2,184	15	Brecht/ Meisel
21. The song of Widow Begbick's drinking truck	1089		51	Dessau
22. What a bit of all right in Uganda!	1093			
Five more songs from 'Mahagonny':				
23. The chewing-gum song	adN.182			
24. The 'Johnny doesn't want to be human' song	1128	2,208		Brecht/Weill
25. Alabama song (c.1925)	1127	2,206		Brecht/Weill
26. Benares song (1926)	247	1,120		Brecht/Weill
27. Poem on a dead man (c.1925)	1133			Weill

V–VI   THE FIRST YEARS OF EXILE 1933–1938

LIST OF TRANSLATORS

The translators of 147 and 152 have not been
   identified.
Nos. 24 and 25 were originally written by
   Elisabeth Hauptmann for
   Brecht in English
Other translations are by the editor.